I0772934

Knights of the Octagon:
WEDDING CRASHERS

Colleen Snyder

Copyright © 2024 by Colleen K. Snyder
Published by Take Me Away Books, an imprint of Winged Publications

Editor: Cynthia Hickey
Book Design by Winged Publications

All rights reserved. No part of this publication may be reproduced, stored in a retrieval system, or transmitted in any form or by any means—electronic, mechanical, photocopying, recording, or otherwise—without the prior written permission of the publisher. The only exception is brief quotations in printed reviews. Piracy is illegal. Thank you for respecting the hard work of this author.

ISBN: 978-1-965352-12-0

THURSDAY

The masked figure poured accelerant over the sparkling dreams, wishes, and hopes. Chemicals melted delicate lace tulle. The liquid scarred the shimmering satins. Pearl buttons dissolved. The flash of ignition turned yards of fabric to ash.

The lone shape, shrouded in black, stepped back to admire the work. And make sure everything would be consumed in the conflagration. Leave no hope alive. The arsonist came to save others. Through fire. Through disappointment. Through an abrupt stroke of reality. It would be the only way. And the arsonist knew it.

The store erupted in flames. The vandal slipped out a side window into the humid August night and disappeared.

Sirens keened in the distance. Let them wail. The work was done. Freedom would reign once again.

* * *

FRIDAY

Micah read the news report about the fire at the wedding dress shop. His heart ached for the men and women affected. More than dresses were lost. Fall and winter wedding dates, carefully planned, now came into question. Some events might be held with another dress. But not *the* dress. Not the one the bride-to-be shopped for and chased across three counties and saved for and dieted for…not *that* dress.

He knew because he'd watched Wendy, his fiancée, and Jen, her sister, search for just such garments. The perfect wedding dress. The *one*. He had to admit he thought it all over the top and a great vanity, but he would never say it to them. Women were a mystery to be loved and cherished, not solved.

Micah texted Tav, Jen's intended and his best friend, to see how Jen and Wendy were affected.

Tav texted back. Not their shop. But not helping their anxiety. Need a night at Kensies.

Micah chuckled. Kensies served as the local bowling alley with a punching bag. The women could work out some emotion by beating Tav and Micah on the lanes or with the bag. Their choice.

Micah texted. *Meet there? Seven?*

Sounds like a plan. If Jen is down with it.

Wendy, too. Will text if not.

KO. Knight out. Their ending to all texts. Knights of the Octagon. Because no one had a round table, and Knights of the Oval sounded weird. Together since junior high. Together through…

Micah left the reminiscing and went in search of his eldest son. He found the soon-to-be college student in the den, working on his college prep work. "BB. You free tonight?"

BB looked up from his desk. He pushed his books away. "You got a date?"

"Only if you don't." Micah leaned against the doorframe of the room.

BB grinned. "Not tonight. Tomorrow, though." A slow smile crossed his son's face.

Micah raised his eyebrows. "Oh? Anyone I know?"

BB shook his head. "Not yet. She's in youth group." He closed his books and faced his dad, twirling the pencil in his hand.

Micah approved. "That's a good place to meet people. Tav and I thought Wendy and Jen could use some stress relief tonight. Another wedding shop was torched."

"I saw. What is it now, three in the last month?"

"Yeah. It's tough on people." Micah tapped the doorframe with his foot.

"It wasn't theirs, was it?"

"No. But they probably feel like it's a matter of time before their shop gets hit. I think as soon as the dresses come, they'll be standing in line to get them. Directly off the truck. Without alterations." Micah chuckled, but only just.

BB dipped his head. "I can understand."

"Can you?" Micah tipped his head.

BB admitted. "No, not really. It's a piece of fabric. An expensive piece of fabric. A lot to pay for half a day's entertainment."

Micah waved his hand. "Do not air such a sentiment. You'll liable to be drummed out of the Knights."

"Only if the women take over. We still outnumber them, right?" BB's eyes sparkled.

"Yeah. You, me, Ben, Tav, Luke, and Addison still tip the scales to the dark side."

BB snorted. "Let's keep it that way. You and Tav have been losing your backbones over this wedding." He stood from his desk and walked with Micah into the kitchen.

"Wait until you have a woman of your own."

"It'll be a partnership. Fifty-fifty." BB lifted his head.

"Wrong. But we'll talk about it later. I need to see if Wendy is available tonight."

"And if Quinn lets her off work early." BB stated the apparent problem with Wendy's availability. Quinn served as both her boss and the father figure for the Knights.

Micah growled, "On time for once would be nice." Her overtime hours were building.

"I hear you." BB laughed.

Micah walked back to his office and debated. Should he text? Email? Call? Carrier pigeon? *Too far back.* He texted. *You free this evening?*

Five minutes later, the answer came. *You want a date? Could be. You free?*

Another five-minute gap. Micah moved back to the kitchen to see what he could fix for the boys for dinner if plans worked out.

Free. Off on time.

Micah read the text with surprise. *Quinn getting soft? Hush.*

KO

Micah grinned. The senior knight, Quinn Magary, kept a tight rein on his "self-adopted daughters." Protective. When he wasn't the hard-nosed boss.

BB came into the kitchen with his phone. He slid the cell across the stone bar to his father. "Did you see this?"

"The fire at the dress shop? Yeah, the fire's the reason why we're—"

"Not that fire. The one at Harmony Ranch." BB's disgust filled his voice.

A popular wedding venue. "How bad?" Micah cocked his head to the side. His adopted son wasn't usually this involved with current events.

BB took a seat at the bar, looking out into the living room. Open concept at its finest. "Destroyed. They'll be out of commission for months. Maybe permanently."

This went beyond dresses. This meant entire weddings. Micah stared at the storefront on BB's phone, trying to remember what he knew of the place. He and Wendy had called it, of course. It had been one of the top five venues…

An uncomfortable idea hit him. He ordered, "Pull up the dress shops. Get the names." While BB retrieved the names, Micah pulled several "Best of" lists for wedding dresses. Then for wedding sites.

BB read off, "They hit the White Pearl first."

"Number two shop."

"Lacey's came next."

"Number one."

"After that, Beatty's Boutique."

"Number three." Someone was targeting the most popular sellers and venues. Which meant… "We should call Ginger's Event Center."

"And tell them what? You have an idea about some nutcase torching weddings?" BB's voice sounded incredulous.

"Why do you say nutcase?" Micah's eyes narrowed. He pulled a frying pan from a cabinet under the stove.

"It would have to be if someone thought doing this would stop weddings." BB waved a hand, dismissing the idea.

Micah reached for the box of rice in the pantry. "But is that what's being done? Trying to stop weddings?"

"Or just destroy people's happiness. Same difference."

Micah scowled. "If we have a notion—"

"The police will have the same notion. And if the perpetrator is dumb, they'll try to hit Ginger's and whoever else on the list. If they're going by the same ranking. There are different 'best of' registers." BB stated the problem with Micah's idea.

Micah sagged, deflated. "Yeah, you're right. I might look like the perp myself if I called in the threat and they *did* get hit. 'Mr. Andres, what is your connection with Ginger's Event Center?' I'd have to have a great alibi."

BB chuckled. "Yeah, being out with your best friend, his girl, and your girlfriend might not cut it. The cops would be suspicious of Tav and Jen, too. Better keep your thoughts to yourself."

Micah grumbled. "All right. This time." He retrieved a can of chicken broth from the cupboard.

"You didn't choose one of the top five venues for your wedding, though, did you?" BB traced a pattern with his finger on the counter.

"No, they were all booked for years. None of them on the lists were available at six months out and we wanted to be married before the holidays." Micah snorted. They thought they'd have so much time. Bad thought.

BB smirked. "Enter our Extreme Wizard Quinn, who can arrange anything."

"He's not a wizard. He's got contacts, that's all." Micah poured the broth into the rice and set it to simmer.

"Well-connected contacts. The Hemming's house is quite the setting."

Micah beamed. "Yeah, the women"—he stressed the term—"were very impressed. And pleased."

BB shrugged. "Who wouldn't be? Five thousand square feet of opulence."

Micah held up a hand. "It's understated opulence. It's not gaudy or over-the-top Victorian or anything. It's beautiful. And it will work just fine. Hand me the chicken."

"I still think a wedding at Kensies Bowling Palace would be just as good." BB laughed, took the chicken from the fridge, and handed it to his dad.

Micah leaned over toward his son and stage whispered, "So do I. But I don't get to say that."

BB plopped in the kitchen chair to watch his dad fix dinner. "Did you suggest it?"

"Not if I expected to keep my manhood. I realize this day is for Wendy and Jen. They're trying to put two weddings together so they can have their mom for both and not confuse her with two events."

It was BB's turn to scowl. "Alzheimer's. It's nasty. I hate what it's doing to Mrs. Smothers." He drummed with his hands.

"So do we all. Especially her daughters." Not to mention her foster and adopted sons. Four boys ranging from sixteen to twenty. Early onset slow death. No one deserved that.

But it happens. It happened, and only God knew why. And would one day reveal the answer. Until that time, they would cling to the facts they knew: God is love, and God is good. Everything had to be filtered through those two truths. Micah browned the chicken in another skillet.

Ben, Micah's younger adopted son, raced in from the outside, chased by Mialma, the black lab. She barked and danced and ran after Ben, who hid behind BB. "Help! I have her chew toy."

BB shifted away from Ben. "Then you're all hers. You know better than to take her chewie." Ben circled around his brother, angling to put the bar between himself and the dog.

Micah ordered, "Down, Mialma. Down." Mialma sat, her butt wiggling and her paws dancing. Micah held out his hand to Ben. "Give me the toy."

The boy hung his head. "We were on-ly play-ing."

"I'm sure you were. But it belongs to Mialma. It's

special to her, and you know you're not supposed to take it from her if you don't want her to chase you."

"But I wan-ted her to chase me. I did not want her to catch me." Ben carefully spaced his words. Autism. But his speech had come a long way in the four years he'd been Micah's son.

BB laughed. "Yeah, you're going to have to be a lot faster to get away from her. She'll motor you down."

Mialma whimpered. Micah repeated, "Give me the toy." He held out his hand and waited.

Ben dragged the toy from behind his back and handed it to his dad. Micah took it. He held it out to Mialma. "Gentle."

Mialma reached out and tenderly accepted the toy from her master, turned, dropped it once on the floor, and pounced on it. She flipped it into the air, caught it, and banged out through the door back outside.

Micah rubbed Ben's head. "Okay, buddy. Lesson learned. She will chase you. She will catch you. Got it?"

"Got it."

Micah put a hand on Ben's shoulder. "I'm going out with Tav, Jen, and Wendy tonight. We're going to Kensies, so Wendy and Jen can punch the bags if they want."

"Wen-dy pun-ches hard." Ben smiled and laughed.

"Wendy punches very hard. Quinn taught her well."

"Pop-dad will teach me?" Ben tipped his head to the side.

"He will if you ask him." Micah flipped the chicken in the skillet.

Ben continued to pursue the issue. "I will ask him when I see him. When will I see him a-gain?"

"He's worked hard this summer, especially this past month. A special job he's been given. Hopefully he'll be able to spend some time at home in August before you boys go back to school." Quinn never talked about what he did. And the Knights didn't ask. Better not to know. Quinn Magary was a man of two worlds. He had his work world, where he disappeared for weeks at a time and never spoke of what he would do or where he would be. Then he had the "Pop-dad" side…the relaxed, grandfatherly, fatherly side who loved family and being with family and supporting the Knights in all their endeavors. Their mentor never spoke of his "natural family" if he had one. His comments about the Knights being his sons and daughters and family made it clear. *We're it for him. He's it for us.*

Micah shook off the musings and repeated, "We're going out about seven. Which means you need to be in bed when I get home at eleven. Right? No arguing with BB."

Ben nodded once, his singular nod all anyone ever got. "Yes, Dad. I will not ar-gue with BB. He's my bro-ther, and he takes care of me."

He cast a sly eye at BB and added, "If he does not talk on the phone to Mit-zy all night."

Micah raised an eyebrow. "Mitzy? I thought she was old news." He looked at BB, expecting an explanation.

"She's back in the picture. We're friends." BB shrugged, but his failure to meet Micah's eyes told a different story.

"Okay. What about Miss Youth Group?" Micah couldn't help but ask.

BB hedged, "We'll have to see on that one." He fidgeted with his fingers.

Micah laughed. "Well, don't get them crossed."

BB shifted his weight from side to side. "No, no. No chance. Mitzy is just a friend."

"That's how they all start, son." Micah returned to fixing dinner. He put the browned chicken in the pan with the rice, added creamed soup, and the beans. They would cook together until it came time to eat. Simple meals were the best meals. And BB could take it from there.

While dinner cooked, he dressed for the date. Blue jeans, pullover shirt. Nothing fancy. Slip-ons so he could change into bowling shoes without wasting time. Bowling should be serious business. Especially if he wanted to beat Tav. Which he'd never done. But hope springs eternal.

His *last* duty was to set the alarm as he went out the door. The boys would be in for the night. No chance of Ben running out and forgetting to deactivate the sirens. BB could be counted on to set and reset the system when taking Mialma out for *the* final time. But Ben? Not so much. There had been a few false alarms before Micah determined to leave the system off during the day when Ben was home. The Knights all knew each others' codes. Easier that way. But they still knocked before entering. Decorum, and all that.

Micah drove to Kensies Bowling Alley. It wasn't the original Kensies. The one in Acorn had been destroyed in the earthquake and flood that followed. But the old management rebuilt in Galt, where Micah and the Knights were living. And working and going to school. So much to do to rebuild after the destruction of Acorn and the surrounding area. So many lives lost. The Knights had tried to warn people, but few believed them.

Another part of history best left in the past. Why should he be looking back? Tonight, he should be looking forward. A fun night to get the girls' minds off the wedding and the potential disasters haunting the town. Right. Let's punch something.

Tav and Jen were already at Kensies and had two lanes reserved. Wendy came in behind Micah. He kissed her warmly and deeply, risking a full-body hug. It took his mind off the fires, to be sure. When he came up for air, he grinned at her. "I know that made my day better. Did it yours?"

"Yes. Anything would make this day better." Wendy held Micah's hand as they walked to join Tav and Jen.

Micah dropped his shoulders. "So Mialma could have kissed you, and it would have had the same effect?" He gave her his best impression of Ben's pout.

Wendy grinned at him. "I didn't mean to say it that way.

Yes, Mick, kissing you made my day wonderful."

He nodded. "That's better." He let his smile return.

Tav had sodas and chips waiting. "I think we'll bowl and, after, go out to eat. Agreed?"

In Knight fashion, the four put their fists in a circle, counted silently to four, then raised their thumbs. All in agreement. This would be a good night. Now, if they could all agree on where to go as easily as they had agreed to go, they would have a perfect evening.

Jen and Wendy poured all their anxieties into beating Tav and Micah on the alleys. Then, they took turns on the speed bag. Wendy won the competition. Fastest and hardest. Micah had to wonder which bothered her more, her current assignment with Quinn or the whole anxiety about the wedding. With three months to go on her assignment and four months to go before the wedding in late November, it could be a toss-up. His job was to not add to the stress. Be supportive when he could and stay out of the line of fire when he couldn't.

Wendy suggested they go to Jericho's for BBQ after Kensies. Jen agreed, and they settled it. No arguments. Go with the flow.

As they were waiting for their dinners to be brought out, a news item on the wall-mounted TV caught Micah's attention. *"An explosion at Ginger's Event Center has destroyed the front of the building. Three units are on scene. We have a reporter…"*

Micah's gut twisted. He looked across the table at Tav. His friend scowled. "They need to catch this guy. Or gal. Or group. This is getting ridiculous."

Wendy looked up sharply. "Ridiculous?" Her eyes narrowed, and she slapped her hands on the table.

Micah held up his hand. "No one thinks this is a joke. That's not what Tav meant."

"How do you know what Tav thinks?" Wendy snipped at Micah. "Oh, I forgot. You two read each other's mind."

Tav dipped his head. "If we had minds. I'm sorry if you thought I meant this was at all funny. I didn't. It's dire. People are hurting because of this arsonist. I feel for the ones who've had their hopes destroyed. People are out a great deal of money because of this. Not to mention the months of planning. It's bad."

Wendy settled in her chair. "I'm sorry I jumped. I knew you didn't mean it the way it came out. I shouldn't be as on edge as I am."

Micah squeezed her hand but said nothing. He didn't want his head handed to him. Not that Wendy would do that, right?

Better to be silent and thought a fool than open your mouth and remove all doubt. Micah pointed to the server coming their way. "I think he has our order."

They ate in silence. Four pulled pork BBQ sandwiches, two orders of fries, and coleslaw all around. Baked beans and plenty of napkins. Micah waited until the majority of the meal had been consumed before he brought up his hunch. "I had a feeling Ginger's would be next."

Three heads snapped around to look at him. Micah held up both his hands. "Not a feeling. Not a premonition. But BB and I were looking at the wedding shops, and the ones that have been hit were the top three in the area on the list we looked at. Harmony Ranch and Ginger's are the top two event centers. Wells Cathedral is number three."

"You think we should call someone?" Jen lifted the remains of her sandwich and took another bite.

"BB said if I'd thought of it, the police would have figured it out as well."

Jen shrugged. "Depends on if they're looking at the same list. There are half a dozen 'best of' rankings. Might not hurt to call in and mention it."

"BB thought it might make me look guilty. Like I knew more than I should." Micah dredged a fry in BBQ sauce and stuffed it in his mouth.

Jen threw in, "BB has a point." Tav dropped his head to look at her sideways. Jen stared back at him. "He does. I'm not saying Mick shouldn't call, just that BB's point is valid. It could make Mick look like he knows something."

Tav grimaced at his intended and offered, "We can all vouch for where you were when the fire started. We could probably provide you with alibis for all the fires. Seeing as we all live next door to each other." Micah's friend served more brisket ends.

Micah nodded. "Truth." He grinned. "I love our living arrangement."

"Eight-plex with all the Knights living together in one square block. Long as we don't fall out with each other, it works." Tav pointed a french fry at Micah.

Micah beamed. "And when we get married, Wendy moves in with me, and you move in with Jen to take care of Arlene."

"And you're right there to help with her. The whole band all caring for each other." Tav gave a thumbs up.

Wendy scowled. "I'm not sure 'band' is the right nomenclature for us. I think my brothers might object."

"They're still on the outside. Not full Knights," Tav agreed with her.

Wendy corrected, "Not Knights at all. You have to be a follower of Christ to be a Knight. My brothers haven't made a commitment."

"True, but it doesn't mean they're not part of the family. Or the 'band.' Just means they're still miscreants." Tav went in for more fries.

Wendy tossed her napkin at him. "While I agree with your assessment of my brothers, I wouldn't say that. Seekers may be better."

Micah cleared his throat. "Listeners. Ury is the only one who's shown any real interest."

Wendy held up her hands. "Listeners, then. I'll buy it."

"Will you buy dinner?"

"No."

Micah grinned. "Of course not. It's my turn anyhow." He paid the bill, and the four got up and walked back to the parking lot. Since they had all come in separate cars, they all drove home alone. Micah decided he would take the long way around. He wanted to drive past Wells Cathedral. But would there be a guard on it? Had the police made the connections? Should he call?

He reached for his phone. Pulled over and called the tip line. Anonymous tip line, of course. He relayed his hunch to the automated recording. And left it. He drove the four miles to the cathedral to see if the police had the same hunch.

The building had long been devoid of worshippers. Under new management, the whole thing became an event center. The interior had been reworked, the stained glass refurbished, and it now drew crowds again.

Micah circled the block once. He didn't see any police or guards of any kind. He couldn't be the only one drawing conclusions, could he? Not with it so obvious. He parked his van in the shadow of a sugar pine tree. Darkness deep enough to see the street but not to be seen. He climbed out of the van but didn't shut the door.

What are you doing here? Are you out of your mind? Go home. Leave the sleuthing to the professionals.

A shadowy figure dressed all in black approached the stone façade. It looked right, then left, then right again. Finally, it raised a hand and did something to one of the windows. Black handles were pressed against the glass. The figure outlined and removed the maybe 4-foot by 4-foot piece of glass and set it on the ground.

Glass cutter.

You need to get out of here. Now.

The figure climbed in the window. Micah watched until the figure disappeared into the building. Then Micah got back in his van. He reached to start the engine. A voice at his shoulder hissed, "This does not concern you."

Micah froze. The voice ordered, "Get out of the car.". He felt a cold barrel of steel slide on his neck. Micah obeyed. He stared straight ahead and prayed.

The darkness prevented him from seeing his assailant. The voice whispered, the tone forced and low, "Hands on the van. Don't move. Stand completely still."

The gun barrel slid off his neck. The voice directed, "Stand still. You turn around, you die."

Micah strained to hear footsteps. No sound. Nothing. He stood for a minute.

Nothing.

What seemed like five minutes passed.

Nothing.

Micah lowered his hands. Slowly. Inch by inch. He turned with deliberate motion.

Nothing.

He exhaled. Climbed into his van. Prayed. Started the engine. Drove. Home.

* * *

SATURDAY

Twelve a.m. Micah sat on his couch as Quinn repeated his question. "One climbed in the window of the facility?"

"Yes," Micah repeated his answer. Tav and Quinn sat in Micah's living room. Two too many to listen to the tale of his poor judgment, but so it went. BB and Ben sat in the kitchen, staying out of the conversation but listening. Always listening.

Micah explained, "I called it in. Someone in the back of the car told me it was none of my business. They stuck what I believed to be a gun next to my head. Told me to stand still. I stood still."

"Tell me again why you went to the cathedral?" Quinn paced in front of Micah.

Micah sighed inwardly. "I wanted to play a hunch. With all the vandalism at the bridal shops and the event centers, I looked at what might be next. Wells Cathedral was listed as third in popularity on the list I saw. I thought maybe the police would have figured the same and went to see if I guessed right. I thought they would have people all over the place watching for the vandals."

"And if they'd been staking the place out, you'd have driven right through it and blown the whole thing. Good thinking." Quinn sat in the rocker opposite Micah.

Micah ignored the mentor's sarcasm. "I'm not stupid. I called it in. Anonymously. I didn't try to stop anyone. I didn't make a scene. I called."

Tav sniped, "Next time, call from home. The cops do know what they're doing."

Quinn defended Micah. "But they didn't have the place staked out." He raised his eyebrows to challenge Tav.

His friend waved Quinn off and addressed Micah. "It's 'see something, say something.' Not 'think something, do something.' You could have been seriously hurt or killed."

Quinn added, "Arsonists have no qualms about leaving dead bodies in their wake."

Micah raised his hand. "Okay, okay. I was stupid. I admit it. I wanted to prove I could be right. Ego." He stopped, then added, "I was right. But my execution stunk."

Quinn growled. Micah held both hands in the air. "I know, I know. Next time, I'll keep my thoughts to myself."

Quinn huffed. "Don't stop thinking, Mick. But share your thoughts with the rest of us. 'In a multitude of counselors, there is wisdom,' so the scriptures say. We might have talked you out of it."

Tav huffed. "Or gone with you. With this bunch, it could go either way."

"Thanks for the vote of confidence." Micah shook his head. He looked to Quinn. "Why would they steal the window? Only the window?"

"The glass is valuable. Maybe they're artists and wanted the window for a project. Maybe you stopped them from doing more. Maybe they were the vandals, and you caught them. We won't know until they act again."

Micah suggested, "Now you know the depths of my stupidity. Can you all go home and let me get some sleep? I'd like to forget this whole affair."

Tav's eyebrows raised, as did his tone. "You're not going to report this?"

Micah's shoulders sagged. "I'll think about it tomorrow. I will. Right now, I want to go to bed and pretend my life wasn't threatened."

Quinn pointed at Tav. "To your quarters, Knight. We can harass him in the morning. Let the man decompress." He laid his strong hand on Micah's shoulder. "We'll talk later. Get some rest."

When Quinn spoke, people listened. Tav returned to his home across the quadrangle.

Micah walked Quinn to the door, closed it behind him, and addressed his sons, "Okay, everyone back to bed."

BB hugged him. "I'm glad you're safe, Dad. See you in the morning."

Ben kissed Micah. "Good night, Dad. Sleep well."

Micah watched the boys head to their rooms and shut their doors. He sighed, activated the alarm system, and went to his own room. He shucked his clothes, got on his knees, and prayed, "Thank You, Lord. You saved my life. Put it to Your use. And stop me before I make stupid choices." He paused, then continued, "I know. If I'd pray before I make the choices, I might not find myself with so many impulsive ones. Lesson learned. For now. I love You, Lord." Micah climbed into bed, stared at the ceiling, and counted, "1000. 999. 998. 997…"

* * *

The following morning, BB made breakfast of eggs and bacon and handed it to Micah. "Eat, Dad. You'll need your strength. Your interrogators will be back, I'm sure." He called to the back, "Ben. Breakfast is ready."

Micah sat at the kitchen bar and pushed the eggs around with his toast. The bacon wafted its aroma into his fogged brain.

The teen served a plate for himself and Ben. He laid Ben's plate on the bar top and took his to the dining room.

Someone knocked at the door. BB disabled the alarm

system, then opened the door to allow Wendy in. Micah gave her what he hoped was a disarming smile. "Good morning, beautiful."

Wendy ignored the compliment. "I heard you got held up at gunpoint last night."

Micah swallowed the sigh he wanted to make. He continued to smile. "I wasn't held up. I stumbled on a break-in at Wells Cathedral. The thieves told me not to get involved. At gunpoint. End of story."

Wendy grimaced. "Have you filed a police report? They'll want to know what you saw."

"I didn't see enough to be helpful. I saw a figure. I saw it cut out the glass. That's it."

"It might be enough to break the case. I've seen crimes brought to justice with less." Wendy sat beside Micah on the retro metal bar stool. The green one.

Micah continued his protest. "But this isn't like anyone got hurt. They didn't do anything to me. They didn't even threaten my life. They just said it didn't concern me, and I should not turn around. How does that constitute a threat?"

Wendy growled. "Andres, you're being deliberately evasive."

"No, I'm being logical. I don't have anything to say the police can't already figure out." He continued pushing the eggs around with his toast, not eating.

"They should be the ones to decide." She turned to BB. "Agreed?"

BB held up his hands. "I'm not arguing with you. I know better." He attended to his plate of breakfast.

Wendy pointed to Micah's plate. "Those your eggs?"

Micah stuffed them in his mouth.

Wendy smirked. "Good man."

"You want some? I'll fix them for you." BB pointed to the kitchen.

"No, I'm good. I'll eat at lunch." She shifted in her seat.

BB measured her up and down. "Have to fit in the dress,

right?"

Wendy sneered at him. "Smart aleck. Right. The dress." She sighed. "I'll be happy when this wedding is over." She picked a piece of bacon off Micah's plate, broke off the tiniest piece, and placed it in her mouth. She chewed, swallowed, and frowned.

Micah lifted her hand. "We can simplify the ceremony, you know."

"How? It's a double wedding. Everything is twice as complex." Wendy stared out the window over the sink.

"We still have time to make it easier." He kissed her fingers.

"I repeat, how?" Wendy turned to face him full-on. BB turned to face him, too. As Micah's best man, the youth had a vested interest in the goings-on.

Micah drew a circle with his fingers. "The wedding party hits the road. We find a chapel somewhere, we exchange our vows in front of each other, and we're done. Simple."

"What about the relatives? The distant relatives? The friends? The co-workers? The two hundred or so people who we've invited to come? What do we do about them?"

"Throw a party after. But we take the pressure off you and Jen."

Wendy smiled and ran her finger down Micah's cheek. "I love you, Mick. We'll be fine. We can make it the way it is. It'll be over before we know it."

"Just know I love you."

They kissed.

From the back, they heard Ben. "No kis-sing. Not un-til you are mar-ried." The diminutive chaperone appeared in the dining room. Ben's self-declared rule stated those who weren't married should only kiss on the cheek. In deference to his sensibilities, Micah and Wendy tried to remember not to kiss in front of him. Outside Ben's presence would be another story.

A crash shattered the front window. Micah ran to the living room, ducking down lest something else come flying through. A brick lay on the carpeted floor, surrounded by glass shards. A paper had been wrapped around the missile, tied with string. Micah didn't pick up the brick but cut the string. With the tip of his knife, he dug the note out from under the stone. Careful not to touch it, Micah unfolded the message so he could read it.

Not your concern. Stay out of it. Or else.

Micah stared at the paper. *How do they know where I live?* But what did "stay out of it" mean? He wasn't in it. His part ended last night. Didn't it? What more could he do?

Tav came running from his house at the sound of glass breaking. He picked the note up with a tissue and read it. Tav stared at Micah. "Twice warned? Interesting."

"Do we call the police? Or does that count as being 'in it'?" He touched the brick with his foot. Mindful of leaving no prints or grinding glass into the carpet.

Wendy put her hands on her hips. "Of course, we call the police. Someone is threatening you." She gave Micah her fiercest, no-nonsense look.

"It's not really a threat. It's a warning. All I have to do is nothing, and I'm safe." The words sounded weak even as he said them.

"You believe that?" Wendy's tone sounded incredulous and carried more than a tad of heat.

Micah held up both hands. "I don't know what else I'm supposed to do that involves whoever this is. I called in the anonymous tip last night. The bad guys warned me off. Anything else is…" He trailed off. "I don't know what this is about. Someone make it make sense."

Tav thought a moment. "I'd say you don't do anything. We'll get the window fixed, and we say it's over."

Wendy scowled hard. "That's ridiculous. Someone is making threats. Someone who knows where you live. You need to call the police."

Tav ducked his head. "Okay, maybe. I don't think these guys are exactly masterminds. There might be some prints the police can lift." He raised his palm. "Up to you, Mick."

"Great. Leave the decision to the waffler."

BB packed Ben to spend the day with his friend Charlie and left to drive him. After, BB would go to his job at the coffee shop. A part-time position to fill the days before leaving for college.

Micah grunted. "Fine. We call the police. Let them decide if it's something important."

Wendy nodded. "Agreed." She pulled out her phone and dialed the non-emergency number for the police. "I want to report a vandalism."

Twenty minutes of waiting and explanations later, she disconnected the call and sighed. "That hurt. Trying to get them to connect the dots. I guess the paperwork from last night's anonymous tip hasn't hit the computers."

Micah shrugged. "Police work moves at the speed of molasses. Justice moves slow, they say." Did it mean he'd have to look at the broken window for days? Undoubtedly, the police would be out before the day ended. Wouldn't they?

"But it needs to move faster if they want to prevent crime, not simply investigate it after the fact." Wendy's frustration echoed in her tone.

Micah touched Wendy's hand. "It's fine, Wendy. This will all be resolved. God has it. We're in His hands. We'll get through it."

Micah watched the tension drain from Wendy's shoulders. "Right. I know. I hate attacks on my family."

Tav agreed. "We all do. We all get defensive when it gets personal. I'm not discounting this could be more serious than we think. But until something more happens, we have to move on." He pointed to the window. "Plywood or plastic?"

"Plastic. I like being able to see the road. So does Ben."

It would be easier for the youth to have sunlight. Light helped keep Ben centered. The more Micah could keep things the same, the better Ben did. The upcoming loss of BB to college would be a trial they would have to manage together. But the support of the other Knights would make it better, if not easier.

"Plastic it is. I'll see if anyone here has some, or go get it from the store." Tav began texting.

Wendy pointed to Micah's phone. "Call your insurance company. The sooner you report this—"

Micah cut her off. "Deductibles. I'll pay for it myself. After the police do whatever they're going to do. Though I think vandalism is low on the criminals-to-catch list."

"But it's connected to the arsons. That should move it up on the 'need to look at seriously' register." Micah saw the tension in his fiancée's face rising again.

"You'd think. We'll have to see. We don't know if the police will even agree it's connected."

Wendy looked at her phone. "Jen needs me for a few minutes. I'll be back." She pointed at Micah, then Tav, and walked out.

Micah studied his friend. "You want to do some forensics, considering the mounties might not?" He walked around and looked at the living room.

"What kind?" Tav measured the window with his phone. Yes, he had an app for that.

"Physics."

Tav groaned. "Physics is more BB's strength."

"I know. We'll have him check us. But let's figure the average human throwing the brick. Where would they have been when they threw it? Were they in a car or standing on the street? We can canvass the street for cameras to see if anyone caught anything." Micah looked out the broken window to the houses on the far side of the street.

Tav grimaced. "Mick, you do know what the phrase, 'Stay out of it' means, don't you? It means you leave it alone.

Quit playing detective."

"But if I can help find the perps faster, we can close this out."

"And if the perps find out you're helping the police, they could close you out. Or your family. Remember, they do know where you live. They probably followed you home last night to see where you are. Do you want to go into hiding for the next few weeks?"

Micah glared at Tav. "Low blow, man."

"Not really. If you want to get all in this investigation, the perps are rightfully going to think you're trying to help find them rather than sitting it out. I believe the police can figure things out on their own. I do. Maybe not as fast as you would like, but at least without your help. And it will make the perps happy enough to leave you alone."

Micah sagged against the couch. "But it would give me something to think about besides how mad I am at myself for getting into this mess to start with."

"And getting further involved will only make it worse. You trying to play detective is a bad idea. A really bad idea. Leave it alone."

Micah's brain rumbled. "You think they'll bring a forensics team? To measure the trajectory of the brick, the amount of shatter, the tensile strength of the glass, and how much force it would take to shatter it?"

Tav put a hand on his friend's shoulder. "I think they're going to send someone out to look at the note. Then, tell you there's nothing else they need from you, and you can clear the glass and go on with your life. I don't think vandalism warrants much attention." He ducked his head to the side. "I realize it's not just your house that's involved. There are all the other places, as well. And we're talking thousands of dollars. Maybe they will. But I doubt it. Give it a rest. Or I'll tell Wendy on you."

"You wouldn't." Micah's tone sounded aghast.

"I would if you don't behave. Let it go, Mick. It really

doesn't concern you. Not beyond those who stole the glass. And broke your window. We know those are the same people. We don't know if they're the same people who damaged the dress owners' shops. They could be unrelated." Tav returned to his measuring.

"You don't actually think that, do you?" Micah eyed his friend sideways.

"Of course not. But it's not my call. I'm not a trained professional, and I don't play one on TV." Tav smiled a straight-lipped smile.

Micah slumped down on the couch. His shoulders drooped. Maybe Tav had it right, and he should leave it alone. Maybe. Maybe he could *think* about the calculations. But he'd have to know the trajectories, the distance the glass traveled, the weight of the brick, and the tensile strength of the glass (single pane or double?). Also, the average strength of both a man and a woman…

A woman. The person at the window last night had been a woman. He knew it. The profile fit. Thin. Spry. Definitely a woman. He sat forward to tell Tav and stopped. Stay out of it. Let the police figure it out. Right. Not his job. His job was to be alive to show up at the wedding venue. Right. Leave it, Andres.

The police forensics team arrived an hour later. The technicians took pictures of the broken glass, the glass on the rug, and the position of the brick. They bagged and tagged the brick and the note (and the strings the note had been attached with. Get everything essential.) They didn't take any measurements, but they did photograph the outside of the house and the road. Micah didn't have the opportunity to give them his opinion of the gender of the perp at the cathedral, however. No one asked, so he didn't offer. Stay out of it. Right.

After the forensics squad left, Micah looked at Tav. "See? I can follow orders. I didn't say a word. Didn't ask any questions. Nothing that could be perceived as participating in the case. Did I do good?"

Tav grinned. "You did good. I'll be sure to tell Wendy what a well-behaved boy you were."

Micah muttered under his breath but made sure the words were unintelligible. He did not want to be held accountable for idle whispers. Bad enough to think those things. Why get disciplined twice?

Quinn came later in the morning. He carried a notebook with him. He nodded to Micah first. "Nice to see you in one piece. Being threatened at home takes things to another level."

"Thanks, Quinn. That makes my day." Micah turned from his task of holding the plastic tight across the opening while Tav stapled it in place.

"Maybe this will." Quinn leaned against the porch rail. "I did some calculations this morning. With almost complete certainty, I can say our perpetrator was a female. Maybe five-eight, a hundred-twenty pounds. And she's left-handed."

Tav groaned and hit his head with the palm of his hand. "Quinn! I've been working all day to keep Mick from getting further involved in this. Now, you want to fill his head with possibilities? Get him deeper into the mess he's *not* supposed to get involved in?"

Quinn chuckled. "No, that's why I did all the calculations. And why I'll be the one to take the heat from here on out." He glared at Tav. "And yes, I've informed the police of my findings. And it's not my effort. It's the calculations of my technicians." He raised his eyebrows.

Tav sighed. "Fine. So long as Mick is out of the loop."

Micah frowned. "Do I get a say in this?"

"No." Quinn and Tav echoed one another. Quinn continued. "You're out. It's the best way to keep you safe. Not to mention BB and Ben. Think about them." The man's face smiled. His eyes didn't. Quinn pointed to the street. "I'm off to shop for Grace. She wants pasta for dinner, and we're out. I thought I'd tell you what we found first. I'll keep you posted with anything else we learn." The man sailed down the street to the corner market on his wife's errand.

Micah growled. "So stupid. Why did I ever go out there?"

Tav clasped Micah's shoulder. "Quit rehearsing the past. It happened. Now we move on, got it? The old is gone. The new has come. Or is coming. Breathe and enjoy the rest of the day off."

Micah groaned. "Day off? I've got clients who need taxes taken care of. They left me a message about needing an extension filed. Immediately."

"So they get filed a day later. I'm sure you didn't wait until the last day to record them, right?"

"I don't play those games. I always make sure they've got a week's leeway." Except Howard sprang this on him last night. After he'd gone to Kensies. The joys of being self-employed. Of course, if it was a choice between working Saturday and a date with Wendy, the date definitely won.

"Now they have six days instead of seven. It'll be fine, Mick." Tav stretched. "How is the forensic accounting going with Quinn?"

"We're still chasing the bad guys. It's amazing how many criminals can be taken down for not filing taxes when the authorities can't get them on any other charge."

"Good reminder to file mine." The men wrapped their repair job on the window.

Micah grinned. "I won't let you forget. I won't let any of the Knights forget."

"Always good to have an accountant around to keep us honest."

And on time. Micah asked, "How are the advanced classes going?"

"I'm within five hours of having the master's done. When I'm done I'll make up my mind which way to take this psychology degree."

"A psychologist might be a good thing for this bunch. Tell us if we're looney or not for doing what we do."

"Following Jesus? Not a chance. Maybe by some people's standards, but not by His. And His standards are all we're worried about, right?" Tav eyed Micah sideways.

Micah nodded. "Last time I checked."

"Keep checking, Knight."

* * *

SATURDAY AFTERNOON

Later that early August afternoon, Micah raked leaves in the front yard. Lots of trees make lots of leaves. The neighborhood had a forest of mature, fruitless mulberry trees. If he wanted to get a jump on fall, he needed to start raking now. Mialma lay on the porch, keeping a watchful eye on his activities. Micah worked toward her.

The black lab sat abruptly and woofed. Micah turned. A barrel of white fluff attacked his rake from the side, shaking and rattling it for all it was worth. Small as the fluff was, it wasn't worth much. Micah reached down and caught hold of the puppy while Mialma jumped off the porch to protect her master.

A young woman ran to him, agitated and yelling. Maybe in her late twenties. About Micah's age. He held the pup out to her. "Yours?"

The woman stopped yelling and grabbed the puppy. She cradled it to her chest and tried to soothe the barking, growling, yipping frenzy. Finally, she settled it and held out her hand. "I'm Carly." She set the pup on the ground.

"Mick." He pointed to the lab, which tried to nose the puppy. "This is Mialma."

"Strange name. I've never heard it before." The woman stared hard at the Labrador as if to put the name to the muzzle and failed.

"It means 'my soul.' She's my son's soul mate." Micah didn't bother to tell her he'd named the dog. It had become true, however, as Mialma would never be far from Ben's side. Except when the boy attended school, and she had no one else to bother but Micah.

"You live here?" Carly looked around at the houses.

"No, I am raking leaves for the fun and exercise." He smiled. She didn't. He tried again. "Yes, this is my house. Do you live near here?"

She waved down the street. "Over a few blocks. I am walking Roger for his exercise."

"You named the dog Roger?" Micah grinned.

"Why not? Better than Mialma." Micah raised his eyebrows at Carly. Carly retracted the statement. "Sorry. I was rude." She hesitated. "Is your wife at work?"

"I'm not married."

The eyes sparkled. Bad news. Micah added, "Engaged."

Carly smiled. "Congratulations. Have you set a date?" Roger and Mialma began the peculiar dance dogs do when first meeting each other. Round and round.

Micah admitted, "A few months from now." Leave it there. He didn't know this person. With his track record, better to be vague. Or more vague than he usually would be.

"Well, maybe I'll see you next time we pass this way." Carly waved to indicate the street.

Micah dipped his head. "Maybe."

She stopped. "Or we could set a play date for your dog and Roger. What did you say his name was again?" A breeze wafted the smell of lilacs from the yard across the street.

"She. Mialma." Micah patted the dog's head.

"Right. Well, maybe they could play. Roger needs some friends, and I could use a few new acquaintances." She raised an eyebrow to go with the suggestion.

Micah shook his head. "I'm not sure it would be appropriate."

"Why not? We're both adults." Carly's eyes narrowed.

Micah shrugged. "I'm engaged."

"I'm not asking to marry you. Just if our dogs can be friends." She sagged. "You have to ask the girlfriend's permission, don't you?"

Micah petted Mialma's head. "No. In a group, we're fine. Alone, no. Sorry." He wasn't.

Carly picked up Roger in one hand. "Well, I guess we won't walk this way." She stopped. "Or is it okay as long as you're in your yard and I stay on the sidewalk?"

Micah laughed. "I'm not trying to be difficult. The dogs can play out in the open. I'll bring you a chair so you can supervise. I'm old-fashioned. I want to avoid any appearance of impropriety."

"Is your girlfriend so controlling you can't talk to strangers?"

Micah leaned on his rake. "It's not her. It's the Lord I serve. I can talk to strangers all I want. I won't put them in a compromising position."

Carly lifted her head. "Ah, you're one of those people." She dragged out the word "those."

"If you mean one of those who love the Lord and are trying to follow Him, yes I am."

The two dogs chased each other around the yard, rolling and playing. Carly watched them for a moment. She sighed. "I understand. I don't have to like it, but I understand." She looked up and down the street. "I don't suppose there's anyone around here who would talk to me, is there?"

"The house on the corner has women who will talk to you anytime. No dogs, though."

Carly whistled for Roger. The pup came, albeit reluctantly. He nipped at her toes. "Stop that! You little rat." She picked him up, used his paw to wave goodbye, and smiled. "I do hope we'll see you again. With your girlfriend."

"Fiancée."

"Right. Her." Carly walked off down the street. She turned and looked at the corner house, then moved off down the way.

Micah looked at Mialma. "Rude, I was. Lost you a playmate, I did."

Mialma climbed back on the porch, huffed, and laid down again.

* * *

SUNDAY EVENING

Flowers were harder to burn. The floral warehouse kept the inventory cold, moist, and fresh. Roses, anemones, dahlias, lilacs…hydrangeas, ranunculus…ferns, baby's breath…all needed a liberal supply of water to survive.

White phosphorous would take care of it. Properly placed and ignited, it would burn anything. The arsonist would be nothing if not relentless in the desire to save others from a fate worse than death itself. Maybe those affected would not see the salvation being offered. But eventually, everyone would welcome it. And thank the arsonist. And praise the tireless effort, knowing it was all for the best.

The sweet-smelling savor of a warehouse of aromatic flowers burning to a crisp rewarded the silent figure who stole away from the inferno. And planned the next target.

* * *

MONDAY

BB leaned against the porch, watching a strange woman with a small dog talking with Arlene Smothers. He spoke into the phone. "Seems odd. I'm going to be calling her Grandma Smothers in another sixteen weeks."

Mitzy laughed over the connection. "You'll finally have a grandparent. Is that weird?"

"A little. Hard enough to call Mick 'Dad' when he's only eight years older than me. Changing from Mrs. Smothers to Grandma Smothers seems somehow disrespectful. But she's Wendy's mom, so I'll be her grandson."

"Four months, huh? How's the planning going?"

"Pretty sure Wendy and Jen have it done. Except for the cake. The bakery has been putting them off. Canceled on them. But I think it's the last item on the list." The woman and her dog walked down the street, leaving Mrs. Smothers alone on the porch.

"Why'd they wait so late?"

"Have you called a wedding baker? A wedding, anything? People are panicked about being vandalized. No one wants to do business right now. You know how it is. You're in the flower business. You got hit like everyone else." BB watched the older woman climb from her chair and head back into the house.

Mitzy paused, then said, "But we supply other places besides bridal. We do event centers, businesses, hospitals Wedding planners and shops rip people off for tens of thousands of dollars, all in the name of vanity."

BB chuckled. "Don't let that attitude get aired around. It won't endear you to many." He paused, then asked, "Will you come with me to the wedding? You know everyone."

Extended silence. "Are you asking me on a real date?"

"Well…yeah. I am. Will you?"

"I…I'd…I'd be honored. Do I have to wear a dress?"

BB grinned. "No. I mean, it's a wedding, but you can wear what you're comfortable in. No one sent out 'formal attire only' on the invitations." Mitzy in a dress? It didn't register.

"I didn't get an invitation." She sounded miffed.

"I'm asking you now. And I'll send you one if you come with me." BB shuffled his feet on the landing.

"Sure. I like hanging around your crowd. They're weird but cool, you know?"

"Tell me about it. I live with them." BB saw Micah walking up the sidewalk with Mialma. "I should get off. Dad is on his way home. He's gonna want to know if my chores are done."

"Are they?"

"Most of them." He chuckled. "Don't tell him. I'll talk to you later, Mitzy."

"Bye."

BB slid his phone into his pocket and straightened to walk alongside his dad and the aging Labrador the last few feet. "How'd the walk go?"

"She's slowing down. I think her hips are bothering her."

BB frowned. "That's not good."

"No. But if we take care of her, she'll be fine." Mick asked, "Chores done?"

BB grinned. "Yes, Dad. Most of them. I still have the vacuuming to do."

"Good enough." Mick looked at his phone. "Ben should be getting home soon. This will be his last summer session in private school. End of this month, he'll start 'regular' school with kids his own age."

Was his dad still worrying about the decision to move Ben to public school? Ben was ready. More than ready. All the special education he'd had the last few years had prepared BB's little brother for this. Mick had nothing to worry about.

Of course, BB delayed starting college until the spring semester so Ben wouldn't have two shocks to his system at the same time. Starting public school and losing BB. But that didn't mean BB worried about his brother. No. Not at all. BB needed the extra time, that's all. Had nothing to do with protecting Ben. Nothing.

Mick asked, "What should we do for dinner? And don't say 'pizza.' Ben always votes for pizza."

BB thought a moment. "How about pork chops?"

Mick pointed to his son. "Great idea. You cooking?"

BB chuckled. "I knew you were going to ask."

"Hey, you're going off to college. You need survival skills. Cooking is one of them. And it impresses women."

"I'll remember." It's all about the women right now, isn't it, Dad?

The school van turned the corner and stopped at the curb. Ben climbed down the steps, ruffled Mialma's fur, and raced home with the dog. BB shrugged. "I know where we rank."

"Got that right." Mick and BB walked to the house.

* * *

TUESDAY NIGHT

Wedding planners were the worst. They designed their whole business around selling lies. "Magical moments." "Greatest day of your lives." "Romance." All fabrications designed to steal money from unsuspecting dreamers.

The arsonist had to be strategic. Most of the agency's client information would be stored on the company server. No one should be able to recreate the records once the vital job had been done. No, the server and all its precious plans and contingencies and "to do" and "done" records must be destroyed. Special care would be required. Of course, if the registry of weddings could be downloaded before the server was destroyed, individual weddings could be attacked. More opportunities to free couples from their illusion of happiness.

The arsonist worked quickly and efficiently. The computers were targeted and efficiently stripped of their information. The conflagration could be started.

Flames erupted in the building. Smoke detectors broadcast frantically. Alarms tripped at the nearest call center. But nothing would stop the conflagration. Black powder fireworks fed the blaze and created havoc for responding units. Unable to approach, the fire department was reduced to preventing the inferno from spreading to other buildings. The arsonist watched in visceral awe. The work proved a thing of beauty. And freedom would win the day once again.

* * *

WEDNESDAY

Micah read on his phone the description of the warehouse fire. The stakes were getting higher. From individual shops to a warehouse supplying hundreds? What did the arsonist want? What could go through the mind of a mad person? Weddings would be delayed but stopped? Or did it go deeper than weddings? Marriages? Marriage? Happiness? Joy? What did the arsonist hope to prevent?

All questions with no answers. Except someone needed to find out. And soon.

Micah shared his introspections with Tav over a chess game. They sat in Micah's living room at the small coffee table.

Tav admitted, "I've tried to think about what the arsonist is doing. And I'm coming up with nothing. I don't know how you stop someone when you don't know what they want. Or don't want."

"What do you think will get hit next?"

"Hopefully, nothing, and the police will catch this person. Or persons."

"You think there's more than one?" Micah moved his knight out of harm's way.

Tav shrugged. "The warehouse had to be a big

operation. For someone to get in and out without being spotted, without any camera footage at all, says whoever it is is very organized. A group would make more sense." He moved his bishop to challenge the knight.

"Don't groups like this usually leave a manifesto or something? A note saying why they're doing what they are?" Again, Micah moved his knight.

Tav continued to press his advantage. He captured Micah's pawn, putting Micah's king in check. "You'd think. If they wanted to be known somehow. Get their fifteen minutes of fame."

The front door opened. Wendy's voice asked, "Is it okay to come in?"

Micah and Tav looked up from the chess board and answered in unison, "Yes."

Wendy scowled. "Why isn't the alarm working?"

Micah smiled at Wendy. "It's working. I turned it off. I'm home. I'm fine. Mialma likes it off. What can I do for you?" He shoved the chessboard away. "I was losing anyhow." As usual. He stood and kissed her on the cheek.

"Are you up for going out tonight?" Wendy chewed a hangnail.

Micah asked, "What is tonight? BB has a Bible study with the church youth group. I have to be home."

"Fran at the bakery called. She felt bad about canceling on us."

Micah added, "Twice." Let her feel bad. It didn't help.

Wendy conceded, "Twice. She wants to make up for it by having us come in tonight after hours. She'll do the tasting on her own time."

Micah shook his head, his lips in a straight line. "No good. I told BB I'd be here."

Wendy sighed. "I know, but it's getting late for them to schedule. They have to have the selections two months in advance. If we don't go tonight, we'll have to find another baker. One who won't mind cutting it fine." She laid her hand on his shoulder. "Please?"

Tav raised a finger. "Do all four of us have to go?"

Micah sniffed. "I don't care who orders the cake as long as I get chocolate."

Wendy patted his shoulder. "Yes, dear. You will get your chocolate layer."

He acted hurt. "Not everyone likes vanilla, you know. There should be alternatives." It wasn't the only reason, but he would give them nothing more at present.

"I understand." She chewed the inside of her cheek and addressed Tav. "I would trust you and Jen to make the decisions for both cakes. As long as we have two cakes. I don't like the idea of one giant cake. It's too risky."

Tav nodded. "Agreed. But I thought more of you and Mick going and Jen and I staying here. Jen can stay with Arlene unless Jen wants the night off, and my brothers and I will take care of Ben. He could come to our place. It's been a while since he's had a 'hang out with the guys' night. And we could video the meeting. Do it over the phone, and Jen can make whatever changes need to be made."

Wendy relaxed only a little. "If the shop will allow it."

"If they want our business, they will. I can't see what the problem would be. You'll be able to taste everything and handle any fine details that won't translate over the phone. Jen can veto anything she doesn't like."

Micah assented. "Sounds like a good plan." He picked up Wendy's hand. "What do you say? You in?"

"I'll talk to Jen. We need to be at the bakery at seven-thirty."

"And request the chocolate. And make sure it's not dry, either. I'd rather have moist—"

"No one is going to allow a dry cake, Mick. Relax."

Micah grinned. "I want my cake and to eat it, too."

Wendy threw a pillow at him. A small one. And she missed.

* * *

At seven-thirty, Micah and Wendy were at the shop looking at representations of wedding cakes. The bakery itself stayed dark. Lights off, closed for the day. Only the kitchen, not visible from the street, had lights on. Wendy explained what they wanted. "Understated elegance."

The representative, Fran, asked, "Do you want a fountain? Ladders? Pillars between the tiers?"

Wendy barked, "No. Just two cakes. Understated. No phoophaw. Four layers each. Fourteen, ten, six, and a four-inch reserved at the top. So we have two hundred and fifty servings. Plenty of cake for everyone."

Fran smiled. "You've done your homework."

"Yes, I have. We have. And we want a chocolate layer." She sat back and gave Micah a tight-lipped smile.

Micah patted her hand. "It's fine, Wendy. It'll all work out. Be cool."

Fran's eyes widened. "You want a chocolate layer? Chocolate frosting?"

Micah could see her reassessing everything she'd already planned. He assured her. "White frosting is fine. But chocolate cake."

"Do you want a chocolate layer for each cake? Which layer?"

Micah looked to Wendy. "Maybe the ten-inch layer? And both cakes."

Wendy nodded. "Right."

"With what fillings?" The woman moved on smoothly to the next issue at hand.

"Your suggestion would be?" Micah deferred to the expert.

"Raspberry for the chocolate. Possibly a lemon chiffon for the rest of the layers. Unless you want to do multiple flavors."

Wendy eyed Jen. "What do you think—"

Glass shattered. Micah grabbed Wendy and shoved her

to the floor. A Hummer smashed through the walls of the darkened bakery. Bricks flew, and metal twisted. Fran screamed as the vehicle accelerated and continued through the building, crushing and destroying everything in its wake. It tore out the oven on its way out the far wall. The wheels screeched, rose on one side, then slammed down. The driver gunned the engine and motored down the street, disappearing around the corner.

Jen's voice screamed over the phone, "Wendy!"

Tav yelled, "Mick! Someone talk to me. What's going on?"

Bricks from the remaining walls crashed down on top of Micah. He couldn't answer. He flung debris to the side, digging Wendy out. His fiancée lay groaning under a countertop. Micah wedged it off her. "Are you okay? What's wrong? Where are you hurt?"

Wendy grabbed at her foot. "My ankle. I think it's broken." She pushed him off. "Find Fran." She leaned against the wreckage. "And tell Jen to shut up."

Micah realized the group was still connected over the video call. Jen's shaky voice came back, "I heard you. What happened? We lost the video."

Micah left the two women to fight it out. He shoveled through the rubble to reach Fran's still body. He leaned next to the baker and checked for breathing.

None. He laid his hand on her carotid artery.

Nothing. He slipped back on his haunches and sighed, "Father. Give her family peace." Anger burned in him. "And her killer justice. I know, mercy and grace. I'm not looking to mete out punishment. But stop this madness, please."

Wendy called out, her voice trembling, "Mick, did you locate Fran? Is she okay?"

He slid back beside Wendy. He cleared his throat. "No. Yes, I found her. She didn't make it."

Wendy stared at the floor. "Now it's murder."

Micah nodded. "Now it's murder."

Sirens wailed in the background. Tav demanded, "Tell me what's going on, Mick. Are you hurt?"

"No." He felt nothing.

"Yes." Wendy corrected his statement. "Your head is bleeding. So is your arm. You got cut." She applied her palm to his head and held it over the cut.

Tav said sharply, "I'm on my way."

"No," Micah snapped back. "The police and fire are coming. You'll only be in the way."

Quinn's voice came over the phone. "I'll be with you in half an hour."

Micah had only one answer. "Yes, sir." He leaned next to Wendy, put his uninjured arm around her shoulders, and laid his head on hers. The only thing remaining was the waiting.

* * *

It took two hours before the trio returned from the remains of the bakery. Micah was bandaged on his head and arm. Wendy had a wrap on her ankle and crutches to help her walk. Both sported bruises and cuts from flying glass. Quinn wore a grim expression as he stalked into the house. He took a seat at the kitchen table, looking at the living room. The assembled Knights waited for the report.

Tav filled in what they knew. "We saw the local news. One fatality and no clue as to who might have been involved." He added, "We saw you on the screen, Quinn. In the background."

Quinn growled. "Junior reporter. Looking for something to fill the airtime. Wanted to know if I knew the people inside. Guess he heard me say I'd come to pick up Mick and Wendy. I gave the police their names, and he made the assumption we were related.

"The bakery owner was killed. Mick and Wendy avoided being hit by the grace of God alone. This is personal now. Someone must have known you would have a tasting this evening. Otherwise, why not hit the bakery before it opened when no one's around? This is about weddings. Most likely, someone left standing at the altar. I'm going to put my team on researching jilted brides or grooms."

Jen shook her head. "How do you plan to find them?"

"Social media. Stories abound about weddings gone awry. We'll see what we can find." Quinn glared at the plastic over the front window.

"Do you think this is directed at us? Or were we simply the unlucky ones?" Wendy settled on the couch with the ottoman under her foot.

Quinn shrugged. "Not enough info yet to know. We're still digging."

Tav frowned. "I don't care why. I care who. What can we do to catch this guy? Or girl."

Quinn frowned. "Odds are it's a woman." He smiled a tight-lipped smile at Wendy and Jen. "Weddings are all about the bride. If someone got left at the altar, it's most likely the bride. And she would be more inclined to revenge."

"Your statement's a bit sexist, don't you think?" Wendy huffed. She nailed the mentor with a menacing glare.

"It's statistics. Take it up with the numbers." Quinn remained non-plussed.

"Well, the statistics say more women than men end relationships. Which should include at the altar." Wendy would not be gainsaid.

Micah decided to de-escalate the almost-fight. "What do we do now?" He settled deeper into the couch next to Wendy.

Quinn suggested, "Everyone go home. We'll meet for breakfast."

Micah tapped knuckles with Tav. "Thanks for taking care of Ben for me."

"Yeah, next time, I'll go." Tav pursed his lips and lifted his eyebrows.

"Next time." Micah huffed.

Wendy glanced at her sister. "We'll have to start calling tomorrow…" She trailed off and burst into tears. "What am I saying? We were nearly killed, and I'm worrying about a cake?"

Micah hugged her and kissed her head. "You're stressing and not thinking. You need a good night's sleep. Go home. Rest. Take tomorrow off."

Quinn glared at Micah. "I was going to say that. Since I'm the boss, I will make it official. Wendy, take the day off. Take the rest of the week off. You need to get your head together."

Wendy sniffled but stood defiant. "Thanks, Boss. I'll be okay."

"After the week off, you will. Go home." His stare brooked no arguments.

Everyone dispersed. Micah walked Quinn to the door. He touched the man's shoulder and kept his tone low. "You think the glass perp has forgotten about me?"

"Maybe not forgotten. But moved on. I don't think it's the same person. Why warn you, then try to kill you? It doesn't make sense."

Micah considered it. "Right."

"Don't suppose you remember what ranking your bakery had, do you?"

"I think it might have been top five." He grimaced. "We finally got in the game. Bad game to be in."

Quinn patted his shoulder. "Hang in there, Mick. We'll figure it out."

"Right. Night, Quinn."

Quinn left. Micah closed the door and turned to look at his sons. "Everyone hit the hay. We're done for tonight."

No one objected. Only after Micah climbed into bed did he remember to pray. He got back out of bed and hit his knees. "Father, thank You for protecting Wendy and me. Be with Fran's family and friends. And Father, please help the authorities catch this person before anyone else is hurt. In Your Name, amen."

* * *

47

WEDNESDAY NIGHT

SMASH!

The arsonist slashed across the countertop of glassware, shattering everything. Chemicals spilled to the floor, splashing and sizzling. Smoke and rage filled the room. Bellows of "NO!" echoed from wall to wall in the unoccupied garage.

How? How had it happened? No one should ever have been hurt. Never. The plan had been explicit. From the beginning, no one would be injured. Vandalism. Property damage. Nothing the police would make a priority. Kid stuff. The authorities had more significant cases to worry about. Cases where people were hurt. Or killed.

Now…now, the arsonist would be public enemy number one.

The shop was supposed to be empty. No one should have been there. The hours were carefully verified. Closed at seven p.m. Even given half an hour to clear out, there still should have been no one at the bakery.

News reports on the television were calling it murder. Death incurred while in the commission of a felony got you a murder charge. All the careful planning. All the meticulous calculations. Ruined. Destroyed.

Along with the arsonist's life.

At least no one got a look at the arsonist. Not one they were reporting, anyhow. The arsonist would not go down alone. If murderer was the new title, let it be well-earned. Plans began to materialize. Revenge would be had. And it would be sweet. In the meantime, work still needed to be done. And the arsonist knew just where to hit next. But first, a call had to be made.

* * *

THURSDAY MORNING

Micah's business phone rang. *Restricted.* Not uncommon for some of his clients. He picked it up. "Andres Accounting."

A voice seethed, "Why were you there? At the bakery. It should have been empty."

Micah looked at the phone. "Excuse me?"

The voice continued to rage. "No one was supposed to be hurt, ever. The shop had closed. You made me a murderer. I'll kill you for what you did to me." The call disconnected.

Micah's eyes lost focus. What? He shook himself to restore functioning in his brain. And immediately dialed 911. "I want to report a threat. And a possible lead to the bakery store crash last night."

He paused. "I'll hold."

And he moved to activate the alarm system.

* * *

Wendy, Jen, their maids of honor, and their bridesmaids all video-chatted. Wendy and Jen sat in their kitchen. Mom read in the living room. A murder-mystery. She loved them. The girls had the door partially closed to keep Mom from hearing the conversation. No sense in upsetting her by rehashing the event.

Wendy listened to Caron and Sami voicing their indignation at the events last night. Sami exploded, "You were nearly killed! Over a cake!"

Jen's ladies-in-waiting were not left out, either. Minnie waved her hands. "How can you be so calm?" Lasha murmured in agreement. The young woman's face sported a shade of anger Wendy had rarely seen.

Jen kept her tone even. "We have Mom to think about. We don't need her upset more than she is. The more we relive it, the greater the chance she'll go over the edge. So let it go. And tell us you found another bakery."

Sami looked at her notes. "From what I can tell, no professional shop wants to do business with our party. Not after the murder. We're bad news."

Caron agreed. "It's like suddenly we're responsible for all the vandalism in town."

Jen sighed. "I know. I know. I get the same feeling. We'll have to find someone who doesn't work for a shop. Put out feelers to everyone we know. I'll ask at church."

Wendy agreed. "Right. I'll do the same. You four get busy and see what you can find. Someone has to make cakes. Possibly in their home. And would be willing to work for us."

The women signed off. Wendy offered with more conviction than she felt, "We'll find someone." She snorted. "Or we'll do it on our own. We might not have towers, but we would have cake." She took a sip of her power drink. Combined with the pain meds, she managed to keep going. Except everything in her wanted to crawl in bed, pull the covers over her head, and bawl her eyes out. It wouldn't help, but it might release some of the emotions.

Jen cackled. "Oh, that'd be fun." She stopped. "It would be fun." Excitement filled her tone. "We're not helpless. We can bake a cake. How hard can it be?"

Wendy stared hard at her sister. "You're serious?"

"Yeah. We can do some of those online decorating

classes. We didn't want fancy stuff anyhow. If we can't find anyone, let's do our own." Jen's eyes sparkled.

Wendy let the idea rattle around in her head. "We might be able to do it."

"First, we need to learn to make buttercream icing." Jen grew sober.

Wendy waved her hand. "Making the icing is no problem. Getting it smooth with no bubbles? That's the trick." She visualized cakes past. Not pretty. Edible but not pretty.

"So, we'll go shopping for the equipment, and we'll see who has the creative eye." Jen sneered at her sister.

"And the steady hand." Wendy scoffed. "What do you think Mick and Tav will think?"

"As long as Mick gets his chocolate, I don't think they'll care. Just one less worry." Jen searched the internet for the hours and location of the shops with the broadest selection of cake decorating tools.

Wendy lowered her head and shook it. "I hope we know what we're doing."

"We're going to find out. Come on. It'll be our contribution to the wedding." Jen patted her shoulder. "Our personal touch. Everything else is preprogrammed and designed. This will be all us."

Wendy derided. "It certainly will be."

"Should we tell the boys?" Jen stopped her internet search and looked at her sister.

"Let's take the classes first, then tell them. We'll only say we've got it covered."

"Are we telling the whole truth?" Jen's eyebrows raised.

Wendy shrugged. "Yes. Maybe. One way or another, we'll have cake. Even if it's flat. Tav loves your baking. Maybe we don't get the fancy filling. But we still have cake."

Jen held out her fist. Wendy fist-bumped her sister. "Done." She looked at the time. "I'm going to call Mick.

He's ignoring work to spend time with the boys today. I want to see what he's planning on doing, and then I'll leave him alone for his 'male bonding time.' I'm sure Ben will appreciate it."

She punched in his number and waited. And waited. It went to voicemail. "Can't answer now. Leave a message."

She shrugged. "Me. Love you." She hung up. "Okay, that was a bust. You think Mom is up for a game of Rummikub?"

"We'll try it. She likes to play. I think she can still match the colors and numbers. She may have trouble with the gold and orange."

Wendy dipped her head. Her heart hurt. Mom was disappearing. But there were flashes of her personality. The wedding was still four months away. Would Mom make it 'til then? And be able to appreciate seeing her daughters get married? What had Micah said?

Wendy chewed her lip. "Jen…what would you think about moving this wedding?"

"You're worried about Mom, right? I see her slipping, too." Jen gazed in the direction of the living room.

"Why can't we just have a small ceremony, get married, then have the large one later? Since the invitations are all out for later. We can have an intimate wedding, and Mom would see us and know us."

Jen tapped her fingers on the desk. "We have a problem with the dresses. They aren't here yet and won't be for another two months."

"So, we buy some off the rack for the one now, and we have the special ones for later. At least the attendees' dresses are ready and have been delivered. One less thing to stress about."

"Who do we invite to this small gathering?" Jen sounded almost in favor of the idea. Almost.

Mick called it eloping. Maybe they wouldn't run away, but it would be close. "It would be the Knights and our ladies. We can still have everyone stand in. The guys can rent the tuxes early, and we can have them and their plus-ones. All the long-distance relatives and friends and coworkers can come to the big party."

Jen seemed hesitant. "Let me think about it. We probably should ask the guys. They might have something to say about it."

Wendy sneered. "We could call a meeting and put it to a vote."

Jen shook her head. "I think this should be between the boys and us. We can fight with the Knights for the right date like we did before. But a pre-wedding wedding should be for the four of us to decide."

Wendy grinned. "I'm being sarcastic. It was just a thought."

Jen texted Tav. *Need to talk about moving the wedding. Call me.* She nodded to her sister. "Let's go see what Mom is doing."

"Right. We've left her alone long enough."

They walked to the living room. Jen walked. Wendy limped. She refused to use the crutches. The X-rays said hairline fracture. The wrap was good enough. No crutches. Too restricting.

Mom's chair was empty. The front door was closed. Wendy searched the bedroom while Jen took the bathroom. Nothing. No sign of her in the house.

Jen jerked open the back door to look at the patio.

Still nothing.

Wendy hobbled out the front door. "Mom!" Tears choked her cry.

* * *

THURSDAY AFTERNOON

Micah mowed the grass. Tav weed-whacked the fence line. Lots of yard work to be done. When you have eight houses all backed around one open space, the landscaping requires constant attention. Ben labored in the backyard, blowing leaves from the bushes across the way to the houses on the north of the quadrangle. Quinn blew them back.

Ben came behind his dad and fumed. "Dad! Pop-dad is cheat-ing. He is blow-ing his leaves to our side of the yard."

Quinn yelled across the field, "Just sending them back to you, Ben."

Ben lowered his leaf blower. "Can he do that?"

Micah laughed. "Well, he's doing it. But so are you. You'll have to see who has the bigger blower."

Ben stuck out his lower lip. "Pop-dad does." He looked at Micah, a wistful look in his eyes. "Can we buy a big-ger one?"

Micah grinned and shook his head. "No, we can't. But maybe the two of you can blow the leaves in the same direction into one pile. Try negotiating instead of fighting."

Ben continued to pout. "But I like to blow the leaves across the field. It is fun."

Micah put a hand on Ben's shoulder. "Maybe not for the

guys on the other side of the field. They have to rake them." He squeezed Ben's shoulder. "You'll have to work it out with Pop-dad."

Ben glared across the backyard. "I will." He picked up his leaf blower and marched across the quadrangle to challenge a grinning Pop-dad. Micah smiled.

At that moment, his attention jumped from his task to a moving flash. A white puffball raced down the street and attacked his feet. The man turned off his mower for safety's sake, reached down, and corralled the barking puppy. He looked up the street to see Carly walking with Arlene Smothers. The women held arms. Both were talking and smiling.

Micah's heart jumped. What was Arlene doing out with Carly? Did Wendy and Jen know? He stuffed the pup under one arm and jogged up the street to intercept the two women.

Arlene cocked her head and looked at Micah. "Micah. I met a new friend."

Micah smiled carefully. "I see."

Carly assured him, "I saw Mrs. Smothers walking down Cherry. I asked her if I could join her in her walk." She held his eyes in understanding.

Arlene pointed to the sky. "I wanted to feel the sun on my face. I went out on the porch, but the shade trees were in the way. So, I walked down to the sidewalk and followed the sun where it shone the most."

Carly kept her voice light. "And then I met you about five blocks from here. You told me you lived in the quad." She raised her eyebrows at Micah. "I remembered the place from my last walks this way. But I had to have Mrs. Smothers show me exactly which house she lived in."

"I told you. On the corner, dear." Arlene looked at the area and laughed. "Oh, I see. It's all corners. That makes it more difficult." She looked from house to house, her face unsure.

Micah kept his tone gentle. "You live in this one." He

pointed to her home. "I'm sure Wendy and Jen are very concerned about you."

Arlene's face went blank for a moment. "Wendy and Jen?" Then she lifted her head. "Of course. My daughters."

Wendy burst from the house, yelling, "Mom!"

Arlene waved her hand. "I'm right here, Wendy. No need to shout."

Wendy joined Carly and Micah. Tav laid down his weed whacker and came to join the group. Jen raced from the house and made it a sextet. Wendy took her mom's hand. Micah watched his fiancée choose her words and emotions carefully. "Mom, Jen and I were very worried when we couldn't find you in the house. You were reading in the living room when we walked into the kitchen."

"Yes, but I wanted to go onto the porch for a bit. I know you girls are busy, so I didn't want to bother you. I went out to get some sunshine."

Jen swallowed hard. "I know how much you love the sun, Mom. It's never a bother for you to tell us what you want to do." She shifted from foot to foot.

Carly took Roger, the pup, from Micah and caught Wendy's eyes. "I'm Carly Jenkins. I live over a couple blocks. I'm a licensed"—she tipped her head to the side—"bonded caregiver. I met your mom a few streets over."

Wendy caught her lip between her teeth. She nodded. "I appreciate you bringing her back." Micah watched Wendy's eyes as she studied Carly.

Jen took her mom's arm. "Why don't we go on the porch? You can tell me what all you saw on your walk."

Arlene gave Carly a hug. "You must come over and see me, please? It's so nice to have someone to talk to. My daughters are very busy planning their wedding. It would be delightful to have someone who hasn't heard all my stories for the umpteenth time."

Wendy's eyes filled with moisture. She choked, "We never get tired of hearing your stories."

Arlene patted Wendy's arm. "I know you don't, Wendy. I love you." She turned and walked with Jen back to the house and onto the porch.

Wendy addressed Carly. "I don't want you to think we let Mom wander the streets. We're taking good care of her." Heat tinged her voice.

Carly held up her hand. "I understand. Like a toddler, it only takes a moment for them to get into something…or out of something." She pursed her lips, then continued, "And you can't lock her in the house." She hesitated and added, "Your mom has interesting tales to tell, I'm sure. I would love to come and sit with her on the porch and listen. You can do background checks on me. I'm not a stalker." She looked at Micah and back at Wendy. "I'm new in the area and looking to get established in the care field here. I have references. I can work as many hours as you need." She smiled. "Your mom will know me as the neighbor who comes by to hear her stories."

Wendy looked from Micah to Carly back to Micah. He shrugged, then agreed. "After the background check, I think it would be a good idea. It might give you and Jen a little break from being caregivers and let you be daughters again."

Carly shifted Roger from her right hip to her left and held out her hand. "What do you say?"

Wendy glanced at the house. "I'd have to check with Jen." She shook Carly's hand.

Carly tipped her head. "Are you two twins? You look awfully close in age."

Wendy laughed. "No. We were adopted at about the same time and the same age. Jen is older by a few months."

"I see. Who's getting married? Your mom mentioned you two were planning a wedding."

Wendy sighed. "Trying to plan. We're both getting married." She pointed to Micah. "I'm marrying this guy, and"—she pointed to Tav—"he's marrying my sister. It's a double wedding."

Carly grinned. "I see your problem. Everything is twice as hard. I don't envy you."

Wendy groused, "Me, either." She pulled out her phone. "Give me your contact info. I'll text you if Jen says we're good."

Carly smiled wide. "That will be great. I work independently and set my own hours, so I'm mostly always available." She looked at Micah. "My first neighbor." Her eyes sparkled.

* * *

Wendy and Jen met with Mick and Tav on the back porch. Mom sat beside them, reading her book. The air cooled as the sun went behind the trees. Wendy opened the conversation.

"Jen and I discussed it, and we want to move the wedding up."

Mick's eyes sparked with excitement. Wendy waved him down. "We're not talking about eloping. Get it out of your head."

He grinned at her and settled back in his lawn chair.

Jen picked up the narrative. "Because of certain…developments…we think it best we don't wait four months. We think eight weeks would be a better time frame. We'll do a small intimate wedding with just the Knights and their plus-ones. Then we can have a large wedding for the friends and relations later, in November like we planned."

Tav leaned forward to stare at her. "Are you sure? Will you have time enough to do this the way you want?"

Wendy corrected him. "The way *we* want. This is for the four of us."

Tav corrected himself but qualified it. "We want. But it's easy for Mick and me. We get suits and show up."

Jen scowled. "This is *our* wedding. All four of us. You two have as much input as we do."

Wendy added, "And if we move the date up, we'll need

you two to do more than 'show up.' We'll give you responsibility for different tasks."

Mick lifted his eyebrows. "Which is fair and right. But let me ask you this. Are you going to give us a task and let us do it to the best of our ability and judgment, or are you going to look over our shoulders and tell us how you want it done?" He held her eyes in challenge.

Mick being forceful? Wendy sat back. Scary thought.

It shouldn't be. She either trusted them or she didn't.

Well…she trusted them to complete the task. But to her aesthetic? Could she live with stripes and spots? Floral prints? This would be a once-in-a-lifetime day…

It would be half a day. Four hours in a lifetime of marriage. If the marriage lived or died on the wedding ceremony, there shouldn't be a wedding. Much less a marriage.

All these thoughts crossed Wendy's mind in a matter of moments. She looked at her sister. Jen looked back. She stuck her fist into the circle between them. Wendy did the same. The men followed suit. Wendy silently counted to four, then lifted her thumb. So did all the others.

Mick sat back and asked, "What did we just vote on? You watching over us? Or letting us do it on our own?"

Tav chuckled. "Vote's been taken. You're on the hook no matter what it is."

"I know. I'm wondering, that's all."

This was the Mick she knew and loved. Wendy tapped him with her foot. "You're free to figure things out. We'll tell you what the task is, and you get to execute it. I trust you." She smiled. "For the small wedding. The large one will be under closer scrutiny."

He leaned over and kissed her on the cheek. "I love you, Wenders."

She kissed him back. "Love you, Mick." She sat back in her chair. A slight breeze picked up, cooling the air even further.

Jen cleared her throat. "Trust applies to you two. The brothers get explicit directions."

Tav laughed. "Good thinking. I think Luke and Addison will be fine. Addison has a definite skill at coordinating colors." He picked up Jen's hand. "Do you have a list of projects to be done?"

"Not yet. We were working through our wedding planner book and were still at the four-month stage. Now I don't know what will have to happen."

"Let us know when you do. We'll get to work." Tav's smile reassured Wendy. "We'll get this done, ladies. And in style. You'll see."

We certainly will. But whose style? Wendy cast off the worrying thought. And sat back to enjoy the sunset.

* * *

SATURDAY

Two days later, Micah stood out front throwing hoops when he saw Luke pull up with Tav in the car. Micah waved at the Vaughn brothers. Luke motioned to his brother and called, "Tav wants to try on and reserve the tuxes. We're all free tonight."

Micah walked over to join them. "Works for me. What about Addison?"

"Tav thought just the grooms and best men right now. The others can go when we decide what we're wearing."

"Quinn?"

"We need him to come, yeah. But he's your problem."

Micah grinned. So he had to convince the boss to go tonight. He could give Quinn a choice. Quinn could wear the tux or wear his military dress uniform. Which would endanger Micah's life for mentioning, but hey…Wendy was worth it. Micah had seen Quinn and Grace's wedding pictures taken on the beach in Hawaii. They'd eloped. Smart. Very smart. Still, it wasn't too late, was it?

Except they practically were. Eight weeks would fly by. Ready or not.

Micah thought a moment. "Are Jen and Wendy coming tonight?"

"It's a guy's night. Girls aren't invited." Luke grinned.

Tav disappeared into the house. Luke leaned against the car.

Micah raised his eyebrows. "So, they have no say in what's chosen?"

"Nope."

Micah patted Luke on the back. Tonight was looking up. Micah went in search of BB to tell him the plan.

He found his son deep in conversation with Mitzy. Micah waited until BB disconnected the call. "We're going for tuxes, and we have to convince the boss to come."

BB offered, "You want me to talk to Quinn?"

"Sure. He won't tell you no. Can't turn down his grandkid."

BB chuckled. "Then have Ben ask. Quinn'll never say no."

"Truth."

BB went anyhow. And Quinn agreed to go with them, if only "to keep you boys out of trouble and make you take this seriously. No messing around."

BB relayed Quinn's directive to Micah and sighed. "So, no purple tuxes."

Micah laughed. "No pinstripes, either. We'll be fine." He paused. "We'll take Ben with us. I know the fittings are for grooms and best men, but Ben won't cause a problem. I hate him being left out of things."

BB shrugged. "I don't see a problem. He doesn't take much room. He'll be fine. I don't know anyone who's going to object."

"Good. I'm going to go tell Ben, we'll both get cleaned, and we'll see you in a bit."

BB raised his fist and tapped knuckles with his dad.

* * *

At six-fifteen, Micah found BB on the phone. Micah eyed him sideways. BB mouthed, "Mitzy."

Micah shook his head and tapped his wrist as if tapping a watch. BB nodded. Micah moved off to find Ben. His youngest sat at the table sketching faces. Micah picked up a drawing of Quinn and studied it. He laid it down. "Is that how Quinn looks to you? Always frowning? Why do you think he looks so serious?"

Ben put away his sketch pad. "He has a mon-ster who fol-lows him a-round. That is why he is se-ri-ous all the time."

"You think we can help him get rid of the monster?" Micah didn't know what monster Quinn had. Maybe his job? Could it be what Ben saw?

"He has to give it a-way." Ben signed the picture as he always did. He placed the drawing in his portfolio.

"Then someone else will have the monster?" Hmm. Sounded ominous.

Ben dropped his chin once. "Yes." The charcoal pencils were positioned with extreme care, points up, in their own case. Meticulous. Everything where it needed to be.

Micah put his arm around Ben's shoulders. "Come on, Ben. We're going to go make the girls happy."

"It is good when Wen-dy is hap-py."

"Yes. Yes, it is."

* * *

The reservation said seven p.m. for six men. The concierge welcomed them at the door. Quinn made the introductions. "We have four ushers and a groomsman who will come in for a fitting later. These clowns are the best men." Quinn pointed out BB and Luke. The mentor took Micah and Tav by the arms. "These are the grooms." He pointed to Ben. "He's a very important groomsman." Ben preened a little.

Micah read the man's name off his tag. "Brooks. We appreciate your help."

Brooks glanced from man to man. "Two grooms?"

Tav nodded. "Two brides. Works out well that way." He shifted his weight from foot to foot.

The man smiled. "Ah, a double wedding. How exciting."

Micah kept his comments to himself. The less said, the less painful the evening would be. Brooks asked, "And when is the wedding?"

Tave looked at his phone. "Seven weeks."

Brooks's head jerked. "Sir, you can't expect—"

Tav waved him down. "What we expect is to rent something basic for a private ceremony. We'll do the blowout wedding later. We have a deadline to meet."

Micah explained, "The brides' mother is losing her battle with Alzheimer's. We want something she can participate in and remember."

Brooks nodded. "I see. Very commendable. Let's see what we can do for you. I'll call around to other shops if I need to."

The man opened the door to the showroom. "Come in here, gentlemen." As they passed through into the inner sanctum, Brooks asked Quinn, "And what is your role?"

Quinn quipped, "Zookeeper." Brooks snickered. Quinn added, "I'm standing in as father of the brides."

"But you're not?" The man cocked his head.

"It's complicated. All the relationships are complicated." He pointed to Micah. "He's marrying this man's sister." Quinn indicated Tav. Brooks nodded. Quinn continued, pointing to Tav. "He's marrying Micah's bride's sister. Who isn't his sister."

Brooks lifted his head. "I don't see. Adoption?"

"Lots of it. Leave it there. I try to." Quinn gave Brooks a sardonic smile.

Brooks's eyes crinkled. "Wise counsel. Okay. Let's see what we can do."

After an hour of looking and trying, the group settled on classic black tuxedos with two-button jackets, a vest, pinch lapels, and satin stripes down the pants. Classic lines and available in every size. The group voted. Five thumbs up.

Quinn abstained. Shoes were left to the individual to provide. Black. No tennis shoes. Then again…

Tav suggested, "It would be original. Black tennis shoes."

Micah put a thumb up. "I'm in."

Quinn glared at the two. "No."

Micah sagged. "But they'd be comfortable."

"No."

Tav demanded, "Vote."

Quinn raised his eyebrows. "No. End of subject."

Micah looked at Luke for support. Luke shook his head. "The zookeeper has spoken. We wear dress shoes."

Micah scowled. Tav pouted. But Quinn smiled. "I promised I'd keep you two in line. I keep my word."

Micah grumbled, "Can't argue with that."

Tav added, "Wouldn't do any good if we did."

They finished their business. As the group left the establishment, Tav stated, "We're going to Lucy's for ice cream. No vote needed, right?"

Six thumbs went up anyhow. Voted and carried. Quinn drove the van to the south side of town for the best ice cream in the county. The party was lively. Well-behaved but lively. Micah called to see if Jen and Wendy wanted to join them. The ladies declined. Micah scowled as he turned to Tav. "They're busy at home. Practicing. I don't know what, but they're practicing."

Tav grinned. "Dance moves?"

Micah chuckled. "Better be me. I have no rhythm in my feet."

Tav snorted. "You have no rhythm any place else, either."

Micah scowled and made a fist. Tav did not look intimidated. Micah considered taking Tav to the ground in his best wrestling move, but with Quinn around, he thought better of it. Besides, they still had another Vaughn brother. Tangle with one, you tangle with the whole trailer park.

They ate ice cream, insulted each other, then headed home. They were a few blocks from home when Luke's SUV suddenly swerved to the left. Luke jerked the steering wheel, overcorrecting to the right. He swerved again and came to a stop under the burned-out street light. The one they had complained to the city about replacing. Months ago.

Luke breathed hard. "Blow out."

Everyone climbed out. Luke bent down to inspect the tire. He studied it for longer than necessary. He called Quinn to check the damage out.

Quinn looked, then straightened. "Everyone back in the van. Now." The sharpness in his voice meant business.

As Micah climbed in, he studied Luke. "What's the problem? What did you see?"

Luke settled into the driver's seat. "The rubber is bent in. Like something pierced it." He stared around the darkened area. "Like a gunshot."

The hair on the back of Micah's neck stood up. He, too, began scanning the area. Sniper? Kid with a dart gun? What?

In the dark, there would be no telling and less seeing. Luke started the engine and began rolling the injured SUV home. As they turned the corner, shots rang out. Quinn yelled, "Down! Everyone down!"

The windshield exploded. Glass shattered and fell inward. Five bodies slipped to the floor of the vehicle, using the seats for as much protection as they could offer. Luke bent over and steered the car away from home. He flipped around the block, shredding the tire. The shooting stopped. Luke dodged and ducked around the neighborhood and out of it until Quinn tapped his arm. "Switch."

No one rose from the floor. Quinn took over driving. Luke slid below the shotgun seat in hopes of staying out of the line of fire. Quinn circled the SUV through the darkened corner again. Nothing. He stopped.

Still nothing.

He waited.

Still nothing.

Quinn put it in gear and drove home.

Wendy and Jen came out to meet the group. Jen's eyes were wide and white as she grabbed the back door. Tav tumbled out first. She grabbed him and sobbed, "We heard gunshots."

Wendy circled Micah, BB, and Ben in a singular hug. Tears streamed down her cheeks. She didn't speak. She kissed Micah full on the mouth.

For once, Ben did not protest.

* * *

Another shelf of glassware met its demise. Shouts of, "Who? Who is after Andres? That's my job! Mine! I will kill him. No one else."

The arsonist kicked a box across the warehouse floor. Pummeled it. Smashed it into pieces. "I want him to see me when he dies. I want him to know I'm the one who ended his miserable existence the way he ended mine."

The black-robed figure made a phone call. "Who? Who is interfering? 'I don't know' isn't good enough. Find out. Now. Today."

The arsonist slammed the phone down in frustration. There were other targets to be annihilated. Other defenseless people to save. It was time to get back to work destroying illusions. Freedom called.

* * *

SATURDAY NIGHT

Quinn glared at the assembled Knights. They met in his home instead of Mick or Tav's. "Everyone. Phones in the box." Eight cell phones piled into a secure box. Quinn closed it and moved it to the bedroom. He came back and addressed the occupants of the room. "This isn't random. This is directed at you. I want to know everyone you've talked to in the last month. Especially about the wedding." Quinn glared at everyone in the circle. He tried to lower his anxiety threshold. But these were his kids. Self-adopted, but still his.

He pointed to Wendy, then Jen. "Starting with you two."

Wendy threw both hands in the air. "We've been working on the wedding for months. Who haven't we talked to?" She sat on the floor beside Micah. Jen sat on the couch with Tav.

Quinn shook his head hard. "Not good enough. Who outside your circle? What vendors wanted your business, but you went with a competitor?" He turned to the men. "Who did you tell about the fittings tonight?"

Mick stared at his shoes. "No one."

"No one." Tav echoed Mick.

BB admitted, "I told Kenmore." The teen glanced around the room as if looking for someone to condemn him.

Quinn let him off the hook. "Unless he had a reason to tell someone else, I think we can give him a pass. He owes you his life. I don't think he's forgotten."

BB relaxed. "We don't talk about it. I won't let him talk about it."

Quinn banged the table. "Think, people. Someone knew we were out last night and where we were going. The tire blow-out served as a diversion. You five were the prime targets. There has to be a connection."

Ben sat beside his father on the floor, silently staring at the carpet. Quinn debated having Mick leave him out of the discussion. But Ben's being in the van made him part of the possibilities. He needed to be included, even at the million-to-one chance this was about him.

Grace glanced at Quinn. "Bring me one of your whiteboards."

Quinn went to the back and returned with a whiteboard and markers. "What are we drawing?"

"Circles." Grace drew a circle with the Knights in the center. She began filling in the attacks and who they were directed at or impacted.

When she had finished, Quinn stared hard at the board. He added lines from the center to the incidents. No pattern developed. The dress shops, the event centers, and the floral warehouse remained outliers, unconnected to the Knights. Beyond being wedding connected.

Mick pointed to one of the circles. "How did I go from being uninvolved to being a prime target?"

Quinn pointed to the center of the circle. "It's your wedding." Mick gave Quinn a jaundiced eye. Quinn ignored it. The mentor wanted connections, no matter how tenuous.

Jen frowned. "Unless there are different perpetrators."

Wendy cocked her head. "Like the wedding crasher is different from the ones trying to kill the guys?"

Jen nodded. "Could be. Though why anyone would be after us remains a mystery."

BB asked, "All of us, or specific ones?" Good questions. Which needed answers Quinn didn't have. He paced a few more steps.

Grace drew her lines again. "Mick and Wendy were at the bakery."

"Which the perp thought was empty." Mick's tone carried heat as he added a pertinent fact.

"But they threatened you, so you're top on the list," Quinn reminded Mick.

Mick protested, "Six guys were in the car that got shot."

Quinn scowled. "And I'm discounting it being your boys, BB or Ben." He rubbed Ben's head. Ben looked up and smiled into Quinn's eyes. Quinn felt an unfamiliar tug at his emotions. *God, I love this boy. Protect him. Protect all of them.*

Tav shook his head. "I made a spontaneous decision to go out tonight. How could anyone know?"

Quinn shrugged. "Not hard. Phone tap. Listening to conversations over the phone. Spy. Shadow. A determined perp can find ways to accomplish their plans." Except who? And why?

Mick's eyes narrowed. "How do we catch them?" He stopped. "Wells Cathedral didn't get hit, true?"

"True. Either you scared the perps off, or the break-in wasn't about vandalism. Beyond the window."

Mick didn't buy it. "So, the window became the object of interest?" His tone spoke of his incredulity.

"Thieves come in all makes and models. Some artist needed a centerpiece. I don't know. But it seems like it's not part of the pattern."

"Pattern?" Wendy eyed the whiteboard.

Grace pointed to the circles. "Doesn't connect to anything else. It wasn't damaged beyond the window. And the perps were quick to keep you from getting involved. So yeah, it's not part of the pattern."

BB pointed to the board. "Okay, look. The wedding

gowns could be separate. The event venues could be connected to the wedding dresses. So could the bakery. But this last event had to be planned. We were the objectives. With Dad being head of the list. And Tav running second because it's their wedding."

Tav glowered but didn't respond.

Quinn gazed around the circle. "Any other discussion? Someone see something we haven't?"

No one raised a hand. Quinn tapped the table. "I propose we set a false trip and see what happens. Tav, Mick, as of now, you're going to visit Mercury Park on Wednesday. You're checking out the pavilion there to see if it would be suitable for a wedding. I'll have some of my operatives— excuse me, my people—at the location to see who shows. I want you to tell only those you would usually tell in the manner you would tell it." He stopped, then added, "Which will be by text, I know." He looked around at the assembled young people. "I want this to be as normal a few days as possible. We can't throw any more variables into this. Be smart, people."

Wendy objected. "But if we all talk, how will we know who the bad guys are?"

"This is to verify Tav and Mick are the targets. We'll narrow down the suspects after."

The crowd broke, retrieved their phones, and went to their respective houses. Nice thing about living in a quadrangle. No one had far to go.

Grace waited until Quinn saw the others out, then sat beside Quinn on the couch. She laid her head on his shoulder. "You really think their wedding is the target of all this?"

"No. I think it's deeper. We just can't see the connections yet. This park thing is a smoke screen for the boys and girls to think I'm doing something about all this."

"Aren't you?" Grace pulled away in surprise.

"Not as much as I would like, no. I've got a project at

work that will take my time." Quinn's voice darkened. His mood darkened as well.

Grace's eyes narrowed. "Away from family?" She laid her hand on his arm.

"Yes." Quinn left it there. And knew Grace would, too. They embraced.

Quinn picked up his ready bag from the living room closet. He rifled through the contents to make sure he had everything. He looked at Grace. "Keep them safe while I'm gone." He clasped her in his arms again. "Keep yourself safe."

"I will. You too. Don't get lost."

He kissed her long and hard. "I love you, Grace Magary."

She kissed him again. "I know."

Was it humor or tears in her eyes? Quinn slipped out the door. It closed behind him.

* * *

MONDAY

Late in the day, an unknown car pulled into the driveway. Micah studied the occupants from the recently replaced front window but didn't recognize the two figures. Wrong house? He walked to the porch to see if he could help.

A boy and a girl, both in their mid-to-late teens, stepped out of the car. They seemed hesitant. Micah watched them join forces, square their shoulders, and march up the walk.

He opened the door before they could knock. "Hi. Can I help you?"

"Are you Micah Andres?" The boy shuffled his feet, his hands behind his back.

"I am." Micah wondered what school activity they were promoting. Over the summer? Probably band camp.

The girl drew in a deep breath, let it out, and said, "We're here to apologize."

Micah looked at the silhouette of the young woman. Five-eight or so, maybe a hundred and twenty, thirty pounds. He'd bet the farm she'd be left-handed. "For what?"

She glanced at who was undoubtedly her brother. She turned back to Micah and held his eyes. "Breaking your window. And threatening you."

Micah raised his chin. "I see. Why don't you come in and tell me about it?"

The teens exchanged glances. "Uh…we…"

Micah smiled. "I won't hold you hostage, and I won't call the police. I forgive you for throwing the brick through my window. I'd like to know what you were doing with the glass from Wells Cathedral, however."

The teens hesitated. Micah said, "My son BB is home. He's eighteen. Went to school at Wexford. Played on the soccer team."

Brother and sister looked at each other. The girl shrugged at her brother, then nodded to Micah. "Sure."

He waved his hand for them to come inside. The girl came in first, and her brother followed.

BB stood in the dining bar area. He cocked his head as the two entered. Micah explained, "We have visitors. They want to tell me about the window."

BB grinned. "Confession is great for the soul."

The boy lowered his eyes. "Yeah, well, maybe. But we saw on the news what happened at the bakery. Then again last night. We didn't want you to think we were part of any of that. We're thieves, not killers." The young man pulled a galvanized pipe from his pocket. "This is the 'gun' I used."

Micah chuckled. "I never thought you were connected. Why warn me off, then try to kill me? It didn't make sense." He raised an eyebrow. "Names would be nice. And this is my son, BB."

The girl's eyes danced from BB to Micah, but she extended her hand. "I'm Jerranne Farley. This is my brother Grayson." She looked around the room. "Nice place. I always wondered what these houses were like."

Micah pointed to the couch. "Have a seat. You want something to drink? Soda? Water? Power drink?"

They both sat, their backs rigid. "No, thank you." Jerranne seemed to be the older sibling and took the lead. "When the congregation sold the church, they had a lot of talk about the windows. Most of them were purchased as memorials for church members who died. Some of the families objected to the sale and the continued use of the windows. They wanted to remove the stained glass honoring their loved ones, but the church was sold 'as is.' The new owners thought it would be cool to have the glass. It made the place more 'unique.'" The girl scowled.

Micah dipped his head. "I've seen other places have that happen. A church became a restaurant and still had the commemorative glass." He sat in the chair opposite the couch and leaned forward.

Grayson picked up the story. "The families tried everything they could to get the special pieces returned. The group who bought it said no. A court battle left the windows with the building. Some of the families were quite old, and the greats and grandparents were devastated." He stopped and said, "Including ours. Great-grandpa had dedicated a window to his daughter, our grandma, who died in childbirth. She was his only child. It crushed him to see her memory being 'desecrated' every week."

Micah glanced over at BB. His son appeared to listen closely. Checking for veracity? Good practice. "Yeah, I can understand how hard that would be."

Jerranne shifted on the couch. "He's not the only one who felt this way. Other families are thinking of taking matters into their own hands and stealing the memorials back." She stopped, then added, "Like we did."

Micah chewed on his lip. His eyes narrowed. He turned to BB and asked, "How busy is Kenmore?"

A slow smile crossed BB's face. "Never so busy he can't take on new projects."

Jerranne glanced from Micah to BB. "What are you talking about?"

Micah tapped the coffee table. "What if there were ways to satisfy both groups? What if you got your original windows back, and the building owners got some unique art in return?"

Jerranne's eyes widened. "What art?"

Micah motioned between himself and BB. "We know a very talented artist who works in glass. His creations hang in more than a few homes around town. I wonder if we could convince the building owners to give the memorials in exchange for fresh, unique art. They might draw more people who otherwise wouldn't come because of the 'church' feel of the place."

The young woman's face lit up, then darkened. "We can't pay what he probably wants."

BB snorted. "The man practically gives things away. Don't say no for him."

Grayson bumped his sister's shoulder. "Maybe? Worth an ask."

Jerranne looked at Micah. "What do you get out of it?" Suspicion tinged her tone.

Micah shrugged. "Satisfaction. Your great-grandpa gets his daughter's memory back. You're off the hook for an expensive window, and everyone is happy."

"Except you're out money for your front window," Grayson stated the obvious.

Micah stared at the teens. "Glass is cheap. I would ask you to volunteer at the Central Kitchen on a weekend, though. Honor system."

Grayson nodded. "Yeah. We can go there. I know where it is. They do good work." He glanced at his sister, glanced back at Micah, and asked, "What about the police?"

"I'm not pressing charges. You'll have to work it out with the owners of the Cathedral. But if Kenmore goes with you, with some of his art, they might only want volunteer work, too. But I can't promise."

Jerranne stood. Grayson followed. The young woman extended her hand. "Thank you for being so understanding, Mr. Andres."

"Thank you for coming and admitting what you did. Took a lot of courage." He shook hands with both teens.

Jerranne lowered her head. "Well, we didn't want to be

associated with whoever took out the baker. They committed murder."

Micah inhaled a long breath. Could this be the time for a Gospel lesson? No difference in sin? All guilty before God?

No. Not now. God would have opportunity later. The Spirit confirmed his choice with peace. The field wasn't ready yet. But he could plant a seed.

Micah walked the two Farleys to the door. "I forgive you like Jesus forgave me. You can take anything else up with Him."

Guilt tinged Jerranne's face. Her countenance clouded a moment, then cleared. "Right. I'll talk to Him about it."

The two climbed back in their car and drove off.

BB fist-bumped his dad. "Well done."

"We'll have to tell Kenmore he's 'giving away' his services. And we'll pay him to do it." In his head, Micah began calculating the size of the windows and how much glass would be needed to replace them. Hmm.

BB grinned. "Yeah, he knows the game. Maybe this time, he'll cut you a break. Since he'll be getting free publicity. Windows in Wells Cathedral? That oughta bring in the business for him."

"Let's hope so. Kenmore deserves a head start. He's a good kid." Who lost his dad in the earthquake two years ago. One of those who didn't heed the warnings. Sad. Very sad.

BB's eyes shone. "I'd adopt him. If he didn't already have a mom and a family."

"And he wasn't older than you." Micah wrote notes on the whiteboard.

"Right." BB laughed. He turned serious and asked, "What do you think will happen during the sting at the park?"

Micah shook his head. "I don't know. I can't even guess. I hope the perps get caught, and we can be done with this." He snorted. "Would be great if the wedding crasher would come forward like the kids did and confess."

"With a murder charge against them? I doubt it." BB pulled a power drink from the refrigerator. He opened it and downed half the contents.

"I didn't say I thought they would. Just it would be nice if they did." Yeah, and donkeys fly, too.

"Truth." BB stretched. "I'll call Kenmore. He needs to get his show ready."

"Do that. I'm going to go tell Wendy we can cross the window thieves off our to-worry-about list." Micah erased Wells Cathedral from his whiteboard.

"Maybe it will improve her mood." BB stopped, then added, "Something needs to. She's so stressed lately."

"Her and Jen both. I hoped when we moved the wedding up, they would be more relaxed about it, but something seems to be off." She had a shadow in her eyes Micah couldn't decipher.

"Maybe it's the surprise they keep talking about." BB swallowed the other half of his drink and dunked the bottle into the recycle bin.

"Maybe. I'll go ask her." He should. They hadn't exactly sat and talked in a while. Maybe now?

"Good luck with that." BB tapped fists with his dad, then walked to his bedroom.

Micah sighed. "I'm gonna need it." He gathered his courage and walked to the Smothers' house.

Arlene and Carly sat on the porch. They swung on the porch swing as the day wound to a close. He smiled at the two women as he climbed the steps to the deck. "Evening, ladies. You're looking well."

Arlene stared at him for several moments. He could see her mind trying to connect to his face. Carly acknowledged, "Hello, Micah. Did you come to see Wendy?"

Relief flooded Arlene's face. She laughed slightly. "Micah. How good to see you."

Micah gave a grateful nod to Carly. He spoke to Arlene.

"It's good to see you, too. I came to talk to Wendy. Is she home?" *Do you remember her?*

"Wendy. My daughter. Yes, she's here. She's inside with Jen. She's my other daughter, you know." Arlene lifted her head in satisfaction. The sun illuminated her creased face.

Micah nodded. "I know Jen."

"She's getting married to Tav. And Wendy is getting married to Micah." She paused, then asked, "Do you know him?"

His heart ached. "Yes, I know him. I'm Micah."

"Of course you are. I meant the other Micah. The one with the two boys. He adopted them like I adopted Wendy and Jen." Arlene sat a little straighter.

Micah swallowed hard. "The other Micah. Yes, I know him. He's a good guy."

"He's marrying my daughter, Wendy, you know." Arlene swung with supreme contentment.

Carly held Micah's eyes. Tears glinted in her eyes. Micah felt them as well. His voice caught. "Yes, he is. Can I speak to Wendy for a few minutes?"

Arlene nodded. "Of course. She's inside with Jen. My other daughter. Do you know Jen?"

"Yes. I know Jen. She's marrying Tav."

Micah leaned in and kissed Arlene on the cheek. He felt Carly's hand squeeze his arm as he passed her, opened the door, and walked into the living room.

Wendy came out from the kitchen, a dish towel in her hands. She wiped her hands and put the towel on the table. Wendy laced her hands behind Micah's neck. She kissed him warmly and melted into his chest for an embrace.

Micah nuzzled her hair. He hugged her, then stepped back. "Whatever we're waiting for, we need to hurry."

Wendy looked into his eyes. "You talked to Mom? She's having a bad day, that's all, Mick. She acted fine this morning. She'll be fine again in a little bit. Her evening meds haven't kicked in yet."

"If you're sure. We can move it to tomorrow if we have to."

Wendy shook her head. "No, we can't." She led him to the couch. They sat. "Jen and I have to get dresses yet." She sagged. "I know. We've been a little preoccupied. But we're going tomorrow." She held Micah's hand. "I'd feel better if I knew we were going to be safe. If Quinn's people catch this vermin Wednesday, we can relax and really celebrate."

Micah exhaled slowly. "I understand. It's hardest on you and Jen. You're living it. I'm only watching it from the outside. If you say we wait, we wait."

Wendy reached over and kissed him. "Thank you. Did you come over to make my day better?"

He smiled. "Yes, I did. I thought you'd like to know the people who broke my window came to confess."

Wendy's face lit up, then darkened. "Let me guess. You let them off the hook."

"Not exactly. The Farleys were a couple of teenagers."

"Out looking for fun?" Sarcasm laced Wendy's tone. She stepped back from Micah and crossed her arms over her chest.

"No. Let me finish." Micah marshaled his story. "They were trying to retrieve a memorial stained-glass window their great-grandfather had dedicated to his only daughter. Long explanation. They confessed so they wouldn't be identified with the people who killed Fran at the bakery."

"And what are they doing besides seeking your forgiveness?" Wendy tapped her foot against the floor. But she did uncross her arms.

"They're going to the police and to the building owner. We're going to offer to exchange the memorial windows for fresh art from a local vendor who does magnificent glasswork. Free to the owner, and any family who wants their windows back can get them."

"And who pays for all this?" Wendy scowled. Hard.

Micah shrugged. "I know a guy."

"Sure you do. Some independently wealthy philanthropist who does nothing but give money away." Wendy flipped the dishtowel across the table.

Micah dropped his head to the side. "Eh. I wouldn't say that. He's fairly frugal and has made some wise investments. But he does enjoy giving as the Lord directs."

Wendy snorted. "Why haven't you ever introduced me to him? I've never heard you talk about a rich friend." Hands on hips.

Micah stepped back and looked at Wendy side-eyed. "All our friends are rich, Wenders. You're living in a quadrangle with wealthy people."

Wendy frowned. "I know you, Tav, and Luke won the Magary Chase prize back when. You split a million dollars six ways. Even given really great investments, you're doing good. But rich? Comfortable, maybe."

Micah took her hand. "I thought we'd have more time for me to tell you this part before we married, but everything is moved up. I needed Quinn's permission to tell it, but here goes." He looked down, looked around, then held her eyes. "Quinn gave us an extra $500,000 each because of the way things happened, losing Jeremiah."

Wendy's eyes went wide as dinner plates. Then narrowed to slits. "Quinn gave you? Not the Chase?"

Micah nodded. "Quinn gave it to us. Quinn is a very wealthy man. Very. And he's very generous with his giving. You know he subsidized us living here."

"Subsidized how?" Wendy dropped onto the couch and twisted to look in the direction of Quinn's house.

"We each bought the houses from him for a dollar." Micah sat beside her.

Wendy smacked the couch. "Oh, come on. No one does that."

Micah asked, "Didn't your mom tell you?"

Wendy rolled her eyes. "Of course, she didn't tell me. I

don't handle the finances, but I saw her budget. She clearly had 'mortgage' marked. And it wasn't nothing."

"Jen handles the finances?"

"Yes, and I handle the medical." Wendy shook her head, then yelled, "Jen! Get in here."

Jen came in from the kitchen, drying her hands on an apron. "What are you yelling about?"

"Micah's trying to weave some story about Quinn selling us these places for a buck. Do you know anything about that?" Wendy's tone filled with accusation.

Jen shrugged. "Yeah. Mom told me when we moved in here."

Wendy's jaw dropped. "But the budget. The mortgage…"

Jen leaned against the wall. "It's Mom's way of saving. She put in an amount she could live with if she had to pay a mortgage. She subtracts it each month and moves it to a savings account for major repairs, or college for the boys, or anything else that comes."

Wendy turned to stare at Micah. He nodded. "Quinn is quite wealthy and quite generous. But he doesn't let people know about it."

Wendy stared at the floor. "So you really are the rich friend paying for the glass art?"

"If the event center goes for it. The Farleys agreed to work at the soup kitchen for a couple weekends. I thought we—you, me, Tav, and Jen—could all go together and work. It would give you a break from wedding planning. I think we all could benefit from a 'focus reset.' We're getting too wrapped in the pageantry." He squeezed her hand. "Me included. I think a weekend off would do us good."

Wendy held Micah's eyes. "Why didn't Quinn ever tell me?"

"He doesn't tell anyone. Don't feel left out. Quinn doesn't want people to treat him differently because of the money."

Wendy swallowed. "I'm going to beat him about the head and shoulders." She grinned. "Rat. All this time, I've been buying the coffee at work?" She picked up her phone and punched in numbers. "Grace? Is Quinn around? I've got…oh." Wendy sobered quickly. "I understand. Right. Is there anything you need? Why don't you come over for dinner with us? We can have a girls' night in. You can help us play games with Mom. Sure. About seven? Great. It really helps us. Thanks, Grace. We'll see you in a bit."

Micah watched Wendy disconnect the call. His stomach knotted. "What is it?"

"Quinn left. The Office called."

Micah lifted his head. "And?"

"And he's gone. No one knows for how long."

"He'll be back for the wedding, Wendy." Micah picked up Wendy's hand. "Quinn won't miss walking you down the aisle. He gave his word. He'll be here."

Wendy looked at Micah. "Is this what our life will look like? Me disappearing for days or months at a time? You not knowing when—or if—I'll be back?"

"If you want it to. We talked about you continuing to work at the Office. I know that's your career. I'll stand by you, Wendy." He kissed her hand.

Wendy's eyes darkened. "I have to think." She touched Micah's cheek. "I have to think hard." She stood, stepped toward the kitchen, then stopped. "I always thought I'd work until the babies came." She nailed Micah with a fierce glare. "We did talk about babies."

Micah stood. "Yes, we did. We said if the first one is like you, we'll have two or three."

Wendy grinned. "And if it's like you, we stop with one. I remember the discussion."

Micah risked a warm kiss. "We'll work it out, Wenders. We will."

She kissed him back. "Go home. I'll talk to you later. We're going to have a ladies' night. Eat ice cream and talk about men who keep secrets."

Micah laughed. "Talk about women who don't ask questions."

Wendy huffed. "Maybe a little of that, too. I love you, Mick."

"Love you."

He walked back to his own house. As he passed Carly, he nodded. She saluted him. Arlene continued talking.

* * *

THURSDAY

The word came down Thursday afternoon. Wendy got the call from the Office. The sting at the park had gone without incident. A mirror image of Tav's car had driven to Mercury Park. A Tav look-alike got out, walked around, looked in the pavilions, sized up the seating possibilities, and generally made his presence known. Nothing happened. No one approached him. When the Micah look-alike arrived, and the two of them were together, the shooting started. A sniper on a hill rained down bullets in their direction. Quinn's people returned fire, and the shooting stopped.

Wendy relayed the message to the various Knights assembled at Mick's house. Grace, Luke, Tav, BB, and Addison, listened intently. Ben spent his time drawing pictures. Mick remained silent as she finished her report. "They didn't find anyone, but they did get a partial plate number from a fleeing vehicle. They'll try to trace it down and let me know what they find."

Tav asked the obvious. "And this all tells us what?"

"You and Mick are the focus of the attacks. The attacker may concentrate all their attention on you two." Wendy clasped Mick's hand. She wished she could read his mind. What would the confirmation of their suspicions do to him?

Mick drew in a deep breath. "What do you want me to do about it? If they're targeting me, they're leaving others alone. It could be considered a good thing."

Luke snorted. "Not if it means you get killed. Rule One. We don't trade lives, remember?" Luke sat on the floor, leaning against the couch for support.

Mick shrugged. Wendy interrupted the argument before it could become one. "What if you went into hiding?"

"For how long? We've got a wedding in seven weeks. I don't think the bad guys are going to forget us for long. Sooner or later, we have to do something about them. I vote for sooner."

Tav's eyes narrowed. "What are you suggesting?" He bent to look at Mick, partially obscured by the corner of the kitchen.

Mick's voice carried heat. "I'm suggesting we catch these guys. Or girls."

Wendy nodded. "We all want that outcome. How?" She squeezed his hand.

Mick pointed out, "We still have the leak in our midst. I say we use it. Divide into four teams." He pointed to Tav and Luke. "You're team one with Addison. Wendy, you, Jen, and Grace are team two. Your brothers are team three, and the boys and I are team four."

Mick rose to his feet and began pacing around the living room. "Each one of us is going to say there's a…a bachelor's party on…Wednesday. Team one will say it's at Kensies. Team two…um…Blackberry's. Team three will say it's at Marshon's, and team four will say it's at Walker's. We'll have the police stake out each place, and whichever gets hit, the police will be waiting. They catch the perps in the act, and we've got our bad guys."

Mick looked around the room and issued a challenge. "Now poke holes in it." He dropped on the couch and waited.

The silence lasted several moments. Wendy didn't want to be the first to speak. Someone had to see the flaws. Glaring flaws. Mick was reaching, she knew. But someone had to say something.

Tav leaned forward. "It's a good plan, Mick."

Not what Wendy wanted to hear.

Tav continued. "I like your thinking. Little problem of innocent people being in the line of fire at those places." He sat back in his chair. "And finding enough look-alikes to fool the bad guys."

Mick shook his head. "We make sure it's a private party. No one will actually be at the location except the police. We rent the entire facility."

Silence again. "Will the police go for it?" Luke raised his question.

"If they want to catch this bunch or person, they will. Remember, they're after someone who killed an innocent woman. They should want to clear the slate." Mick defended his idea.

Tav reminded him, "They want to clear all their slates. It's a matter of the availability of personnel and priorities. I'm not saying it's not a good plan." He turned to Wendy. "Could you round up some of Quinn's contacts for an operation like ours?"

"I don't have Quinn's contacts. I don't even have my own. I'm an intern. I think Quinn keeps me around to keep me out of trouble." Wendy smiled a tight-lipped smile.

Mick squeezed her hand. "I doubt it. Quinn doesn't put up with charity cases that don't pull their own weight. He'd have canned you long ago if he didn't think you had value."

Wendy lowered her head to Mick's shoulder. "Thanks, Mick. I love you, too."

Grace spoke for the first time. "It's the truth. Quinn used to go through interns weekly. He appreciates your work." She scowled. "And if he hasn't told you, I'll remind him when he gets back."

If he gets back. The thought taunted Wendy. She shelved it. Back to Mick's plan.

Grace still spoke. "I think Mick's plan could work. If the police don't like it, we could hire security teams to take down the attackers."

"And if they have as much luck as the team at the park? We still won't know anything." Tav remained skeptical.

Mick retorted, "We'll know where the leak is coming from. At least it's something. We can plug the hole or use it to our advantage."

Tav sighed. Mick tensed. Wendy could feel his frustration. She leaned into his shoulder. "We all want this monkey off our backs, Mick. We all want these people caught and put away. Yours isn't a bad idea. We need to make it work, though. And not get anyone hurt. Or killed. Again."

She left it for him to chew on.

After several moments of silence, he asked, "Can we at least try my idea with the police? If they turn it down, we can fall back and regroup. But can we at least contact them with the plan?"

Tav called the vote. "All in favor of taking Mick's plan to the police?"

Seven thumbs went up. Tav stated, "Carried. Mick, since it's your plan, do you want to bring it to them?"

"Let me look like the madman? Sure, why not." Mick's eyes darkened. But it had been his plan.

Wendy bumped him. "Not a madman. But this is becoming personal."

"Because they're after me. When the caller said they would kill me, it became very personal." He threw his hands in the air.

Tav reached across and grasped Mick's arm. "God has this Mick. You're not in it alone. If you want someone to go with you, say it. You've got a room full of volunteers waiting for the word."

Mick looked around the room, then nodded. His face relaxed a bit. "I know. Like all of you, I'm stressed. I'll talk to the police on Monday. And I'll do it alone. You all have work to do."

The tension in him relaxed. Wendy felt it in his shoulders, his chest, his hands. Saw it in his face. She kissed him tenderly…

…to hear Ben's, "No kiss-ing un-til you are mar-ried."

Wendy jumped, grabbed the youngster, and kissed him all over his face and neck and back. "I'll give you kissing, Ben Andres! I'll kiss you and kiss you and kiss you, and you can't do anything about it!"

Ben giggled and squirmed and protested. "Wen-dy! Stop! Help! BB help!"

BB laughed. "You're on your own, little man. You crossed the wrong woman."

Wendy let Ben go. He continued to giggle and laugh. He stood in front of Wendy and said, "You can kiss on the cheek. I will let you."

Wendy ruffled his hair. "Thank you, Ben. That's very kind of you." She kissed Mick on the cheek. And watched all the anxiety in him disappear. He kissed her on the cheek as well. Everything back to normal. Except for a crazed vandal and a killer who might or might not be the same person. Or persons. Wendy sighed silently.

* * *

FRIDAY MORNING

The police were less than enthralled with Micah's plan but agreed to hear him out. When Micah finished his explanation, the detective pushed back his chair and looked at his partner. "What do you think, Spellman?"

Detective Spellman dropped his feet from his desk. He glared at Micah. "We don't care you have someone passing information, nor do we care who. But we do care about catching this criminal. Especially after they graduated to murder."

Detective Heller corrected his partner. "Manslaughter."

"In pursuit of another felony, it's murder." Spellman took a drink of cold coffee, crinkled his face, and spit it out into the trashcan beside his desk. "Bah. Yesterday's."

"Murder, then." Heller shrugged. He rolled a pencil between his fingers.

Micah ignored the debate. "How can we help bring this person in? We're involved. We can work together." Micah handed his notes to Detective Heller. Heller took them and began looking over them.

Spellman shook his head. "No, but we can use your source. Let me ask you a question, Mr. Andres. Why would your leak's information be credible now since it wasn't at the park?"

Micah talked fast. "The leaker will want to prove they have good information. Not like at the park. Something solid to give the bad guys."

"Makes sense. Maybe. Maybe the killer goes underground." The detective scribbled on his desk. Not on paper, on the desk.

"The person who called me made it clear they were coming for me. One way or another, they won't quit. If they were unhinged before, they're over the top now." Micah debated his ace in the hole. He hadn't discussed it with the others. No need. They would have voted him down. But here, now… "And I'm willing to be the target."

Spellman guffawed. "You're a tax accountant. What would you know about standing for someone to shoot at you?"

Micah glared at the detective. "It wouldn't be the first time." Might be the last… *Sorry, Wendy.*

Heller tossed the notes Micah had given him on the table. "No dice. We don't use civilians. They panic, they think they're Rambo, they do stupid things and get our people killed. We'll look at your ideas. And if the team thinks they're valid, we'll use them. If not, we'll chase this animal down the old-fashioned way. With regular police work."

He stood, signifying the meeting had ended. Micah took the hint and rose to his feet. "Will you at least let us know what you're doing?" *Can I salvage that much from this visit?*

"So your leak can tell the perp? I don't think so. We will keep you posted, and we will talk to you if we need your help. Otherwise, you'll hear about the arrest when it happens. Thank you for coming in, Mr. Andres." Spellman nodded his head.

Micah shook hands before he walked out. He didn't want to shake hands. He wanted to tell the self-assured officers what he thought of them. But doing so would not match his "What Would Jesus Do" bracelet. He left the office and climbed into his van. Returning home, he'd hear a whole lot of "I told you so" comments. But he tried. At least he'd done that much.

As he pulled onto his home block, he saw Carly walking away from the Smothers' house. His gut twisted. Could Carly be the contact? The spy? Could she be using Arlene?

His face burned with anger. How could anyone—

Do not be swift to accuse your neighbor...

Right. Proof. They would need proof. So far, Carly had been nothing but kind, helpful, and loving even, toward Arlene. And she'd passed the background check with flying colors. It had to mean something. Didn't it?

He parked and walked over to Wendy's house. He knocked. Jen came to the door. "Hey, Mick. How'd it go downtown?" She kept the door partially closed.

"About like we expected." Micah's face must have told more than he wanted.

"That bad, huh? Let me get Wendy." She closed the door, leaving Micah outside. Secret project again. Still. Always, it seemed lately.

Wendy came out on the porch and closed the door to the house behind her. "How did it go?"

Micah huffed. "It didn't. We're useless civilians. We might have a good idea, but the police will be the ones who decide if it's worth doing or not. In the meantime, we should stay in our sandbox and play." He stuffed his hands in his pockets.

Wendy frowned. "They didn't say that."

"Not word for word. It's a rough translation. They don't think we can help. They did say they don't care about our 'leak.' They only care about catching the killer."

Wendy put her arms around him. "I'm sorry, Mick. It was a good idea. The plan is a good one. If they can't see that, then..."

"Then what? The killer walks? Or continues to stalk me?" Bitterness filled his tone. "I'm a tax accountant. What would I know about being shot at?" Micah stood rigid against Wendy's consolations.

"Did you show him your scars?" Wendy jostled him.

Micah scowled. "No. It wouldn't have mattered. It would prove their point…I don't know how to stay out of the line of fire." Micah leaned against the wall of the house. "We're going to have to do this on our own."

"Shall I call all the guys together?" Wendy stepped back to look him full in the eyes.

"And fight it out like we did last night? I hope someone has been thinking about it." He couldn't keep the defeat from his voice. And his heart. And his mind.

Wendy ran her finger down the side of his cheek. "We'll work it out, Mick. We will. We're the Knights of the Octagon. Solving problems is what we do."

"Right." Still no conviction.

Wendy kissed him long on the mouth. He drew strength from her. Squared his shoulders. Nodded once sharply. "Right. We solve problems." *Now, believe it.*

"Together. Remember that part. We do them together."

Micah smiled at her. "I hear you. No running off playing a martyr. I won't make you a widow before you're a bride." He slipped his arms around her neck.

"You better not. I'll make Jesus send you back." She leaned forward to kiss him again…

The door opened, and Grace exited. She raised her eyebrows at Micah and Wendy. "While Ben's away? Hmm?"

Micah shook his head and held up his hands. "No, ma'am. Honest. What are you doing here?"

Grace's eyes lit. "I was visiting with Arlene on the back porch."

Micah's eyes narrowed. "Oh?"

Grace nodded. "Absolutely." She raised an eyebrow. "How did the meeting go?"

"About like everyone expected. The police aren't

interested in helping us or our helping them. Civilians don't know what it's like to be shot at." The bitterness returned to his tone.

Grace patted Micah on the shoulder. "Call the group. We'll figure something out."

Wendy muttered, "I wish Quinn were here."

Grace nodded. "So do I, dear. But until he is, we'll have to muddle through with just the nine brains we have." She narrowed her gaze and mock-glared at Wendy. "Contrary to his popular opinion, his brain only counts as one. We'll work it out."

Grace kissed Micah on the cheek and walked toward her own house. Wendy grinned. "I guess she told me."

"I guess she did. She's right, though. I'll let everyone know. We should spend time coming up with solutions. Then we can meet and not just brainstorm all night." And leave him to come up with another idea they would shoot holes in. Let someone else take the heat.

"Sounds like a plan."

Jen's voice called sharply, "Wendy! Quit spooning, and come help me."

Wendy chuckled. "And you think Ben is bad?" She called over her shoulder, "I'm coming. I'm coming." She kissed Micah one last time on the lips, then disappeared back into the house.

Micah walked to his home. Grace spoke the truth. They would figure it out. And finish the threat once and for all. Have the wedding, get married, and live happily ever after.

Right.

* * *

TUESDAY

Wendy defended her pronouncement over the phone. "I'm sorry, Sami. Like I told Caron, we need to do this as quickly and as painlessly as possible. Mom is getting more and more confused. Having too many voices will muddy her understanding of what's going on. We want her to enjoy the moment. Or at least be present mentally. Jen, Grace, Mom, and I are going to Garvey's to get gowns for the pre-wedding wedding. Yes, you'll be wearing the gowns we picked out. I know, you'll have to wear them twice. But it'll save you money from buying a different one for the big ceremony."

The woman sighed. Without making her feelings known aloud. "Garvey's has the largest selection of ready-to-buy, ready-to-walk out the door with dresses." She nodded, knowing Sami couldn't see her. "Right. I know. Hundreds of brides will have worn the same styles and patterns. At this point, it doesn't matter. Speed matters."

Wendy walked in circles on the porch. "No, we have Grace to supervise Mom. She'll keep her engaged while we try on dresses. No alterations. We have to be strategic. Right. Okay. I'm sorry. There will be time to make it right for the next wedding. But we've got less than seven weeks, and we need to get this done." Wendy fiddled with the stray hairs escaping from her bun. "Uh-huh. Okay. I've gotta go. Love you." She disconnected the call and looked at Jen. "Your turn."

Jen grumbled. "I hope it goes as fast. Lasha can be a talker."

Wendy huffed. "All your friends are talkers."

Jen raised her eyebrows. "Why do you think it is? I'm quiet."

"They love you because you're quiet. They get to talk and talk, and you say, 'Uh-huh,' and all is well."

Jen lifted her phone and punched in the numbers. "We'll see." She waited. "Lasha. Yeah, no. Listen…"

An hour later, Wendy, Jen, Arlene, and Grace arrived at Garvey's Bridal Shop. Esther, the concierge, led them to the style possibilities. Jen favored the cap sleeve. Wendy wanted a three-quarter length. They compromised with a short sleeve. Jen preferred the empire gown; Wendy wanted to go with the A-line. They resolved the argument with Ro-Sham-Bo, and the A-line won. Both agreed on the square-neck option. Having narrowed down the styles, all they had to do was find a gown to fit the bill.

It took more of the morning (and early afternoon) than anyone liked to find the right combination. Then came trying on the gowns and modeling them for Grace and Mom.

The third gown made the cut. So did the fifth. Wendy retried the third and smiled. She turned to Jen and said, "I love this one. It's even comfortable. Not too much foof. Elegant." She twirled in the three-mirror setup, examining herself from all angles. "Yeah. I like this one."

Jen tried on the fifth gown again. She twirled as Wendy had but frowned. "I like yours better. Let's make sure they have it in my size."

While Esther went to find one in Jen's smaller size, Wendy glanced at Grace and asked, "You want to pick one? You could surprise Quinn as soon as he gets us to the altar.

You could come out, march down, and renew your vows where the Knights can see you."

Grace shook her head. "No, this is your day. No theatrics."

Jen protested, "It wouldn't be theatrics. It would be real. And we're sharing everything anyhow…Mom, Quinn, brothers, the Knights… Another bride wouldn't be out of order."

Wendy added, "And you wouldn't have to match ours." The thought of seeing Grace and Quinn together in wedding attire made Wendy smile.

Mom seemed to follow the conversation. "Yes, Grace. You would make a beautiful bride. Quinn would love it."

Wendy pushed, "Besides, you didn't know us."

Grace swung her head from side to side. "Well…"

"Come on, Grace. It'll be a secret. You and Quinn renewing your vows in front of the Knights would be amazing." Wendy begged. "Please?"

Jen repeated, "Please?" She folded her hands in pleading. "Pretty please?"

Grace sighed. "Fine. For you." She giggled. "Quinn is either going to love the idea or kill me for being talked into this."

"He can blame us. But I think one look at you in a gown, and he's going to forget any objections." Wendy twirled around again for effect. No, she wouldn't use the petticoats. No foof. Simple. Like Wendy.

"I guess." There wasn't as much reluctance in Grace's eyes as in her tone.

The search for another gown began.

And lasted half as long. Grace chose an empire, off-the-shoulder gown. And looked stunning. The woman made a slow turn in front of the mirror. Wendy clapped. "Yes! You're beautiful. How could Quinn get mad at this?"

Grace's eyes shone. She looked at the reflection, then at the girls. "Are you sure? This is your day."

Wendy qualified the response. "Our day. The Knights. And you and Quinn are as much a part of this as we are. So, do it. For us?"

Grace checked her reflection one last time and grinned. "Okay." She wrinkled her nose. "Our secret."

The three women hugged. Mom looked on from the side.

As the women paid for the gowns, she chattered, "I'm so happy this went well. After the bakery incident, I'm afraid something awful would happen again."

Esther began placing the gowns in long bags. "What happened at the bakery?"

Mom blurted out, "Wendy was nearly killed! Some terrible person drove a car through the window and almost hit her and Micah. The poor woman who helped them with the cakes died. How could someone be so cruel?"

Esther shook her head. "That's awful. You're so lucky." The scowl on her face deepened.

Wendy said, "God is good."

The concierge muttered darkly, "He wasn't good to the woman who died."

Wendy offered, "We don't know why things happen the way they do. God is still good, even when people choose to do bad things. We can't blame Him for everything."

Esther shrugged. "Whatever." She rang up the bills and handed the receipts to the women. She asked, "Did you all come together? I see your addresses are close."

Mom smiled. "Oh, yes. We all live next door to each other. Even the boys are just around the corner. It makes it so nice."

"It must be convenient." Esther laughed. The scorn in her voice seemed out of place.

Wendy took her receipt, looked at it, and said, "Wait. You didn't charge me for the veil. You only charged for the gown."

Jen checked her ticket as well. "Your mind must be on

something else. You missed mine as well."

Grace added, "You're three for three. Maybe something is wrong with the machine."

Esther sagged, "I'm so glad you checked! I'd be fired if three veils went out the door without payment. The system must not have recognized the code I put in. Thank you for bringing it to my attention." She reran the transactions.

Wendy scanned her receipt again and dipped her head. "That's better. I would love a free anything, but not at your expense." It could have been a costly mistake.

Jen checked hers, as did Grace. She nodded to Esther. "No harm, no foul. Have a good day, Miss."

Wendy stuffed the ticket in her purse. "Thank you for all your help. We'll take the dresses."

Esther waved at the gowns in their jackets. "Oh, since you're buying off the racks, and these gowns have been tried on before, we offer dry cleaning service, and we will deliver the dresses to the venue. Most brides appreciate not having to worry about the gowns until the actual day."

She got out a pen. "If you'll let me know the venue address, I'll have them—"

Wendy declined the offer. "No, we'll take them now. I want them in my hands until the day of. Then there's no chance a business might be hit, and we'd lose them."

Esther sniffed. "I don't see that happening. We're too big. We could replace three-quarters of our inventory and not bat an eye."

"How fast? That's the key. We need these. Soon." Jen tried to end the conversation.

"How soon?"

Wendy did what Jen couldn't. "Soon. Thank you for your help." She gathered the dresses from the table and headed for the door. Jen scooped up the bottom half of the flowing bags, keeping them from getting caught in the door on the way out. Mom and Grace followed behind.

Outside, Mom chastised Wendy. "You were rude to the

woman in the store. She wanted to talk."

Wendy nodded. "Too much. I don't trust when people ask lots of questions about weddings and the timing and place. Too many events have been destroyed for me to tell the world about our plans."

Mom laughed. "I'm sure she is safe, dear." She stopped, then said, "Wendy. You're my daughter, Wendy. And I'm sure she is safe. After all, she works at a store that does weddings. Why would she risk losing customers?"

Jen groused, "You mean gaining more. I highly doubt if these places have insurance to cover dresses lost at venues that were firebombed. Or the deposits women had to pay, only to have to postpone because of the arsonist destroying their gowns."

"It's bad all around." Wendy stared at the ground. "Who would know more about planned weddings than a bridal consultant?"

Grace threw in, "Wedding planners."

Wendy shook her head. "And they got hit, too. Who is this person?"

Jen added, "Or persons. It could be more than one."

Wendy opened the door to the van. The women laid the precious garments on the back bench of the van. Wendy climbed into the driver's seat. Jen helped Mom into the shotgun position. Grace and Jen slid into the second row. Wendy breathed a sigh of relief. One "to-do" item moved to the "to-done" list. One down…and no idea how many more to finish. Would this wedding ever be over and they get to the "ever after" part?

God knew. And He kept His secrets. For now.

* * *

WEDNESDAY

The following day started with Mom being on the porch. Alone. Wendy opened the front door to let in some air and found Mom sitting in the rocking chair. Wendy tried to keep the frustration from her voice. "Mom. You're not supposed to come out here unless I come with you."

"But you were in the bedroom getting dressed. I didn't want to bother you."

"It's not a bother, Mom. You're never a bother. You have to tell us when you want to go outside. You could fall down the steps or on the porch. Please. Don't come out unless you tell us."

Mom gave a deep sigh. "I'll try to remember. I can't remember things like I used to."

Wendy smiled, but the corners of her mouth turned down. "I know, Mom. But you can remember not to touch a hot stove. And you can remember Jen and my names. I need you to remember not to come outside alone."

"I'll try, honey. For you, I'll try." She headed into the house.

Grace came strolling up the walk. She stepped on the porch and lay her hand on Wendy's shoulder. "Bad day already?"

Wendy frowned. "All the days lately are bad. It's not

her fault. I know she can't remember things. It's not knowing which things she can remember and which things she chooses to forget that make it hard."

Grace nodded. "I can see where it would be difficult."

Wendy led the woman into the living room. "How are you, Grace? With Quinn gone...you doing okay?"

"I just stopped in to see what I could do to help you. With the wedding being so soon, I thought you might need some extra hands."

Wendy stared at her for a long moment. She bit her lip. "Can I let you in on a deep, dark secret?" She glanced at the kitchen with its current disaster.

Grace smiled. "At this point, I think you better." She patted Wendy on the shoulder.

"Jen and I are trying to bake and decorate our own wedding cake. And it's not going well." Understatement of understatements.

"The baking or the decorating?" Grace tipped her head to the side.

"Yes." Wendy led Grace into the kitchen, where Jen stood up to her elbows in buttercream. The young woman looked up as Grace walked in.

Grace raised her hand and waved. "Reinforcements are here."

"We don't need reinforcements. We need saviors." Jen threw the piping bag to the counter and brushed the bowls to the side. Moisture filled her eyes.

Grace laughed. "I'll be the judge of that." She eyed the tiered cake sitting on the table. Grace's eyebrows went up. She covered her chin with a hand and studied the confection. "Not bad. A little wonky. Taller on one side, and a dip in the middle." Her eyes crinkled. "Sort of like the four of you."

Wendy snorted. "About right." She sagged. "But it's not supposed to look like that. It's supposed to look crisp and clean and even. Like a real wedding cake."

Grace rolled her sleeves. "I've never done a cake before.

But I've reconstructed many an ancient structure. Let's see what I can do to help."

An hour later, they had the cake leveled and even. The icing, however, continued to be a problem. Until Arlene came in and asked, "Did you stabilize the frosting?"

Jen turned her head. "Stabilize?"

Wendy laughed. "Nothing and no one in this kitchen is stable, Mom. What are you talking about?"

"It's a way to make the icing decorations last longer. And taste better." Mom's eyes were clear and bright. How long would it last?

Long enough. Wendy should be grateful. She lifted a *Thank You* heavenward. "Show us."

A fourth set of hands joined the endeavor. After fixing and finagling and fiddling with the recipes, they soon had a beautifully iced two-tier cake. The women stood back and admired the creation. Wendy gave it a critical eye. "Okay, fine. The brothers can eat this one. But how do we scale up to feed two hundred?"

Grace pointed her spatula at the cake. "You don't. You add one more tier with support. You feed however many, and the rest get slices from a single-layer rectangle cake." She winked. "Seen it. Ate it. Tasted just as good as the round cake."

She patted both Jen and Wendy on the shoulders. "Remember, the first cake is the one just for the Knights, your brothers, and everyone's plus ones. You're only talking thirty people at most. You can find a baker for later, I'm sure. You've done amazing in this short of time. So give yourselves a break. You got this. You bake and decorate it the day before, put it away, and bring it out the day of. Voila! Cake!"

Jen's eyes drooped. "What about all the other decorations for the event? Flowers, runners, music? We haven't planned those."

Grace pointed to the table. "Get some paper, and let's

figure it out right now. Then we can cross those off your list."

Wendy huffed. "We don't have a list. Things have been so rushed, we've lost track of what needs to be done and what doesn't." She tapped her foot. "The guys have agreed to help. We are supposed to tell them what we need done and trust them to do it."

"You need a wedding planner notebook."

Wendy walked to her bedroom and reappeared with a booklet in hand. "Had one. Everything lists three months or more out."

"We modify." Grace shook both women. "We can do this. You can do this. And you'll be just as married as someone who planned for two years. Remember, that's what counts."

Jen and Wendy exchanged glances. They both nodded. "Right. The ceremony. Not the party around it."

"Okay, let's see what you've got."

* * *

THURSDAY

Micah received a text from Tav. *Going downtown. You, Me. Meet by car.*

Why?

Now.

Micah grabbed his backpack and scurried to meet his friend. As he climbed into the waiting SUV, he glared at Tav. "What's the hurry?"

"We're going to the county office to get our marriage licenses. We had time with the original date, but now, we're pushing it." Tav started the engine.

Micah thought about it. "Drive." He pointed up the street.

Tav pulled into his lane. "Don't tell the girls, though. I don't want them thinking we forgot something this critical."

"I think they've got enough worries right now. This project they've started is really hammering them." He looked over at Tav. "You have any idea what it is?"

"Not a clue. It involves archeology and architecture, but beyond that, they're not talking. I tried to bribe Ury, but he didn't go for it. Said his sister would kill him. No money is worth Jen's wrath."

Micah put his arm on the window ledge and chuckled. "I got the same response from Peter. The girls have definitely put the fear of someone in them."

"Yeah. I thought only Quinn could do that."

Mention of the mentor turned the discussion to a precarious place. "You think he'll be back?"

Tav checked twice for traffic and pulled onto the freeway. "If he's alive and able, he will be. He gave his word. He'll be here."

Micah relaxed in the shotgun seat. "He looked good in a tux. I'm sure Grace had something to say about it."

"Yeah, tux or parade uniform." Tav sat straighter in the driver's seat. "I look kinda sharp in a tux." He swaggered as much as he could from a sitting position.

Micah huffed. "I didn't notice. I was looking at BB and Ben. They cut quite the figure." Seeing his sons in tuxedos had made Micah's heart swell with pride. BB would be his best man, as Luke would be Tav's. Double the fun.

Tav nodded with approval. "I have to say, all the Knights clean up well."

They bantered back and forth until they reached the justice of the peace's office and went inside. They waited in line, paid their $100 license fees, and headed for the door. Micah grinned as he put his in his bag. "Best C-note I've ever spent."

Tav shoved him. "This is the only time you've spent so much in one place. You're too cheap—"

BOOM!

An explosion went off behind them. The concussion wave threw them out the door and into the street. Shrapnel of shattered glass, concrete, marble, and steel rained down. Micah landed on top of Tav, partially shielding him from the destructive shower. A deafening ring droned in his ears. He could hear nothing but the humming. He rolled off Tav. "Are you okay?"

Tav's mouth moved, but no sound reached Micah. He grabbed his ears, yanked at them, and repeated, "Are you okay?"

Tav held his ears, shaking his head back and forth. He

pointed to the building behind them. Smoke and dust and debris filled the air. The smell of explosives clogged Micah's nostrils. Dazed and wounded people streamed from what had been the doorway but was now a gaping hole. Micah spun to his feet, paused to let the world settle, then went into action. Until the first responders arrived, he and Tav would do what they could. He ripped his shirt in half to apply a bandage to a man's bleeding head. Micah ordered, "Hold this." Strange not to hear his own voice. He grabbed the next person who came out of the building. The man collapsed, his back ripped open by shrapnel.

Tav caught him as he fell and eased him to the ground. The man spoke something, then went still. Micah heard nothing. Tav put a hand on the man's neck. He looked at Micah and shook his head. Micah grasped the next person he saw and began staunching the blood flow from an artery where an arm had been.

He lost track of what happened after that. It was chaos and disorder and turmoil and madness. First responders arrived but were outnumbered by the wounded. Micah and Tav continued to help where needed. An EMT gave Micah orders. Micah waved both hands. "I can't hear you." He signed it as well, grateful once again he'd learned ASL in junior high school. All the Knights knew it. Speaking in sign had come in handy more than once. Now, it could be life-saving.

The man signed, "Hold this."

Micah grabbed the IV bag and held it high. A fireman came and took over. Micah shuttled to another paramedic working alone. He voiced what he hoped sounded like, "I can't hear."

The man grabbed Micah's hand and motioned for Micah to hold compression on a chest wound. Micah held his hand tightly over the injury until the paramedic gestured for him to release it. The man applied a more stable bandage. He nodded to Micah. Micah rotated off to find someone else to help.

After what seemed like all day, there were no more bodies to care for. All the injured needing transport were taken away in ambulances or squads. The dead were covered and transported to the morgue. Tav and Micah's wounds were bandaged. They wandered among the clean-up crews, thanking people and shaking hands. And still, Micah could hear nothing but the ringing. Tav grabbed him. He spoke words Micah could not decipher. Micah pulled at his ears. "I can't hear you."

Tav signed, "Concussion wave. I can't hear either."

Micah waved him off. "My ears are ringing. They'll be better tomorrow." Tav took Micah's arm and led him to a paramedic who had put away his equipment. Micah watched Tav's mouth move. The medic stopped what he was doing and gave his attention to Tav. He had Micah and Tav both sit leaning against the squad. The medic examined their ears, frowned, and wrote something on a notepad. "Possible ruptured eardrums. Go to ER or your primary physician."

Tav nodded, then signed to Micah, "No ER. We'd be there for hours for nothing. We'll wait and make primary appointments."

Micah nodded. Tomorrow. Everything would be better tomorrow. He looked around for his bag and found it lying on the ground under a pile of debris. He dusted it off, pulled out the marriage license, and waved it in the air. He grabbed Tav in a bear hug. He signed, "How did you know? How could you possibly know?"

Tav signed. "I didn't know. I figured today would have been a good day. Must have been a God thing. When God nudges, you best listen."

"Yes, you should." Micah looked around at the evidence of the carnage. "You think the arsonist has an accomplice?"

"If there is, they aren't afraid of killing. Hitting a county building? That's big time. And will bring in the state troopers. I can't believe someone would target something this vital. This isn't about weddings anymore. Maybe it never was." Tav continued to sign.

Micah nodded. "Let's go home. Maybe we don't tell the girls we were here."

Tav disagreed and signed, "Knight's code. They'll see it on the news. I'm sure we'll be on it."

Micah had seen several film crews in attendance, though he had paid them little attention. Aside from ducking them whenever possible. He sagged. "Great. I'll never be allowed to go out again unaccompanied."

"Not with me, anyhow. I'm the bad influence." Tav shoved him toward the car. "We'll go home and make audiology appointments. As soon as we can. I'm sure it will be two weeks at the earliest. But at least it will be something."

Micah's mind whirled as they drove home. Hearing only the loud ringing made thinking difficult, if not almost impossible. He could hear his thoughts, but barely. This had to be temporary. Had to be. But what if it wasn't?

* * *

Arrival at home proved less traumatic than Micah feared. No one was around. He and Tav slipped into the house. Ben was at school. BB was working. Wendy and Jen were at home with Arlene, allegedly shopping for bakeries online and on the phone. They would be occupied the greater part of the day, Micah hoped. After a short discussion, the two men showered at Micah's rather than risk being alone and unable to hear any intruders.

Tav and Micah talked through ASL. The next most accessible mode of communication for anyone who didn't know sign language would be talk-to-text. All the Knights knew ASL, but outside their circle, it would be more complicated. Micah stared out the window. He turned to face Tav. He signed, "Should I break up with her? Give her an out? Wendy didn't sign on to marry a deaf person."

Tav punched him hard in the shoulder. Micah rubbed his arm. "I'll take that as a no."

Tav nodded. His signs were crisp. Sharp. "No one says you're deaf. Or going to be deaf. Your hearing is impaired right now. Give it time."

But time was something they were running out of. Micah stared back out the window. Should he give her the out? Let her decide?

What if the roles were reversed? Would you still love her?

Micah sat straighter in the chair. Was he saying he loved her more than she did him? She only had a conditional love and not a "real" love? Did he dare say such to her?

Uh, no.

Then she will want to marry you right like you are. Deaf or not. If she doesn't, she wasn't the one to begin with. Right?

Micah chewed on that one. He wanted her to be the one. Loved her. Wanted to spend his life with her. What if she didn't…

Stupid. Wendy had agreed to marry him. She could have said no. This wasn't about a wedding. It was about a marriage. A forever love. They had it, or they didn't.

They had it. Micah looked over and smiled at Tav. He signed, "I'm done being stupid. She'll love me as I am." He sat back in the chair and relaxed.

Tav held up his fist to tap with Micah. Micah pumped his. They would be all right.

The two men were preparing lunch when Grace popped her head around the corner. Her mouth moved, but Micah couldn't hear her. Grace's face bore a look of deep concern. She took hold of Tav, hugged him, and did the same with Micah. She shook her head, all the while saying things neither man could understand.

Micah held his marriage license. He spoke, "We went

downtown for our licenses. How could we know about the bomb?" He could only hope the words were right.

Grace lifted her head skyward. Tears filled her eyes. She put both hands on her face.

Micah pointed to a seat. The woman complied and sat. Tav began signing. "We went downtown to get our marriage licenses. As we were coming out, the place exploded." Tav stared at the floor. "Three people were killed. Another four are critical."

Grace signed back. "Are you two okay?" She stopped, then signed, "Why are we signing?"

Tav signed, "Micah's got a ringing in his ears. He can't hear anything except that." He paused, then admitted, "I can't either."

Grace stared at Micah, and her eyes narrowed. Her mouth moved.

Micah stared back.

Grace signed. "Nothing?"

Micah gave her a straight-lipped smile. He spoke, not knowing what his voice would sound like. "Nothing. I can hear my thoughts, but that's it. Lonely place to be, believe me."

"What did the doctors say?" Grace signed with distinct motions.

"We haven't seen one yet. We want to wait—"

Grace grabbed her phone and punched in a number. Micah couldn't read her lips, but the dark expression on her face said buckets.

Grace hung up and signed, "Doctor's appointment in forty minutes. Get in the car."

Tav held his hand. "We can wait—"

Grace pointed to the door. "Car. Now."

Micah read her lips as well as her hands. He looked at Tav and signed. "Who put her in charge?" His eyes crinkled in jest.

"We did. Quinn's gone, so she's it."

Micah sighed. "Fine."

Grace pointed to the door. "Out." No translation needed on that one.

The three piled into Grace's car. She drove to an unmarked three-story building with no windows. Grace parked in front of the only visible door and signed, "Follow me. You see nothing. You hear nothing." She sneered at them. "Not a problem, right?"

Micah scowled but nodded.

Grace led them into an open-concept building with stairs and offices suspended from the walls and ceilings. Micah averted his eyes from the equipment at the center of the floor that stood all three stories tall. He didn't want to know. He did, but he didn't. Better not to. They'd been with Quinn, and now Grace, long enough to have learned. Don't ask, so you can't tell.

They climbed two flights of stairs to an office with a closed door. Grace opened it and called something. A man in a lab coat with a name embroidered on it rose from a desk and grabbed Grace in a bear hug. He held her at arm's length, then embraced her and kissed her on the cheek.

Grace signed and talked at the same time. "My friends were standing too close to an explosion. Neither of them can hear."

Doctor Emunson sat Micah down on an examining table. He pulled out an instrument and examined Mick's eardrums. He muttered something Grace translated as, "Yep, busted. Both of them." He looked a little longer, then took Micah by the arm and led him to a chamber no bigger than a closet. He pointed to a chair. "Sit." Micah obeyed. The doctor put headphones on Micah and looked at Grace. Grace explained to Micah, "He'll play tones. If you hear anything, raise your hand. Right ear, right hand. Left ear, left hand. Got it?" Micah nodded. Emunson closed the door. Grace and Tav sat.

The session took nearly ten minutes. Micah raised his

hand halfway once or twice but dropped it as quickly. Maybe he thought he heard something? After a while, he began hearing tones that weren't there. Or were they? He couldn't tell.

Then it was Tav's turn. Same procedure.

Finally, Emunson leaned back, took off the headphones he wore, and explained, as Grace translated, "I can't say anything for sure yet. They need to let their eardrums heal. It may take a few weeks. Once they have something to hear with, we can assess them again." He cocked his head. "How close were you to the explosion?"

Tav signed but also answered, "Directly behind us. Mick stood in back of me. The concussion wave knocked us both down."

Micah nodded. "We were outdoors, or it could have been worse."

Emunson wrote something on a pad. "I'm going to prescribe some drops to keep you from getting an infection. Go home, take it easy, and check with me if anything changes."

Grace hugged the doctor and said something without interpreting it for Tav and Mick. Probably just as well. Quinn had a great many friends from all walks of life who were now Grace's friends. And just as demonstrative.

The older woman drove Tav and Micah home. She gave them strict orders. "No leaving." Grace gave them a catbird smile and signed, "You get to tell the girls. Good luck."

Tav grumbled, "They always accuse us of not listening. Now we have an excuse." He signed it for Mick.

Mick chuckled and nodded. "Truth."

Grace left. Micah debated hanging with Tav but finally signed, "See you later. Good luck with Jen."

"Same to you with Wendy."

Would he need it?

* * *

THURSDAY AFTERNOON

Tav fist-bumped his friend and went to his own home. He set his phone on vibrate. Then sat on the couch to watch the front door. Even with the alarm, it was eerie thinking someone could come in unannounced and unnoticed. Tav wouldn't even hear the alarm. *Lord, You have to bring me through this. Whatever the outcome, help me stay faithful. And grateful. I'm alive. Others aren't. Thank You for sparing Mick and me. Help me make the most of the time You give me.*

Exhaustion—emotional and much as physical—overtook him. He closed his eyes and slept.

To be woken by Luke shaking him. Tav sat up in a fog. Luke's mouth moved, but Tav heard nothing. The memory of the explosion flooded back. He sagged, then said, "I can't hear you. Lost my hearing in an explosion."

Luke signed, "I saw the footage. Is Mick the same?"

"Yes. The doctor says we'll know more in a few weeks. After the eardrums repair themselves."

Luke gave him the side-eye. "Will they?"

"That's what we're hoping for." Tav shivered. "People died, Luke. A guy died in my arms." He pounded the couch, looked at the ceiling, and let the tears flow down his face.

Luke put his hand on his brother's shoulder and let him cry. Tav vented all the feelings he'd stuffed inside so he could help others. Now, they wanted out. He wailed…or thought he did. He had no way of knowing if sound came out or not. He shuddered, shook himself, scrunched his shoulders, then sighed. All the tension flowed from his body into the floor through his shoes. He let out a second long breath, looked at Luke, and nodded.

Luke squeezed Tav's shoulder, then signed, "You two. You're always in trouble. Why did you go downtown?" He sat on the arm of the couch by his brother.

"To get the marriage licenses. Just in time, too." Tav shuddered again. They'd come so close to not getting the licenses… The shock remained real. And present.

"Did you have a premonition?" Luke's eyes widened.

Tav stretched to shake off the tremors. "Had a fear. The girls would kill us if we didn't get the certificates."

Luke scoffed. "Now, you have an excuse not to listen." He smirked.

"It won't fly. Wendy and Jen know how to sign." Ben remained the only Knight who couldn't sign. Micah worked with him, but the process proved slow.

Tav appreciated his brother's attempt to lighten the moment. "We'll work it out."

Luke squeezed Tav's shoulder again. He stomped his foot and questioned Tav with a glance. Tav nodded. "I felt that."

Luke gave him a thumbs-up. He clomped to the kitchen. Tav grinned. Gotta love a brother who cares.

* * *

Micah rested on the couch and hoped he'd feel someone coming in the door. He wouldn't hear the alarm. Vibrations from the door slamming woke him from an unintended nap. He looked to see BB standing in front of him, gesturing wildly. Micah touched his ear and turned his head. He added, "I can't hear you." He signed as well, not knowing if his voice had been clear.

BB's eyes widened in fear. He signed. "What happened?"

Micah rehearsed the events in short form. Very short form. Micah didn't want to relive the moments. Bury them deep. He'd examine the feelings and memories tonight before bed when he and the Lord could process them together. He asked his son, "What were you mad about?"

BB waved it off. "Nothing compared to you. I got my grades from last quarter. I got a B in chemistry."

Micah chuckled. "And that's a bad thing?" Compared to what he'd been through, a B in chemistry would be welcome. Of course, with his grades in school, a B in anything would have been welcome.

"I wanted all As." The young man threw his report to the side. He grabbed a power drink from the pantry and chugged half of it.

Micah grabbed BB in a bear hug and signed, "Love you, son." If BB wanted to talk about school, let him talk. It took Micah's mind off the morning's carnage.

BB set the drink down to sign, "I know. But I wanted all As."

BB turned to the hearing problem. "How bad is it? You'll get it back, right? It's just a ringing. How soon will you be able to hear?"

"It will depend if the eardrums repair themselves. We'll know in a few weeks." Micah repeated the company line. We will know in a few weeks. Right.

BB's eyes widened. "Weeks? What if they don't?" His signing grew vigorous.

"I'm taking it a day at a time, BB. One day at a time. I can't get ahead of this." *Only God knows, and He ain't saying. Not yet, anyhow. But I'm trusting You, Lord. You have this. You have me, hearing or not. I know You do.*

"Have you told Wendy yet?" BB continued to sign.

"No. She's with her mom. They're still looking for another baker."

"Right. The cake. I should ask at church. Maybe someone can give me a recommendation." BB made a note on the envelope with his grades.

Cake. Yeah, let's talk about cake. "That would be great. Maybe someone private would be better. Less conspicuous." Micah leaned against the kitchen counter.

BB stated the obvious. "Less of a target."

"Right." We're all targets, it seems. But who's doing the shooting? Or bombing?

"The perp must really have something against marriage." BB scowled in disgust.

"Or weddings. I'm hoping the police can figure something out." And soon.

"Yeah. You go sleep in your room. I can watch out here. I'll tell Ben."

Micah didn't argue. The weight of the day made his head pound. That, he could hear. Constantly. He made his way to his room, stretched out on the bed…

Then couldn't turn off his brain. Weeks. Weeks of not hearing anything. Lord, what are You handing me? I know Wendy will be with me, but what is this? A simple wedding, and instead, Tav and I nearly got killed. Twice. Are You saying this is a bad idea? Are You trying to tell us no? Why now? Why not before we asked? Why not during the months before now? I don't understand. I prayed. I did. I said if Wendy wasn't the one, stop me before I asked her. Or have her say no. But You didn't, and she didn't.

I'm going to fight for this, Father. Until You say a clear "no." Right now, all I have is opposition from some jaded nutcase. That's not You. Speak clearly. I'll listen.

Micah closed his eyes and slept.

* * *

While the four foster brothers disposed of the culinary evidence, Jen and Wendy decided they needed Tav and Mick to weigh in on some of the decorations. This wedding had to be a "we" thing, not a "you make all the decisions alone" thing. Jen called first and got Tav's voicemail. Wendy thought it strange in the middle of the day, but oh, well.

A text message notification sounded on Jen's phone. Tav. *Hey. What's up?*

Jen texted back, *Call me.*

Can't. Come over.

Anyone home?

Luke. Your propriety is covered.

Our propriety is covered. Truth. KO.

Jen smiled. "I'm going over to Tav's. The brothers are together, so you could come too."

"You need moral support?" Wendy put the decorating bags in the sink to soak. Lots of dish soap to cut the grease of the shortening.

"Another voice would be nice." Jen sounded like she might be pleading.

"Fine. We can tell Mick what we decided, and he'll go along with it. He always does." *That came out cattier than it should have.*

Jen glanced at her sister. "Do I detect a note of dissatisfaction?"

"No. No. He's easy-going, that's all." *Sometimes to a fault.*

"And you would like him to be more forceful?" Jen continued to push. Or pry.

Wendy shook her head. "No. Mick is Mick. I love him exactly as he is. No changes."

"That's good because if you're going into this thinking you'll make him into what you want, you're in deep trouble." Jen put her hands on her hips and stared at her sister.

Wendy fought back. "I know, Jen. I know. We've done all the marriage counseling. I accept Mick for who he is. I love him, warts and all."

The two women walked to the Vaughn home, all two houses away. Jen knocked. Wendy stepped behind her sister, expecting Tav to answer and a warm embrace to follow. Luke answered, however. He hugged Jen, then Wendy, and motioned them into the living room.

Tav sat at the desk, his phone in his hand. He looked and smiled. Wendy saw something behind the smile. Something serious. Something that worried her. The minor cuts and bruises were new as well. What happened?

Jen went over and kissed him. "Hey, Mister. What kind of day did you have?"

Luke signed across the room. Wendy's eyes widened. Tav's voice sounded lower and louder than usual. There was a slurring that hadn't been present before. "Mick and I had a problem. We went to get our marriage licenses. There was…" He stopped, breathed deep, then continued, "…a bomb at the office." Tav motioned to Luke. "Mick and I lost our hearing when it exploded."

Wendy sank into the chair. She covered her mouth with her hand. Emptiness washed over her. Followed by incredible sadness.

Jen stood, her head cocked. "You what?" It was as if she hadn't heard him right.

Luke translated. Jen glanced from Luke to Tav. "He can't hear me?"

Luke said, "No. He can't hear anything right now."

Jen began signing fast and furious. Tav responded in kind. Wendy didn't try to follow the conversation but caught Luke by the arm. "Tell me everything that happened."

Luke took her by the hand. "There was an explosion. Tav and Mick were outside, or they might have been killed. Three people were. Our brother and your man spent the morning rescuing people. They're heroes. Or so the news will paint them."

"But their hearing?" Wendy shook her head. Mick lost his hearing? This couldn't be happening. The wedding…they had a wedding.

"The concussion wave broke their eardrums. The

audiologist who examined them says an eardrum usually can repair itself in a matter of weeks. We'll know more after that."

"And if the eardrum doesn't repair itself?"

"They have surgical procedures which can be done. This isn't permanent, Wendy. Not yet. Not if God wills." Luke studied her hard. Like he waited for a response.

Wendy stared at the ground, lost. Mick could be deaf. Could be permanently deaf. How could she live with it?

She pulled herself up. What a stupid question. She'd live with it like she'd live with any other quirk about Mick. She'd love him, and they'd get through it. She looked at Luke and met his gaze. She nodded. "But if it is, we'll live with it."

Luke squeezed her hand. "Good woman. Thank you. You could text him."

"I'll go over. This needs to be an in-person conversation."

Luke hugged her. "I love you, sister. You're special."

"I hope that's a good kind of special."

"It is. Believe me." He looked at Tav and Jen, who remained in expressive communication. After another five minutes, Jen reached in and kissed Tav on the lips. Warmly. Extensively. A "Ben would break it up" kiss. Luke tapped Tav on the shoulder and signed, "Enough. Save it for after the wedding. In six weeks."

Tav responded with a sneer but sat back from Jen.

Wendy walked to Mick's house and knocked on the door. She readied her phone to text when BB answered. He hugged her. She felt the tension in her son-to-be and took extra time to return his embrace. "It's all going to be okay, BB. It is. Mick will get his hearing back."

BB held her eyes. "Or he won't." The pain in the younger man's voice cut Wendy.

She nodded. "Or he won't." She needed to reassure him. "And it will still be okay. He'll work with what he has, and we'll love him just the same."

BB drew in a deep breath. "Right." He looked down and looked back up. "You think I should delay starting school? Wait until next fall?"

"No." The young man had already started projecting ahead. She had to help him see the future hadn't been changed. His future, anyhow. "Your dad would kill you. And me for letting you. It will be fine, BB. We're getting married in six weeks. You're starting school in the spring. I'll be here for him."

BB led her into the living room. Mick sat at the table. Ben texted from his tablet, and Mick signed and typed. Ben followed along and tried to copy the sign language. They both looked when Wendy and BB came into the room.

Mick stood and enfolded Wendy in his arms. Ben let them kiss, then tugged his dad's arm to break it up. Mick bumped Ben with his hip in play but stepped back.

Ben frowned. "The rules have not changed. Af-ter you are mar-ried, you can kiss for a long time. Not un-til."

BB laughed. "That was an 'I'm glad you're alive kiss.' Those are allowed to be longer." He signed to his dad what Ben had said.

Ben nodded once. "O-kay."

Wendy and Mick went to the couch. They sat and talked via sign for several minutes. Wendy talked, Mick listened. Or watched her hands. She signed, "I love you. Nothing changes. We're still getting married. We're getting married in six weeks. It's as close to eloping as we're going to get."

She held his eyes. "Your hearing makes no difference. We will be fine. You understand?"

Mick's eyes shone. He held her hand and kissed it. He signed, "I would say I'm sorry, but you would hit me. I love you, Wendy."

"I love you, Mick."

* * *

THURSDAY NIGHT

"A bomb? A bomb? Who uses a bomb? And for what? You killed three people, and you missed Andres! How is that possible?"

The arsonist shouted into the night. Of course, there was no one around to hear. But yelling released the frustration.

"This isn't happening. It's not. Andres is mine. No one else's. I don't know who you are, and I don't care. All I care about is getting Andres. My retaliation. Mine."

But if the arsonist had competition…if someone else wanted to get Andres and didn't mind taking out others as well…that created a problem. One the arsonist didn't want.

The arsonist's face drew into a scowl. Eyes narrowed. Lips tight. Face tense. Action needed to be taken. And fast.

The arsonist entered the numbers. A phone rang. And rang.

A voice answered. "Hello?"

"I need names. School names. Teacher names. Bus driver names. I want them now." The phone slammed against the floor. "I will get Andres."

* * *

The group spent the next few days outfitting the Andres and Vaughn homes with assistive devices so Micah and Tav could know when someone knocked, rang, or entered the house. Lights in all the rooms were rigged to come on when a body entered. It made Tav and Micah feel as safe as they could.

The partial license plate numbers Quinn's people recovered at Mercury Park turned out to be from a stolen car. It had been abandoned and partially burned. Nothing further to go on. Micah felt the report was too short, too matter-of-fact. Surely the Office could pull more information than "stolen." Were they withholding information? Knew more than they were telling? None of the thoughts did anything for Micah's confidence. But he resorted to what he knew. God was in control. God loved Micah. Nothing would happen God didn't know about first. Micah remained as safe as he always had been. Right. Now, live like it. With courage. Steadfastness. Resiliency. Get up, get to work.

Micah pulled out the forensic accounting he did for the Office. Hunting bad guys made the time go faster. He could bury his head in numbers. And wait for his hearing to return.

If.

* * *

WEDNESDAY

On Wednesday morning, a light over the front door alerted Micah someone had knocked. Micah looked through the front window and saw two men in suits standing on his porch. He got his phone and opened the text-to-talk feature. Then he deactivated the alarm system and opened the door.

Man number one held a badge and an ID card. He spoke something Micah couldn't hear. Of course. Micah texted, "I'm deaf. Can you sign?" He activated the voice app.

Officer Perry shook his head. Officer Gainey nodded and signed, "I'm here as an interpreter. We know you lost your hearing in the explosion."

Micah waved the men inside and to the bar, where they both took seats. Officer Perry took out his notepad. He asked, and Gainey interpreted, "Why were you at the county office on Friday?"

"My friend Tav and I went down to get our marriage licenses. We're both getting married in five weeks." *Not soon enough.*

"Did you plan this trip?" Perry asked, and Gainey signed.

Micah spoke, unsure what his voice would sound like. He also signed. "Totally random. Spur of the moment. We knew it was getting close, and we'd forgotten to get them earlier. Tav suggested we go, and we did."

"Did you tell anyone in advance?"

"No. Not a soul. He called, I went over, got in the car, and we left."

"How long were you at the office?" Officer Perry took notes, copying down Micah's answers.

"It took about an hour to get the licenses. Several people waited in line ahead of us." *They were the lucky ones.*

"What happened next?"

What happened? What happened? I lost my hearing. That's what happened. "We walked out. We'd only just cleared the building when the bomb went off. We tried to help as many people as we could until the first responders showed."

Gainey nodded. "We saw the reports. You did good work out there." His signing was rough, as if he hadn't used it in a while.

Micah shrugged. He spoke and signed at the same time. "We did what we could." *Could everyone quit trying to make us out to be heroes? You do what you have to. That's all we did. Anyone else would have done the same.*

Perry looked at his notes. Micah saw his mouth move. Gainey translated for Micah. "Is there any reason someone would want to kill you?"

Micah's immediate thought went to the Farleys. They'd been the first ones to threaten him. But no, that situation had been all wrapped up. Wells Cathedral had taken Kenmore's art pieces in exchange for the memorial glass. Jerranne and Grayson had worked three weekends at the soup kitchen and did community service to satisfy the police. Case closed. However, there was one other threat. Micah hoped his voice carried the right tones. "With a bomb? No. I mean, yes, someone's threatened to kill me, but I figured it would be more personal. Not hitting random people." *Certainly not a bomb. Who uses a bomb?*

Perry's eyes narrowed. "Tell me about it." He continued taking notes on his pad. But wrote with more intensity.

Micah detailed what had happened with the arsonist since the incident at the bakery.

Perry shrugged. "Unfortunately, we don't have any proof the arsonist might have been involved with the death at the bakery. Other than your suspicions, of course. We're still following leads, but going from crashing a car to a bomb is a real stretch." Perry looked skeptical. Gainey signed for Micah and added, "Our explosive ordinance personnel say the bomb was too sophisticated to be something thrown together by a layperson."

Micah narrowed his eyes. "The threats I received were real. I don't see why someone like that gets a pass." His signing took on a forcefulness he hadn't intended. Or maybe he had. *Are they not taking the threats seriously? They don't care about my life?*

Gainey lifted his hands. "Lack of hard evidence. That's the problem. Until we get a confession or forensics to tie the two crimes together, we pursue it, but it's a low priority. And we don't see your arsonist as savvy enough to construct the bomb that destroyed the justice of the peace office. Bombing a county office is serious stuff. We need to prioritize for the public safety."

Micah let the information rankle around a bit. And it did rankle. But he buried his frustration. "Do you have any other victims who look like targets?" *Meaning it wasn't me they were after? That's a nice thought.*

"We're still investigating. We'll keep you informed." Perry spoke, Gainey signed.

The men stood and shook hands with Micah. Gainey signed, "I hope you get your hearing back. We know where you are if we need you."

Micah walked the men to the door. He closed it behind them and sighed. Did he believe the arsonist could be the bomber?

If he was honest, no, he didn't. The phone call blaming Micah for Fran's death, and the desire to seek revenge, said murder hadn't been in the arsonist's plans. Not wanton, indiscriminate murder. His murder, maybe. But not the kind that takes out innocent people and doesn't even guarantee Micah is killed. More prone to a face-to-face encounter.

Which left who? Who would be after him? Or Tav? Or maybe just wrong place, wrong time, and the target was someone else? Always possible.

That's what the police were for, right? Let them figure it out. *Walk away, Andres. Go file taxes.*

Micah sighed and went back to his office.

But the thought wouldn't go away.

If the arsonist wanted to kill him face to face, who shot the van? Micah hadn't been the driver. The arsonist specifically wanted Micah, not the whole of the Knights. Which meant…

The shooter was someone else? Someone after the group, not just Micah?

But did that mean the bomber was after both Micah and Tav? Whoever they were, they didn't seem to mind collateral damage.

Did Quinn have anything to do with it?

Micah sat at his desk and drew circles on his whiteboard. If the shooting and the bombing were connected…and the arsons and bakery were connected…

Micah dropped his head to the table and pounded it lightly. Too much. Too much to think about.

What about praying? Unique thought, I know, but hey…

Micah sat. He pulled his phone from its holder and began texting.

Prayer vigil. My house. Seven p.m. All call.

"All call" meant everyone should come. Drop everything and be in attendance.

The responses came back swiftly.

Tav. *I'm in.*

Luke. *I'll be there.*

Addison. *Gotcha.*

Jen and Wendy were slower to answer. *Will coordinate with the brothers. KO*

Grace chimed in. About time. See you.

Which left BB and Ben. Micah hated asking BB to watch his little brother and miss the prayer vigil. Maybe Ben could stay with Jen and Wendy's brothers? He'd talk it over with Ben when the boy got home from school.

In the meantime, he should straighten the house. And make sure they had plenty of coffee. They would need the strong stuff.

* * *

WEDNESDAY NIGHT

Tav, Luke, Addison, Jen, Wendy, and Grace arrived. The group settled around the living room in chairs and on the floor. Micah offered kitchen chairs to anyone who wanted them, but no one did. The floor worked. Tav sat at Jen's feet. Micah did the same with Wendy. Ben sat on the couch beside Wendy and Grace. Luke and Addison took the recliner and rocker, respectively. Only after everyone had been offered a drink (and all declined) did Micah start the meeting.

He signed, "I've been trying and trying to make this make sense, and I can't. Are there two separate parties after us? We know about the arsonist, but shooting the van? Bombing a county office?"

Luke's face darkened. "Bombing a county office takes this to a whole 'nother level. This goes beyond anything they've done before. Which makes me think the two sets of crimes aren't related."

"If the bomber was after you two, he had to know you were going to be at the county office." Wendy pointed out the obvious.

Addison signed, "Not necessarily. The bomber would know you needed to get the licenses sooner or later. They could have planted the bomb some time ago and waited for the perfect time to set it off."

Tav's eyes narrowed as he looked at his brother. "And you know this how?"

Addison shrugged. "I've been working with Quinn some. Summer job."

Luke signed, "Why didn't we know about this?" Micah appreciated the fact Luke kept it so Micah and Tav could follow all the conversations, not just the ones directed at them.

"If Quinn says don't tell, you don't tell. I didn't."

Tav rolled his eyes. Luke shook his head. Addison stretched in his chair.

Micah waved his hand. "They still had to know we were going to be there. We didn't even know we were going to be there. Tav texted me on the spur of the moment."

"So, we still have our leak." Wendy scowled, and her eyes darkened.

Tav disagreed. "Can't have. Not about this. We didn't tell anyone where we were going. We didn't. Addison and Luke were out shooting hoops."

"BB was working, and Ben was at school," Micah added, absolving his two of any possible guilt.

Jen signed, "Is it possible someone is tracking you? Especially you, Mick?"

He threw his hands in the air and signed, "It's possible, but how? Which is why I want to have this prayer vigil. We need wisdom and guidance."

Hands went silent. Mick looked at Ben and signed for BB to tell his brother, "We're going to pray all night. It would be good if you went over to stay with Arlene."

Ben pouted and spoke. BB translated. "He says he can pray, too."

"But we're going to pray for a long time. All night. You would have to be quiet all night."

Ben gave his single nod. "I can be qui-et. Like I am at Bi-ble stu-dy. I want to stay." He lifted his head and added,

"I will take notes." BB passed Ben's answer to Micah.

Micah laughed and rubbed the younger boy's head. "It's not that kind of prayer, buddy. But okay, you can stay." BB translated for Ben. Ben beamed and ran to his bedroom. He came back with a pen and notebook.

Wendy placed pillows on the floor for anyone who needed something to kneel on. She and Tav also set out glasses and cups. Micah signed, "Who's making the coffee?"

Tav answered, "Since we need to stay alert, I figured you would."

Micah grinned. "You know it. That's my job. Keeping people awake."

He went into the kitchen and started the first pot. He would need to make several more through the night.

Luke and Addison took positions on the floor with their backs against the couch. BB and Ben took chairs from the table and placed them in the living room. Wendy and Grace took the recliners. Tav signed, "We're here to petition God for our situation. And praise Him for His goodness to us." He gave Jen a straight-lipped smile. "Some of us will be silent. Feel free to speak as God moves you. Mick's coffee is optional."

Micah sneered. He had already filled his mug. He missed Quinn. Quinn could match Micah cup for cup. And prayer for prayer.

Tav signed, "Let's begin."

Everyone turned to their own altars and their own prayers.

Two hours in, Wendy went to check on her mom and brothers. She slipped out and in without anyone missing a beat.

Four hours in, Ben fell asleep on the floor. Micah carried him to his room and put the boy to bed. Jen left and returned. Tav poured himself a third cup of coffee. Micah made a fresh pot. And still, the prayers continued.

At five a.m., the back door opened. Micah noticed the

light saying someone had entered but ignored it. Backdoor meant Jen or Wendy. Someone who knew the code, anyhow. Micah continued with his prayers. And praises. He didn't forget prayer is as much about giving thanks as it is about asking for requests. Maybe more.

He knelt by the couch. Luke and Addison had moved to the kitchen table. They were sitting reading the Scriptures, speaking in sign to one another. Micah put his head down. He became aware of a figure kneeling beside him but didn't bother to look to see who it was. Didn't matter. All that mattered was his own connection with the Lord. Only when he came to a break did he sit back on his haunches and look around.

Quinn knelt beside him, intent on his own prayers. Micah's eyes widened. He had to resist the urge to hug the man. Not yet. There would be time when the praying was done.

And the praying ended at dawn. Not by arrangement but by the Spirit of the Lord. Luke and Addison leaned over the table, asleep. Jen sat passed out in one of the recliners. Grace slept in the other. BB lay on the floor, also napping. Tav had stretched out on the couch. Quinn continued to kneel in prayer, however. Micah weaved among the bodies to the kitchen. He dumped out the hours-old coffee and made a fresh pot. After the long night of prayer, he thought about weakening it but decided the others might appreciate something with a kick to it.

The smell of fresh coffee woke some of the dead. Quinn came first into the kitchen. He chest-bumped Micah and signed, "How is it going?"

"I'm glad you're back. We need you." He paused, then admitted, "We expected you to be gone longer. Why back so soon?"

Quinn poured a cup of coffee from the still-filling pot. "I'll let everyone know at the same time. Saves having to repeat the story more than once."

Micah nodded and signed, "Gotcha. Glad to have you back anyhow. It will take a worry off Wendy and Jen."

Quinn swallowed the coffee and saluted Micah. "Excellent as always."

Tav wandered in from the living room. He rubbed his eyes, rubbed his face, then did a double-take. He pounded Quinn on the back. He signed, "Welcome home. I didn't see you come in."

"No one did. That's how I planned it."

"Assignment finished?"

"We can discuss it later. Let's wake this crew and discuss what everyone heard last night. After, we can talk about why I'm here."

"Solid idea." Tav roused his brothers, then kissed Jen on the cheek.

She stirred, opened her eyes, and smiled. She signed, "How did you know I was dreaming of you?"

"Aren't you always?" Tav gave her a little boy's innocent look.

"No." She stretched and moved to the kitchen to wait for coffee.

Micah grinned. Way to destroy a man's confidence, Jen. He knelt beside BB and jostled his shoulder. He waited until his son looked at him, then signed, "Time to get up. Past time. You should have at least gone to bed."

BB straightened his neck and shoulders. It looked painful. He shook his head sharply and signed, "Truth. Next time."

Micah gave him a hand off the floor. BB came to his feet and headed to the washroom. Micah tapped him on the shoulder and signed, "Check on Ben while you're back there." BB gave him a thumbs up.

Ben came in to join the group at the kitchen table. He immediately grabbed Quinn around the middle in a bear hug. Quinn gazed around the room and signed, "What a motley bunch. I've seen corpses who looked better than this group."

Micah didn't bother to read the responses. He knew they would be on the theme of "We love you, too, Quinn."

Quinn pointed to Micah. Micah signed for BB to interpret for his brother, then stated, "One last prayer. Thank You, Lord, for all You spoke to us. Now, give us strength to carry out Your commands. In Jesus's Name, amen." He looked around and asked, "Who wants to share what you heard last night?"

Tav raised his hand, then signed, "I heard 'don't quit.' I received assurances I'm right where I need to be." He reached over and squeezed Jen's hand. "We are getting married. Jen will be my wife. Nothing will prevent that from happening." He paused, then admitted, "I think it applies to school as well. I won't quit going, either."

Jen lowered her eyes. Her lip trembled slightly. She signed, "I heard the same thing. But I was afraid it was my own voice telling me what I wanted to hear." She snorted. "I'm also thinking all this wedding planning is overrated." She pointed to Quinn and Grace. "Eloping looks better and better."

Quinn and Grace high-fived one another.

BB lifted his hand. "I heard stand fast. Be strong and have courage." He ducked his shoulder. "I'm not sure if that's about the wedding or about what's coming with leaving for college."

Micah signed, "It could be both."

Luke motioned around the circle. "I heard the same. Stand fast. And I know it applies to everything I'm doing. Or thinking of doing."

Micah asked in sign, "Which is? If you're ready to share." What did the younger man have in mind?

Luke shook his head. "Not yet. Still in the thinking stages."

Addison took his turn. "I heard be ready. I don't know for what, but be ready." He grinned. "The exact scripture that came to mind was 'gird your loins.' I'll take that as be ready."

Micah chuckled. He signed, "Yeah, I think so. We don't do much loin-girding these days."

Luke eyed his brother. "Do you have any clue as to what? I know you said you don't know, but do you have an inkling what it might be about?"

Addison signed, "It might have to do with living on my own." He motioned to his disabled side. "I'm still looking for work. Being on disability is fine, but I know I can do more. Maybe God has something for me to do."

Micah nodded. Luke and Tav both fist-bumped their brother.

Quinn signed, "Mick? What did you hear?" He refilled his coffee mug. And started a new pot.

"Peace. Walk in it. Live in it. Spread it." He hung his head. "I haven't been the best ambassador for peace in a long while. I'm tied in knots about all that's going on. First with the wedding, then with all the vandalism and the front window being shattered and the attacks and near-murders. Peace isn't something I've thought of. I needed the reminder of Who is in control."

Quinn put a hand on Micah's shoulder and squeezed it. He signed, "Hard to drain the swamp when you're surrounded by alligators."

Micah chuckled. At least, he hoped it sounded like a chuckle. "That's putting it mildly." *And in the short version.* He glanced at Grace. He signed across the table at her. "You were here from the start of the assembly. What did you hear?"

Grace's eyes held a hint of moisture. She spoke and signed, "Like others, I heard be ready. But also peace." She dropped her eyes. "I've been fighting. I won't say what. But peace would be good."

Micah nodded. He couldn't reach Grace from across the table but would have hugged her if he could. Instead, he signed, "I love you." She signed the sentiment back.

Micah looked at Quinn. "You want to share?" He made sure BB continued to interpret for Ben. They all needed to hear what the bossman had to say.

Quinn nodded. He glanced around. "Two queries. What am I doing here, and what did I hear from the Lord?" Quinn squeezed Grace's hand. "The first is tied with the second. I heard I am doing the Lord's will. He is with me in my choice. It's the 'right one.'" He stopped and added, "If there is such a thing in His free will. But He is with me." He held the eyes of each person at the table for a long moment. "I'm retiring. Quitting. Whatever they want to call it. But I'm done working on the outside."

Micah watched eyes widen around the room. Including Grace's. He knew his own were saucer size. Quinn Magary quitting his position? Hanging it up?

Micah asked for the assembly, "Why?"

"Because I want to be home. I want to be near my family." Quinn stared at the floor. He signed, "I lost my first family because I put my duty ahead of them." He looked up. "Lost a wife and son. They won't have anything to do with me. Made it clear I could have my job, noble and essential as it might be, or I could have them. I chose the job. I did vital work. Critical work. I couldn't see leaving it. My wife knew what I did before we married. I think she thought she could change me, make me quit. I didn't."

Quinn's eyes filled with water. He brushed them with the sleeve of his shirt. "Even when my son was born, I still kept working. And going out of town. Sometimes for weeks or a month at a time." Quinn's signing became more emphatic. "I had to work. No one could do what I did. No one."

He sat back in his chair. Grace wiped his face. He smiled a straight-lipped smile at her, then continued. "She left with the boy. Said never to contact her. I tried, but she refused contact. Tried with the boy, but even as an adult, he wanted nothing to do with me. I had abandoned him, and he had no forgiveness."

Quinn stopped and corrected his statement. "Has none. I stopped trying about five years ago." He stared at the table and fell silent and motionless. Only after several moments did he begin again. "Then I met you boys." He shook his head. "Worst decision of my life to get involved with you."

Micah, Luke, and Tav all put their thumbs in the air. No one interrupted Quinn's story, however. The floor would be his for as long as it took.

Quinn continued, "And you, Grace, came along and added to the chaos. And I knew I'd found a family. I never thought I would have one, but here you all are." He chuckled. His laughter stopped. "Now this mess with the attempted murders starts, and work wants to send me away. Just when I'm needed most here."

He stopped and corrected himself. "Fine. I'm not needed. But I want to be here. You're my family. I don't want to be separated again. So I quit. Retired. Whatever they choose to call it. But I'm done. And the Lord confirmed it last night. I'm where I need to be."

Quinn leaned over and kissed Grace. A long, warm, ardent kiss.

Ben interrupted. "Quinn and Grace can kiss. They are mar-ried."

Quinn stopped and laughed. He held his arms out for Ben to come to him. Ben raced to Quinn's side, and the mentor caught him in a full-on embrace. "Yes, we are. And we're going to stay married for a long, long time." Ben raced back to his chair.

Grace sucked in her lip. She signed, "Do not quit for me."

"I'm not. I'm quitting for me. I want to be with family. I want to be needed and cared for in my old age. I can't do that from miles away."

Micah reassured the man. "You know we'll always care for you. And yes, I want you around. All the time."

Tav signed. "Ditto. Not only to solve our problems but to share our joys. You're our dad. We love you."

Quinn raised his head and looked at the ceiling. He closed his eyes, pursed his lips, and waited. Addison touched Quinn's arm. The older man reopened his eyes. Addison signed, "Same goes for me. I wouldn't have my brothers if it weren't for you."

Jen signed, "And I wouldn't have Tav, and Wenders wouldn't have Micah. This is all your fault, Quinn. You're stuck with us."

Ben tugged on BB's arm. "Why is Pop-dad cry-ing?"

BB signed but spoke to Ben. "They are telling Pop-dad how much they love him. And Pop-dad is crying because he's happy."

Ben straightened his face. He walked to Quinn and signed the only words he knew. "I love you."

Quinn took the boy in his arms again. No one had to read lips to know what he said. He laid his head on top of Ben's and sat still. Ben put his arms around Quinn.

Micah brushed moisture from his cheeks. He wiped it on the back of his pants. He asked, "Are we done being sappy? Because if we are, we still have a murderer to catch."

Hisses and boos in sign and spoken language came his way. His eyes narrowed. He cocked his head. "Boo again. Longer this time."

Luke and Addison, with Wendy, all booed. Micah looked at Tav. Tav shook his head. Micah turned one ear to the group. Everyone hissed. Quinn signed and ordered, "Low tones."

Micah's eyes widened. He looked at Tav again.

Tav grinned and nodded. "I heard it. The low tones. I can hear it."

Micah signed as well. "I heard it. Like a low rumble. But I heard it."

Quinn pounded on the table. Micah's face fell. "I felt it. I didn't hear it."

The mentor signed, "You're getting the low tones back. That counts. It's coming back for you both. That's fantastic."

Cheers and people pounding on the table filled the kitchen. Micah grinned at Tav. His friend returned the expression. There was hope. Quinn had returned. Their hearing was coming back. It would be a great day.

* * *

T

HURSDAY MORNING

The group fixed pancakes on the griddle in the courtyard for breakfast. Sausages and fried potatoes. Biscuits in the oven. And everyone enjoyed an hour of everyday life. Then they got back to work.

A slight breeze kept the air from becoming stifling. Bluejays squawked at anyone who passed by. Finches fluttered and chased each other away from the bird feeders. Hummingbirds divebombed anyone who got too close. Territorial little buggers. Quinn started the discussion. He signed for Micah and Tav but spoke for the rest. "What do we know?" He held the eyes of his "children" one by one. He had to protect them. But first, he needed to know from who.

"We may have two different groups of villains. One is after Micah and Tav, and one is after anything connected to weddings," Wendy answered first. Quinn smiled inside. He'd trained her well.

"All weddings, or your wedding?"

"Since the dress shops hit had nothing to do with us, I'd say all weddings. At least in the beginning." Wendy continued her analysis.

Tav picked up the narrative. "We think one group is after Mick and me. But why? Who?"

Quinn shrugged. "Interchangeable. If we know one, we know the other. Unless you can think of anyone who might be after you. Who have you made mad? Dissed? Cut off on the freeway?"

Tav threw his hands in the air and then signed, "No one. I can't think of anyone. Not in the past year. I'm sure there are some from the past, but I don't know who."

"So, list the past suspects. The mayor of Acorn." The epicenter of the earthquake from two years ago had been in Acorn. The mayor had been vehemently opposed to the Knights in general and Tav in particular.

"Did he even survive? He didn't heed the warning to leave." Tav stared at the ground. The subject remained a sore one for the young man.

"Doesn't mean he didn't. We should look him up." Quinn dipped his head at Grace. "I'll talk to my ex-people. They'll help me, even though I'm retired."

Grace patted his arm. "Thank you, dear."

Mick grinned. "Bad news when she calls you dear."

"Don't I know it." Quinn kissed Grace on the cheek. He turned back and continued signing and speaking. "Who else?"

Mick offered, "Jonas." Another body from before the earthquake. Who assaulted Mick and nearly killed him.

Quinn heard the grumbles. He grimaced. "We'll have to see if he got out on bond. I'm certain he hasn't come to trial yet. With Acorn destroyed, all the courts and jails had to be moved around."

"We should look Jonas and his crew up." Mick tapped the table. "Who else? Think, Tav. Who hates you enough to want you dead? Any old girlfriends?"

Tav snorted. "You know better than that. Dad kept me so busy with practice that I never had time for a girlfriend. I barely had time for my brothers."

Luke signed. "We know. We remember." Addison nodded in agreement.

Wendy cocked her head. "Wait a minute. What if we're looking at the wrong place." She stared at the ground, then looked up and signed, "The bad guys brought the fight to us. What if Tav and Mick are the targets because they're close to someone else in the group?"

If quiet could get quieter, it did. All eyes focused on Wendy. She hesitated, then pushed ahead. "What if the bad guys are trying to get to Quinn through Tav? Or to any one of you?"

Quinn's eyes narrowed. "By that reasoning, the perps could be after any of us." He stared around the circle. "Who's been naughty?" He stopped. "And I'm not talking about stealing my chocolate." The joke fell flat.

Quinn watched the Knights do some serious soul-searching. He looked inward himself. Who would try to destroy his life by attacking the Knights? Who would care? Granted, he'd put many a perp away. Foiled many plots and kept evil at bay. But those were one and done. Not something that carried forward.

Except—

Quinn waited until, one by one, the assembly declined to know of anyone who would hate them so much they would destroy a friend. Quinn eyed Grace. She shook her head but held his eyes.

Mick held up his hands in defeat. "I got nothing."

Quinn breathed in slowly. "I need to check something out. Someone. It's a long shot, but we're running on long shots."

Tav cocked his head. "Who?"

"Let me research first. When I know, I'll tell you. In the meantime, I want you all on guard at all times. Go nowhere alone, and don't go anywhere unless you have to. Especially with Mick and Tav."

Addison joked, "Tav is lava." Quinn caught his eyes and scowled. Addison shrugged. "Comic relief. Little joke."

"Very little." Okay, so Quinn shouldn't have said that.

Addison hadn't meant to make light of the situation.

Tav signed, "But he's right. Being with me is trouble."

Mick held up a hand, then signed, "I'm not exactly safe, either. Whoever it is wants both of us dead."

Quinn pointed at both men. "Go nowhere. Stay home and stay safe." He sneered. "You got nothing to do for the next month, anyhow. Except stay alive for the wedding."

Tav objected, "I've got my master's to finish."

"I'm sure your professors will prefer you do your work online rather than endanger the entire college. Especially after what happened downtown at the justice of the peace's office."

Tav grimaced but nodded. "I hear you." He added, "Figuratively speaking."

Mick asked, "Does that mean not taking on any new clients?"

"Not unless I clear them first."

"So, is our snitch now working for the second group? The group that wants to kill Mick and Tav? How could they switch like that?" Wendy brought up another issue.

Quinn explained his thinking. "There might not be a snitch for both sides. Let me track down my hunch, and I'll give you our next steps. Besides staying out of bakeries."

Mick and Tav grumbled, even signing. But they agreed, and the assembly broke to clean and put the cooking utensils away. And go about their regularly scheduled lives.

Quinn and Grace walked back to the house. Grace asked, "What are you thinking?"

"I'm thinking being seen that night at the bakery may have been a trigger."

"To whom?"

"I can think of half a dozen possibilities. But the number one would be Lorna."

"Your ex? Why her? She's been out of your life for decades. You haven't heard from your son Denner in five years, anyhow. Why would they come after you now?"

Quinn held Grace's hand as they walked across the quadrangle. "I didn't say it made sense. I said she'd be my number one suspect." He hesitated, then admitted, "And she contacted me after the quake. After we settled here in Galt. In all the confusion after the destruction of Acorn, the letter got bounced around. But she wanted money. Again. She saw Grandfather died, and I had inherited his estate. That meant her current settlement wasn't sufficient for how she wanted to live now, and she wanted to relitigate our agreement."

Quinn opened the door for Grace to pass through. "I told her no." After she entered, he continued, "From a P.O. box. Maybe this is her saying, 'I found you.'"

"What about Denner? He's your son."

"I made generous provision for him. I made generous provision for Lorna. In her thinking, it wasn't generous enough."

They stopped in the kitchen to get cold drinks to take to the living room. Quinn continued his tale. "It's not the first time she's pulled this. She's been relitigating the divorce decree every time I got a promotion or a change in status. The courts told her 'no' the first time…and the second…and the third. She got nasty and tried to have me arrested for various and sundry reasons. Always without cause. But she keeps trying. And threatening to ruin me, destroy me, take everything I own…she's not right in the head."

"But why come after the boys? Why not come after you?" Grace took her seat on the couch.

Quinn slid in beside her and put his arm around her shoulders. "If I die, everything goes to you. I'm guessing she doesn't want to take the chance of you inheriting it all, and she gets nothing. But if I'm alive and she can touch people I care about, she has more of a chance of reaping a reward for leaving them alone. It's a new level of the blackmail she's tried for years."

Grace's eyes flickered back and forth. "That's convoluted, Quinn, even for you. She comes after the boys to get you to give her more money? When would it ever end?"

"It wouldn't. There would never be a payoff sufficient for her to be satisfied. As long as I have anything of value, she'll want it."

Grace shook her head. "You sure can pick 'em, Quinn Magary."

He leaned in and kissed her. "I picked you, you know."

Grace leaned back and looked at him. "I thought I picked you."

"Call it a mutual picking." Quinn smiled, then grew serious. "Help me save the boys. I think she intended the shooting to be an 'I found you' message. The bomb meant she could reach out and touch the ones I care about."

"How do we stop…first, how do we prove it's her?"

"That partial license plate they got at Mercury Park. From a stolen car. Stolen from Lansing, Michigan. Guess who lives in Lansing?"

Grace's eyes narrowed. She studied the floor, then looked up at Quinn. "Is that all?"

"I had my people look into her financials. All that money I've provided for her is gone. She's blown through it and then some. Like I said, nothing I gave her was enough for the lifestyle she wanted to live. And she pulled Denner right along with her. He lives as extravagantly as she does. That's why I stopped giving them the money and put the rest in the will. I figured—wrong—that they would at least learn patience and wait until I died. But apparently, Lorna has figured out a different way of getting her blood money."

"How do we stop her?"

"That's a question without an answer." Quinn drew in a deep breath and squeezed Grace's shoulder.

Grace stared at the floor, then looked up. "What if…?"

* * *

Several hours later, Quinn picked up Tav, Luke, and

Addison and walked with them back to Mick's house. Easier for Ben to be in his own surroundings.

Mick and Tav waited. Quinn settled in the recliner, leaned forward, and folded his hands. He glanced from Tav to Micah and back. He raised his eyebrows. He spoke and signed, "You two are a world of trouble, you know?"

Mick raised his hand. "Say it again. Louder." He looked at Tav. Tav looked back at Mick and nodded. Their eyes had a light in them Quinn hadn't seen in a while.

Quinn repeated his statement.

Both men grinned. And nodded. Mick spoke. His voice remained off-pitch, but he said, "I hear you. I can't make out all the words, but I hear you."

Tav agreed. "It's a drone, but it's audible." He slapped Micah on the back. "It's coming back, Mick!" He finished by signing it as well.

Quinn and the assembled men all clapped and hooted. Mick and Tav took bows and cheered along.

Finally, Quinn waved them all to settle down. He chuckled and signed, "You're still a world of trouble."

Mick grinned and signed back. "Guilty."

Tav nodded. "Same. What can we do about it?"

Quinn narrowed his eyes and glared at Luke, Addison, and BB. "Problem is, if it weren't those two, it would be you three. Four, with Ben."

BB threw his hands in the air. "What did I do?" The teen looked flustered.

"I love you like a grandson. That's the problem." Quinn sat back. "It's the same issue with all of you. Someone, and yes, I know who, wants my money." The schematic of the bomb was the proof he needed. Maybe not proof he could take to a court of law or the police. Yet. But he'd seen the plans of the bomb. Lorna's clockmaker background was all over it.

He gazed around at the group of men. And boys. "They want to use you to get to me."

"By killing us?" Mick raised his hands in disbelief.

"Been done before for less." Quinn nodded. "Grace and I discussed it. Long and hard. The only way to stop the attacks is to eliminate the inheritance problem."

Tav frowned. "We're not in your line of inheritance."

"The attacker believes if they can use you to blackmail me, they can get the money." Quinn's eyes narrowed. He wouldn't go into all the details he'd shared with Grace. The millions he'd given Lorna and Denner. The suits and countersuits. The constant being hauled into court. It had to end. He gave a straight-lipped smile. "But if I give it away, there's nothing they can blackmail me for. No sense coming after you if they have nothing to gain."

Quinn continued. "The easiest way to fix the problem is to give away the inheritance. Then, she has nothing to kill for. If I give it away, they can't kill you to get it back. It's gone. End of story."

Six heads nodded. Tav signed, "Give it away. I know plenty of organizations—"

"I'm aware of them. Already made provisions for them after I'm gone. That's not the issue." One by one, Quinn held each Knight in his gaze. "It's the rest of the money. The money Grace and I are living on. My retirement."

Mick tapped his finger on the table. "You can put it in trust. Distribute it as you will. Then it goes only to the trustees and not to anyone outside."

"I could. I could also give it to my heirs. Give it all away. Then, I depend on the goodwill of my heirs to support Grace and me in the manner we choose to live. Less accounting to worry about." Quinn smirked. "Which means the attacker has no chance of getting any money."

Silence enveloped the room. Five faces reflected the gravity of the offer. Ben drew faces but didn't follow the conversation. The boy would make a court sketch artist one day. Probably could start tomorrow if the law didn't forbid underage employment.

Tav shook his head. "There's got to be another way to do this."

"Not in the time we have. These criminals are after you now. I need to do something equally now. We can go to the bank and arrange the transfer." Quinn looked at the clock and changed his mind. "Will have to be Monday, and I'll have to call my banker tonight to warn him." He smirked. "I like to drop surprises on him in the evenings. He somewhat expects it."

Quinn held Luke and Addison in his gaze. "I need you two to be okay with this. It's going to be distributed between all the Knights. Including Jen and Wendy. I know their portions will be combined with Tav and Mick's. I don't want to have any hard feelings they got two portions, and you only got one."

Luke and Addison both held up hands. Luke laid his on the table, then signed. "Quinn, you don't have to give any of us a share." He said, "Jesus told a parable about a landowner who hired workers for a sum of money. He gave the same amount to the ones who worked all day as the ones who worked an hour. It was His money to give, and He gave it. It's the same with you. You're giving away what you have. You don't have to give any of it to any of us. You could give it all to one or even none. It won't change how much I owe you and love you."

Luke looked at the floor. "That shouldn't be hard to say. I know it. I feel it. It just sounds weird." He looked up. "But I mean it. Thanks, Quinn. For being you." He held Quinn's eyes.

Addison smiled with his eyes. "Ditto without the Bible lesson. You mean everything to us, Quinn. Money or not." The young man leaned forward to keep Quinn in his gaze.

Mick stared hard at Quinn. "The question is, do you trust us to take care of you?" His hands shook while he signed.

Quinn grinned. "That will be the least of my worries,

I'm certain. I know where you all live. Anything I need, I can ask anyone of you for it."

Tav ran his hands over his face. "How much are we talking here? You've already given us generously from the Magary Chase."

Quinn looked at the ceiling and narrowed his eyes. After some thinking and calculating, he ventured, "I guess about ten million."

The Knights looked at each other wide-eyed.

Quinn continued. "Each."

Breathing stopped.

"Not counting Ben's share since he's a minor. That will go in a trust."

Tav gasped. Luke grabbed his chest. Mick rose to his feet and walked out of the living room into the kitchen. Addison bent forward and banged his head on the table. BB slipped onto a chair. Only Ben continued as before. The youngest Knight turned to Quinn. "Thank you, Pop-dad."

Quinn guffawed. He pointed to Ben and looked at all the others. "That. Right there is all the response I want from any of you. Thank you, and drop it."

Tav's jaw dropped. He stared at Quinn. He tried to speak. "I…I…I can't. I can't. I…." Tav swallowed. He signed, "Thank you."

Luke walked over and hugged Quinn. His face looked pale, his eyes wide. "Thank you. It's not enough. It isn't."

Quinn grabbed him by the shoulders. "It is. It's all I want to hear from you characters."

Addison limped into Quinn's embrace. Tears flowed down the younger man's face. Quinn let his own flow. "Love you, Addison."

"Quinn."

Mick made his way back from his foray out of the room. He caught Quinn in a bear hug but said or signed nothing. Tears in his eyes said it all.

BB climbed to his feet. He looked most in shock of the

five older Knights. He stammered, "I don't know how to live like a millionaire."

Quinn's voice came out hard and fast. "You don't. You live like a man. A man who loves his neighbor, his enemy, and his Lord. You live by the mantra, 'What would Jesus do?' You make sure the money you have never has you. You understand?"

BB nodded, then shuddered. "You gotta be around to teach me, Quinn. You're my Pop-dad. You've been showing me. But you gotta keep showing me. Because I'll screw it up. I will. I know me."

Quinn caught the boy by the back of his neck and shook him. "If I believed that, I'd never give it to you. If I thought this would change any of you, I'd never trust you with it. You got it? This gift changes nothing. Except maybe you don't have to worry so much the next time the public utility commission decides to raise electricity rates."

He held his arms out. "I love you boys and girls. I wouldn't do this if I thought it would hurt you or change you in any way. Don't prove me wrong."

A group hug followed. A long, intense group hug. Quinn never felt so free. Or loved.

* * *

The Vaughn brothers returned to their own home. The three men sat on the couch in silence. Tav could guess what was on his brothers' minds. The same as on his.

Luke began to giggle. It started as a chuckle but devolved into almost hysterics. Tav couldn't hear it, but he could see his brother's body shaking. He took hold of Luke's shoulder. "Pull it together, Lucas. You can do this."

Tears ran down Luke's face as he continued to laugh. "I was worried about buying a new pair of shoes for the wedding." He looked at Tav. "Shoes!"

Tav nodded. "I know, bro. I know." A chuckle escaped his belly. "I thought the same thing." He signed, "But we can't be blowing it. We can't live any different than we have been. We can't."

Addison snickered, then signed, "Can we buy the good ramen instead of the twenty-five cents a pack ramen? Once a week, maybe?"

Tav threw a pillow at his brother. Addison caught it and tossed it back. Luke intercepted the pass and rocketed it toward Tav. Tav deflected it. Addison grabbed it and pommeled Luke. A free-for-all pillow fight developed.

Only as the tension lessened did the three men slow their assaults. There was no danger of anyone being injured. Even less of damage to the surroundings. Tav made sure all the furnishings were fight-proof when they moved into the eight-plex. Anticipating love fights had been a no-brainer. Anticipating one for excessive wealth? Not in his wildest imagination.

Once Tav, Luke, and Addison regained a modicum of self-control, they sat and breathed. Tav signed, "Luke, you can finish at any med school. Any med school that will take you, I mean."

Luke disagreed. "We need to stay under the radar. Live like we always have. Except buy the good ramen." He grinned at his brother.

Tav signed his agreement. "But you can still transfer to any college you want. You'll just have to go on a scholarship. And we can make one to fit." He motioned to Addison. "We've done it before."

"True." Addison signed, "I'm going to finish here. No sense changing midstream."

Tav nodded. "Good plan." He lowered his head. "I still can't. This isn't real. It's not." He went to his knees. "Lord, I'm like Solomon. You've given us the ability to do anything, be anything, all for the taking. We need Your wisdom. Show us how to use this gift to honor You."

Luke joined Tav. "Protect us from our base nature. Let everything we do reflect You."

Addison finished. "Thank You for Quinn and Grace. Thank You for trusting us with this gift. Don't let us fail You."

"Amen."

* * *

Micah sat at the table with BB and Ben. Ben continued sketching faces, even those who had left the building. Quinn's look of peace jumped off the page. Micah touched it then signed to BB, "Ask him why is this the first time I've seen him this way?"

"Be-cause he gave his mon-ster a-way." Ben autographed the portrait.

Micah signed to BB, who spoke to Ben. "Did the monster come live with Dad?"

Ben cocked his head and studied Micah for a moment. He looked down and returned to his drawing. "Not yet."

Micah signed, "We'll have to make sure the monster never comes here."

BB corrected, "He may visit, but he can't live here." He made a fist for his little brother. "Right, Ben?"

Ben tapped his fists back. "Right." He started on another portrait. Of BB this time. Smiling.

Micah directed his attention to BB. "What will you do with your share?"

"Set up an anonymous foundation to help others." He shrugged. "What others, right? Have to pray about that. Hard. What about you?" He tapped his hand on the counter.

"Same. Pray. Prayer and more prayer. I don't know. But I'm not doing anything right away. Nothing changes." *Okay, some things change. Maybe a little. Extra tutors for Ben since he's going to be in "regular school." ... Lord, help me set priorities.*

"Nothing?" BB's raised eyebrows challenged him.

"Nothing I'm doing changes. I'm not walking in and quitting my job."

"Good thing because you work from home." BB gave his dad a slow smile.

Micah pretended to swing at his son. "Smart guy. You know what I mean. I'm still going to work on other people's taxes. And estates." He shook his head. "Now I really have to be careful. If I don't handle the little taxes, how will I ever handle the big ones?"

"Yeah." BB chewed his lower lip. "You think the Knights can all keep living together? No one's going to run out and buy a beach house in Bali, right?"

"Maybe one in Monterey. Not Bali. Tropical storms will kill you."

BB chuckled. "Right. No hurricanes or tropical storms in Monterey. How about Cayucos instead? Mialma will be welcome on the beach."

"Better plan. We'll make sure it's big enough for everyone, though. No timeshares to cause fights." *No fights.*

"You really are into early church living, aren't you? Everyone shares everything in common." BB pointed to the Bible lying on the counter.

"It kept down the fights." Mostly. Some of them, anyhow. Except maybe in Corinth…there's always one.

"That, and the Spirit of the Lord being welcome."

"That, too." Right. Where the Spirit of the Lord is, there is peace.

A knock at the door interrupted the Bible lesson. Wendy and Jen stood on the porch. "Can we come in?"

Micah signed, "I don't know. Can you?" Micah grinned at his visitors.

Wendy sneered at Micah. She signed back, "Grammar police. Okay, wise guy. May we come in?"

Micah grinned. "Of course." He waved the two women into the living room. "How can we help you?"

Ben ran in from the kitchen. BB interpreted for Micah. "Wen-dy. Look at the pic-ture I drew of Quinn." The excitement in his eyes flashed. He handed her the portrait of

Quinn, freed from his monster.

Wendy stared at it, and her eyes widened. She looked from the sketch to Ben to the sketch. "I've never seen him like this."

Ben crowed, "I did. Just a-while a-go. When he told us his plans."

"That's a perfect picture, Ben. Are you going to give it to him?"

Ben tipped his head. "Do you think he would want it?"

"I think he would cherish it forever. I think he would frame it and hang it in the living room of his house."

Ben dropped his head. "No. Hang-ing it would be too fan-cy. I would need to draw a bet-ter one for him." The boy's lower lip stuck out.

Wendy shook her head. "You couldn't do a better one, Ben. This will make him very happy."

"I will draw one with Grace and Quinn hap-py to-geth-er." Ben turned to a clean sheet of vellum and began sketching. BB continued to sign all of Ben's utterances to Micah.

"They'll love it." She eyed Micah and signed, "What's different?"

"He gave away his monster." Micah couldn't stop grinning.

Wendy cocked her head. "What monster?" Jen reflected the same curiosity.

"Has Grace talked to you?" *Do the women not know? How had Grace not said anything?*

"Only about our project. You will be happy to know we are almost finished. And we can stop worrying about it."

Micah smiled wide. "Great! So, can you tell me what it is?"

"Nope. Not yet." Wendy gave him a catbird smile. Her face straightened. "What would Grace want to talk about?"

Micah pointed to the couch. "Sit." He swallowed his smile and straightened his shoulders. He could do this.

Signing helped hide the excitement. If his hands would stop trembling.

Wendy and Jen exchanged glances, then sat together on the couch. "What's this about?" Wendy's cocked her head. Her eyes narrowed.

"About Quinn and his monster." Micah leaned against the wall, his hands busy signing. "Quinn believes the attacks on the van and at the justice of the peace were calculated by his son and ex-wife. Designed to eliminate any competition for the Magary Estate."

Wendy turned to Jen, then looked back at Micah. "But…"

Micah nodded. "We're not competition. Except Quinn feels his wife is using us as blackmail to get Quinn to give her more money. In order to keep us from being targeted, Quinn is giving away all of his money. Or the bulk of it."

Jen leaned forward. "To who?" She glared at Micah. "And don't you correct my grammar."

Micah smiled. "Not this time." He pushed off from the wall. "To us. The Knights. He's giving his whole fortune to all of us. In return, we will pay his and Grace's expenses going forward. His ex and her son have no claim on money that's gone. Killing any of us doesn't advantage them. Our share will go to our heirs. They gain nothing."

Wendy sat silent for several moments. "How much is Quinn talking about?"

BB burst out giggling and walked out of the room. Micah tried to straighten his face but only managed to make it worse. He swallowed hard, cleared his throat, and signed, "Ten million dollars. To each of us."

Jen scoffed. "Get out of here."

Micah shook his head. "Can't. It's my house. And I'm serious."

Wendy's eyes went blank. She looked at him and turned her head from side to side. "No. No. Not possible."

Micah knelt in front of her and took her hands. He

squeezed them, then signed, "It's true, Wendy. It's real. Quinn wants to meet with his banker on Monday to arrange the transfer of funds. It will take a few days to go through, but he'll make it all certified and legal. You and I stand to receive twenty million dollars by the end of the week."

Wendy continued to be in shock. She breathed out slowly. Inhaled. Exhaled. Inhaled. Exhaled. "Ten million dollars. Each?" Blood drained from her face.

"Ten million." Micah waited for her to react.

She repeated, "Ten." Like she didn't comprehend the number.

"Ten million." Micah caught her eyes. He studied her intently. "Does this change anything?"

Wendy exploded. She jumped to her feet. "Change anything? Change anything?" His fiancée stopped and caught Micah's hands. She stared him up and down. Micah waited. Wendy breathed.

She signed, "No. It doesn't change anything between us." She touched his cheek. "No, it does not change a thing. I love you, Mick Andres. I said it before. Nothing will change my love for you."

Micah exhaled. He didn't realize he'd been holding his breath. He reached in and kissed Wendy on the cheek. "We're going to live like we planned. We're going to pray and ask the Lord to guide us about every penny before we spend it."

Wendy nodded. "Yes, yes, we are."

Jen asked, "When was Tav going to tell me?" Her tone carried some petulance.

Micah defended his brother-at-arms. "We thought Grace told you. She must have forgotten while you were working on your project."

Wendy nodded. "She did say she had something to discuss with us, but a critical need arose, and we had to focus on other priorities." She chuckled. "I guess she got distracted."

Jen jumped to her feet. "I've got to talk to him. Now." She ran out the front door.

Wendy called, "Jen, wait!" But she was gone. Wendy put her hands in the air. "Okay, now I've got to leave."

Micah waved her down. "Sit. Just for a few minutes." He sat beside her and squeezed her hand. "The picture Ben drew of Quinn came after he gave away his monster. The monster was the money. The boys and I discussed the monster would not come to our house after leaving Quinn's. He might sneak in, but he would never be welcome, and we would never let him stay." He looked into her eyes. "I want to promise you the same thing. If you ever see the monster trying to get a foothold here, you are to slap him down and kick him out. Understood?"

Wendy smiled a sad smile. She spoke as she signed, "If you will do the same. If you see me entertaining the monster, you'll throw him out. No monsters here."

Ben nodded without looking up from his sketching. "No mon-sters here. Not al-lowed."

BB repeated Ben's declaration. "No monsters." He grinned wide. "But oh, Wendy. This is huge. It opens so much."

Wendy got up and hugged the young man. "It does. But we'll keep it from holding us. We'll have the money. It won't have us."

"Right."

Wendy looked at Micah. "What about my mom and my brothers?"

"Quinn didn't mention them. But I'm sure he will make provision for them." Micah stopped. "Who has Power of Attorney for her?"

"Jen has financial. I have medical."

"So, it will probably fall on Jen to manage it for your mom, at least." Micah took Wendy from BB and held her in his arms. "She'll be cared for, Wendy. You have my promise."

Wendy nodded. "I know, Mick. You and I discussed this when we were poor working stiffs. I don't expect to change now." She grinned at him.

He leaned in and kissed her on the mouth. Ben cleared his throat. "No kis-sing."

Micah rubbed his son's head. "Just one little one. To seal a promise."

Ben rolled his eyes. "O-kay." He held the sketch of Quinn and Grace beaming. "Will this be good e-nough for Quinn and Grace?"

Wendy took the picture from the boy. "It will be perfect, Ben. And I know just when to give it to them." She grinned at Micah. "We've got a surprise for Quinn. I'll have this framed, and we can give it to them as a wedding present."

"Wedding? For them?"

"You'll see." Wendy wrinkled her nose and kissed Ben on top of the head. "Thank you, Ben." She walked to the door, hugged BB, then left.

* * *

THURSDAY AFTERNOON

Micah watched as BB picked up Micah's phone. He signed, "A voicemail. It's Ben." Micah studied BB's face, watching it go from happiness to confusion to concern. His face darkened. Finally, he nodded, disconnected the call, and punched in a number. Micah couldn't see who BB called, but his words were short, curt, and to the point.

He hung up and looked at Micah. "Ben's in trouble. Quinn is on his way over."

Which said this wasn't for misbehavior. Micah asked, "What's going on?"

BB signed, "He called you Pop-dad."

A chill ran up Micah's spine. Micah was Dad. Never Pop-dad.

"What did he say?" Micah demanded answers. He signed sharply.

"Wait until Quinn gets here. He's coming—"

The door flew open, and Quinn charged into the house. He held out his hand for the phone, punched in some numbers, and cocked his head to listen.

BB interpreted for Micah:

"Pop-dad will pick me up at five-thirty-one, please. Pop-dad will bring my run-ning shoes. I will need them for the race to-night. The new teacher says you must pick me up.

She knows your face. I ex-plained you can-not hear. She says it will not mat-ter. Come to the field house by the basketball court."

Micah signed back. "There are no new teachers. No one starts without being introduced to the children and the parents." He thought hard. *Today was supposed to be field day. They were going to have all the after-school sports to try out. I was supposed to pick him up at five. How did someone get him alone?*

Field day. Volunteers. Friends of volunteers. Less oversight. Less control. The field house? Why there? Unless she has him passing out the equipment, and that's how she's going to get him apart. She'll lock up. With him in it.

Quinn nodded, his face grim. "Ben is sending a message. Meet at five-thirty-one?" His eyes narrowed. He stared into space. Finally, he signed, "Something about the one. One person?"

Micah looked at the clock. "We've got just under half an hour to figure it out. I'm going to the school."

Quinn shook his head. "Too dangerous. I'll go."

"She said she knows what I look like. She won't accept someone else."

"I'll come as your interpreter. Ben said you can't hear. She'll have to expect someone else."

BB offered, "Ben didn't say you had to come alone. He only said to pick him up."

Micah added, "With his shoes. What do you think that's about?"

"Running shoes. For a race." Quinn repeated Ben's words. Spoken and signed.

BB suggested, "He's anticipating having to run. To escape something. Or someone."

Micah scowled. His back tightened, and his fists clenched. "No one is going to hurt my son."

Quinn put a muscular hand on Micah's shoulder. "We will protect Ben." He held Micah's gaze. "We don't trade lives, Mick. Son or not. You'll carry the guilt, or he will. You want that for him?"

Micah shut his eyes. He cursed the one who would cause him to make such a choice. Cursed the situation that brought him to this decision. Cursed the animal who would use a child as bait for a trap. Cursed…all in a single thought. Micah opened his eyes and nodded once to Quinn. His limbs hardened. Resolve flooded through him. Ben would come home. Micah would rescue—

Who will rescue?

Micah snapped back to reality. God would rescue Ben, or He wouldn't. Micah's job was to trust Him. To listen to Him. Follow His guidance. And pray. Most of all, pray.

Brokenness flooded him. Micah sank to his knees and began to sob. Quinn knelt beside him. Micah sensed BB kneeling with them. He couldn't hear them if they were praying. All he could do was pray on his own. And pray and pray and pray.

A sense of time passing interrupted his supplications. He looked as Quinn put his arm around Micah's arms and semi-lifted him to his feet. Micah stood. Quinn signed, "We've got to go."

Micah squared his shoulders. He wiped his face with his hands and dried them on his pants. He took in a deep breath and nodded. He looked around and realized Tav, Luke, Addison, Grace, and Wendy had all joined the crowd. Quinn nodded to him. "They'll stay here and storm the gates of heaven."

Micah fist-bumped the men, hugged Grace, then kissed Wendy. She signed, "I love you."

He signed back. "Love you." Then, out the door, in the car, and down the street to the school. Quinn drove.

They pulled into an empty parking lot. No cars. Not even one.

In his mind, Micah ran through the employees and teachers he knew. Who would be most prone to help in such a cruel deception? Who hated Ben? Who hated Micah enough to use Ben? Questions with no answers. Yet.

Quinn drove around the back of the field house. He parked at the rear of the lot. Micah signed, "What do we do now? Get out?"

Quinn's eyes narrowed. He asked, "What would you do if you didn't think this was a trap?"

"I'd get out and knock on the door."

Quinn nodded. "That's what we'll do. Come on." He paused, then added, "But stay in front of me."

Micah didn't ask why. When Quinn spoke, you listened. The two men got out of the car and headed for the door. The hair on the back of Micah's neck prickled. Were they being watched? Did a sniper have them in the crosshairs of a rifle? Could Ben already be dead?

Micah reached for the only peace he knew. *Lord, please. Help me. Help Ben and Quinn. We are in Your hands, Lord. Your will be done.*

He stepped a little surer. God had this.

They reached the door. Micah knocked hard. Quinn called, "Ben. We're here."

The door opened. A woman, maybe in her early thirties, looked out. She threw the door wider and demanded something Micah couldn't hear.

Quinn stepped forward. He signed so Micah could understand. "She asked who I am." He addressed the woman. "I'm his interpreter. Micah lost his hearing in an explosion. Ben can't understand sign language, so I have to translate for them."

The woman's eyes narrowed. She glared at Quinn, then at Micah. She motioned for Quinn and Micah to enter the building.

Ben stood inside the door. His eyes reflected concern but not fear. Consternation. He hugged Micah and Quinn. Micah watched him say something. Quinn signed, "I am glad to see you, Pop-dad."

Micah hugged Ben again and kissed the top of his head. Micah signed to Quinn. "Tell him to wait in the car." He nudged Ben toward the door.

The woman shook her head. She said something Quinn translated. "The boy stays here with us." She took hold of Ben's arm and pulled him behind her.

Micah asked, "What is this about? Why is Ben here?"

The woman pulled a gun from her pocket and pointed it at Micah. Quinn signed for her. "I'm sure you know. I warned you."

Micah held his hands out, palms up. Micah looked to Quinn. "Warned me about what? Who are you?"

"Does it matter? You've killed me. I intend to return the favor."

"The least you can do is tell me your name." Micah moved slightly away from the woman, putting space between him and Quinn. In case they needed it. First came listening. And praying. Which Micah did.

The woman smiled, but her eyes glowered. "Call me Zelda."

"Zelda. How did I kill you?"

She snapped her response. Quinn translated. "You were at the bakery. The owner got killed. She wasn't supposed to be there. No one was supposed to ever get hurt. I wanted to save people from their worst mistakes. Not murder anyone. *You* made me do it."

Micah stepped back. "You didn't murder Fran."

She backhanded Micah with the gun, slashing his forehead. "Don't tell me what I did or didn't do. She died. That's murder."

Quinn spoke but signed for Micah's benefit. "Manslaughter. You had no intent. A good lawyer would make the case." Micah raised his hand to his head. It came away bloody.

Zelda snarled. "A public defender? Don't make me laugh. I know them too well." She stepped back, forcing Ben to step back as well. "I'll die in prison. I'd rather die out here."

Micah continued to argue. "No one has to die anywhere. If you turn yourself in, you'll—"

The gun lashed out and hit him again. Just as fast, she pointed the gun at Quinn. The mentor held his hands apart and waved them. Zelda pulled Ben in front of her. She mouthed something.

Quinn signed for Micah. "No tricks."

Zelda's eyes narrowed as she glared at Micah. She continued to speak, and Quinn translated for her. "What did you do? Force her to open? Just like a man. Has to have everything their own way. 'Do it like this. Not like that. My way my way my way.' All of you."

Micah shook his head. He spoke what he could. "She called us to come for a consultation. She'd had to cancel twice and offered to meet with us after hours. Totally spontaneous."

"Well, it makes it bad for all of us, doesn't it?" Quinn managed to interpret the sarcasm as well. Zelda kept the gun trained on Micah but eased back and leaned against the wall. She kept Ben between herself and the two men.

Her eyes glared hard. Quinn signed, "The only question is, how will I kill you? Mine will be a slow death behind bars. Maybe yours should be, too. Slow. One well-placed bullet at a time."

Zelda punctuated her words by firing a shot, catching Micah in the upper arm. He spun around in pain, dropping to his knees. Ben jumped forward, but Zelda caught him and forced him against the wall, her arm over his throat, the gun at his head. Micah shuddered and moaned.

Quinn shouted something. Micah saw Ben settle back and stand still. His face froze in shock. Micah dropped his hand from his wound enough to sign, "Tell him to stay still. No matter what happens, he's to stay still."

Quinn didn't repeat Micah's words in sign as he spoke

to Ben. But he did add verbiage Micah knew he hadn't said.

Quinn could end it if Ben wasn't standing between Zelda and himself. The mentor would only risk taking out Zelda if Ben stayed safe. No heroics.

Micah signed, "Would you kill me in front of my son? He doesn't deserve that. It's not his fault. Let him go."

Zelda dropped a hand to Ben's shoulder. "I won't harm the boy. He's free to go when I'm done."

"But he'll have to watch you kill me. How is that not hurting him? And what about my translator? You're going to kill him, too? Your vendetta is with me. Me, not them. Let them go."

Micah couldn't be sure Quinn spoke for him honestly. But Zelda's reply seemed to indicate the mentor had translated Micah's words verbatim.

"He'll be free to go. The police won't be far behind. I fully expect to go to prison for what you made me do. One more murder won't matter. I'm doing your fiancée a huge favor."

Zelda's head snapped to the side. She hid the gun behind her leg and opened the door wide enough for a face to pop into view.

Micah startled. Luke stood there, with wide-eyed innocence. He dribbled a basketball and wore a sweaty T-shirt as if he'd been shooting hoops. Micah didn't know what Luke said. Micah looked to Quinn. Quinn translated, "Young guys out for a pick-up game. Heard what sounded like a shot. Wanted to know if everything was okay."

Micah peered at what he could see through the partially open door and noted BB, Tav, Addison, and Luke all milling around, tossing basketballs back snd forth. Tav stood with a ball on his hip, looking for all the world as if waiting for the game to resume.

Zelda smiled a straight-lipped smile and responded. Quinn translated, "Everything is fine."

BB grinned and pointed at Ben. Quinn signed, "Hey!

That's Ben. He's my friend's little brother. Hey, Ben! Whatcha doing, buddy?"

Ben didn't look up. He spoke. Quinn signed. "Wait-ing on the teach-er to say I can go home."

Quinn continued to sign for the others. "You want to play with us when you're done? We'll wait." BB tipped his head to Tav and the others. "He's a mean ball player."

Tav, Luke, and Addison all signaled assent. BB addressed Zelda. "We'll hang out here for him."

The woman scowled but had nothing to say. She nodded and slammed the door. She looked at Micah and snarled. "This isn't over. I will kill you for what you've done to me. Mark my words."

Zelda held the gun pointed at Ben as she backed out of the room, down the corridor, around a corner, and away.

Quinn followed as quickly and quietly as possible to the corner. Micah watched Quinn go, then grabbed his son and hugged him all he could. He pushed him back and signed, "I love you."

Ben returned the sign. He hugged his dad again.

Micah threw the door open, and Tav and company entered. Luke went to work on Micah's arm, staunching the bleeding. The pre-med student tore the bottom of his T-shirt and wrapped the cloth around Micah's wound. "That should hold for now. We need to get you to a doctor."

Micah shook him off. "We need to not. Did the bullet go through?"

"No. But it's not moving."

"We'll leave it." He narrowed his eyes and asked, "What are you doing here? Who came up with this idea?"

Three men all pointed at Addison. He shrugged. "Worth a shot."

Micah rolled his eyes. "She could have killed all of you." Luke dabbed at the blood on Micah's head, wiping it on the rest of his shirt. It became hard to tell which one of them had been injured.

Tav signed, "From what you said, she was after you. Not an entire neighborhood. The more people she had to control, the less likely it became she would do something."

Quinn came back. "She got away on a dirt bike. We'll report what we know to the police. Maybe they can get something from Ben's sketch."

Luke muttered, "A dead likeness is what they'll get." He put a hand on Ben's shoulder and knelt in front of him. "How are you doing, buddy?"

Ben sighed and let his shoulders drop. "I want to go home."

"That's where we're going." Micah signed, and Luke translated for him. Micah added, "We all want to go home."

* * *

Back at the house, Ben drew a life-like portrait of Zelda. Quinn questioned Ben in gentle tones to see who might have helped the woman gain access to the school and Ben. Luke bandaged Micah's shoulder. He snapped, "You need to go to the ER."

"No. Not 'til we resolve this." Micah remained adamant. He'd go nowhere. Yet.

The Knights discussed the kidnapping. Addison shook his head. "Does she realize how deep she's digging her hole? From arson to manslaughter and now kidnapping? Do you think she really believes she'll get away with it?"

Micah signed, "No, she doesn't. That's why she came after me. She's convinced she'll be caught and put in prison for life." He stared at the floor. "There will be no plea-bargaining her out of this one." Signing stressed his shoulder. He ignored it. Nothing mattered but finding Zelda.

Wendy sat beside Micah and leaned into his good shoulder. "I can't feel sorry for her. Not after she shot you."

Jen dipped her head to the side. "She gets jilted, she overreacts, and things go from bad to worst." Tav's intended gazed out the window. "I wonder if her ex knows how much trouble he created?"

Luke offered, "She still has an insanity plea. Too much stress, and she snaps. It could be a defense."

"Except she was sane enough to plot Ben's kidnapping. That took cool logic and reasoning to pull off." And some help from the inside. Micah felt less charitable. Especially with his head hurting from being struck. Twice.

Luke shrugged. "Not ours to judge. And they have to catch her first."

"Truth." Short sentences.

Quinn came in from talking with Ben. He carried Ben's portrait. He passed it around so everyone could get a good look.

Wendy startled when she saw the portrait. "That looks like Esther, the concierge at Garvey's. She helped us find the wedding gowns."

Quinn passed the picture to Jen. "Does it look familiar?"

Jen tilted her head to look at the drawing. "It looks like her. But Esther had short hair. And she had it tipped in silver. Esther also had a tattoo on her temple. A butterfly, I think."

Wendy nodded. "Yeah. This woman looks like her, but not everything fits." She passed the drawing back to Quinn. "Still, it might be worth mentioning to the police."

Quinn accepted the portrait. He signed, "Mick, you'll need to accompany me to the DA's office to file charges. I think I have all the information Ben can give me."

"Will they want to talk to him, too?" Micah wouldn't allow it. Not at this point. His son didn't need the extra stress.

"Probably. But not right now. We'll make sure they understand Ben's situation. And have plenty of help for him when the time comes."

Micah stood. He kissed Wendy, fist-bumped the others, and departed with Quinn.

* * *

They arrived at the DA's office and made their report.

DA Larkin remarked about Ben's drawing. "And he's how old?"

Quinn spoke but signed all conversations for Micah. "Twelve. He's got the eye."

"He does indeed. We'll want him as a sketch artist as soon as he's old enough."

Micah smiled. Quinn translated, "That's up to him. He may develop other interests by then. He's got a few years."

Larkin pointed to Micah's arm. "You'll have to go get that checked. We need the bullet for forensics. It will help us capture your son's kidnapper."

Micah sighed. "I know. I know. I'm ready."

Quinn patted Micah's back. "All part of the paperwork, my friend. All part of the paperwork."

Micah grumbled. In sign.

* * *

It took another four hours before Micah and Quinn could return home. Ben had gone to bed. BB and the Vaughn brothers waited for them to return. They needed a call to action. Something to end the attacks and bring the killer and would-be killers to justice.

Tav reminded the group, "We have a leak we need to stop." He spoke but also signed. He pointed to Micah. "Your idea of the multiple targets. We passed on it. But what if we made it work?"

Quinn's eyes narrowed. "What idea?" His signing had some snap to it.

Micah explained for Quinn's benefit. "We divide into four groups. We plan to throw a bachelor party. One group says it's at Kensies. One says it's at Blackberry's, one at Marshon's, and the last at Walker's. Whichever place gets hit, we know which group has the ear of the snitch. We can isolate further from there. But it gives us something to go on."

Quinn looked impressed. He sucked in his bottom lip

and nodded. "Brilliant idea, Mick. Why didn't the sum of you act on it?"

"We wanted to involve the police. Get them to stake out the four locations. They declined. And you were gone, so we couldn't ask your people." Micah shrugged. "And now you're retired, so we can't again." Shrugging bothered his arm. So did signing. But he had no choice if he wanted to make sure the group understood him.

"What about civilians?"

"We hire the place out. No one but our people." Micah shortened his delivery.

Quinn raised his eyebrows. "Good thinking. What about women? If Zelda is receiving information, she won't be likely to show at a bachelor party."

Micah thought hard. The painkillers in his system made thinking difficult. But he would do it. "Call it a pre-wedding party. Mixed couples. Everyone can come."

Quinn cocked his head. "Is that a thing?"

"We can make it one." The anesthetics made it seem like a wonderful idea. All his ideas were wonderful. Going to bed would be even wonderfuler...betterer? Good, anyhow.

Quinn chuckled. "I think we can make it work."

Tav clapped his hands together. "How? We don't have police to use as backup."

Quinn shook his head. "You're not thinking it all the way through. The locations are too open and too well-known. After all the trouble you've had, you should be laying low. Any party should be at a secret location. One where no one goes." Quinn's eyes narrowed. "And I know just how to do it." He smiled. Slowly.

* * *

TUESDAY NIGHT

The Knights set the snare. They spent the weekend broadcasting their particular location for Mick and Tav to go out on Tuesday to celebrate their last days as bachelors. But each venue received word if someone came in looking for the party, they were to be told the festivities had been moved. And no one knew where.

The Knights huddled at the Smothers' house to wait for the trap to spring. Would the elaborate ruse even work? Or would the enemy get wind of the trick and stay away?

Who knew the inner workings of the Knights—or at least Micah and Tav? No one made suggestions of who the leak might be. At least not out loud. Carly continued to flitter at the back of Micah's mind. Could she be the leak? Her background checks were squeaky clean. But did it mean anything? Money can tempt the best—

Be not swift to accuse your neighbor…

Micah breathed out hard. *I hear You. She's a thought. That's all.* And it would make things easy if it *was* Carly. No one could fault Arlene for talking. No one could stop her, either. There would be no repercussions to someone else being used. Someone who should know better…

Micah prayed, Please, let them catch someone. One of the two. At least that much. We'll only have to fight on one front, not two. But in Your will, Father. Always in Your will.

At nine, Tav began calling the establishments where the fake parties had been. Kensies: clear. Which let off the Vaughn brothers. Blackberry's: also no suspicious calls about a party. Which cleared Wendy, Jen, and Arlene. And Carly. Micah bowed his head. *I'm sorry, Lord. Thank You for not letting me make a fool of myself and an enemy of a friend.*

Marshon's and Walker's remained. The maître d' at Walker's said someone had come in looking for a party but didn't say exactly who. Yes, he got a description. A woman. She looked like the pictures the police sent out. Didn't get a name, but she left in a blue Ford pickup. No, he didn't know the model or the year. They had their suspect.

And their leak. Walker's had been Micah's responsibility. Micah, and BB, and Ben.

Micah stared at the floor. He ran the scenarios over and over and over. Who had he talked to? Who had he told about the party? And who would have tipped off Zelda—if it was her name.

Quinn gazed from Micah to BB to Ben. He spoke but also signed. "Names. Who have you discussed this with? Who's our leak?" The mentor leaned forward in the recliner, his elbows on his thighs.

Micah searched his mind and came away blank. "I can't think of anyone. I can't. I haven't been out of the compound for the past three days. I'm not having regular conversations with anyone." Or irregular. Or any for that matter.

Quinn put a hand on Ben's shoulder. "Ben. Have you told anyone about the party your dad wanted to have?" Luke did the translating so Micah and his brother could follow the conversation.

Ben turned his head once. "No. No one. I knew there was no par-ty. I would be ly-ing if I told some-one a-bout it. So I did not tell any-one."

Micah sighed inwardly. Silently. Ben's logic was

impeccable. And unarguable.

All eyes avoided looking at BB. The young man protested, "I know what you're thinking. You're all thinking I'm the leak. I didn't tell anyone I wouldn't have told before." He glared at the group. "I swear to it."

Quinn held out his hand. "No one is accusing you of leaking information, BB. No one is thinking anything of you."

Addison snorted. "Yes, we are. We're all thinking we're glad it was you and not us. Because it could have been any one of us. You don't know who is using the information." He moved to stand in front of BB. "I had my money on Arlene and Carly. If it had been, would I condemn her? Of course not. No one is going to condemn you, either. Someone took advantage of you. Who would the most likely candidate be?"

BB shook his head. "I talked to Kenmore, and I talked to Mitzy. That's it. Those are the only two."

Addison's tone stayed calm and even. "If you had to pick one or the other as a culprit, who would you pick?"

BB threw his hands in the air. "I can't pick either of them. Kenmore is as straight as they come. I'd sooner suspect myself than him."

Micah signed at the statement, "He's right there."

BB stared at the floor. "But Mitzy…Mitzy is harmless. She wouldn't do anything to hurt someone in this family. She wouldn't."

Addison raised his eyebrows. "Maybe she's being used as well. Maybe she doesn't know she's giving out information."

BB's face filled with horror. "Is this my fault? Did I bring all this on us?"

Micah put his arm around his son's shoulders. He signed, "No. Not your fault. You were used."

BB stared into his father's eyes. "Should I have known it? Seen it? Suspected it?" Tears drained down his face.

Micah clapped the hurting young man on the back. "No, son. You couldn't have known. Maybe you were used. Maybe Mitzy is being used as well. We don't vet our friends." Yet. "The only person responsible is the woman who caused all this."

Quinn took BB from Micah. The mentor pushed him back to look into his eyes. "You didn't cause it. But you can help end it."

BB wiped the moisture from his face. He nodded once to Quinn. Micah watched resolve steel his son. "What do I have to do?"

* * *

WEDNESDAY

"**Mitzy. Hey. No**, I'm hanging with Ben Friday night. Dad's going out. Yeah, again. The party was a bust. Place was too crowded, and too many revelers. Drunks. So, the guys are trying again this Friday night. Points and Pints out at Rock Island Lake."

(Chuckles.)

"Well, you have to have a boat and a reservation to get there, so they figure it will be safe. No disruptions this time. No, I'm not going. I know, I'm the best man. But I volunteered to stay with Ben. He's bummed he can't go, too. We'll hang out here with Luke and Addison. What? No, they're not going, either. It's just gonna be Mick and Tav. Not the crowd. They want some brother time. They've been together for twelve years as best buds. It'll be weird not being each other's wingman. So they just want to spend some time. I understand. Do you? You got a girlfriend like that? Yeah, it's rare. Guess they got lucky.

"Okay, I'm going to get off here. I'll talk to you later. We're still on for the wedding, though, right? Yeah. Right around the corner. Unless something else happens. Someone's been after Dad…yeah, right. Not in a week or so. But it doesn't mean it's over. Like to think it is. Maybe. I hope. Okay, bye."

BB hung up. He looked at his dad, then Quinn. "Did I do it right?"

Quinn caught BB around the shoulders and shook him. "Perfect. I'll find out what the background check on Mitzy holds. And we'll see if Zelda takes the bait."

"I don't know what to hope."

Micah squeezed his shoulder. "We hope Zelda gets caught and this is finally over."

BB nodded. "Amen."

* * *

FRIDAY NIGHT

Micah decided he needed the night alone. He wanted to spend it in prayer. Praying for Zelda. Praying for Zelda to be caught. Praying for Zelda to turn herself in and not make a bad situation worse. Praying the Lord's will be done. Praying about what would happen in four weeks…

BB and Ben went for a night to Kensies. BB would entertain Ben until ten. Late, but not impossibly late. They could always get pizza. And ice cream.

Micah set up in the living room, where he could see the lights if anyone came in. Yes, the doors were locked and the alarm system triggered. He still preferred to know when someone came in…even someone with the code. No sneaking surprises, thank you.

He set a chair in front of him to use as a kneeler. A pillow for his knees and his Bible on the seat. He began in Psalms working, backward from 150 to as far as he could get in two hours. The last few Psalms in the book were praises. The best way to start a prayer svigil. "Praise the Lord." It would focus his mind where it needed to be. On the Lord, off Micah's problems. Problems that disappeared the longer he read.

He'd reached the middle of the book when a light came on, indicating someone had opened the back door. Someone with a key? Micah looked up to acknowledge a friend, then froze as Zelda walked in. She pointed her gun at him.

Micah sank back on his haunches. *Lord? How does she know our code? What do I do?*

She barked something. Micah held his hands up, then thought better of it. He pointed to his ear and said what he hoped sounded like, "I can't hear you."

Zelda glared at him. She motioned for him to stand. That, he understood. Micah rose from the floor and dropped his hands to his sides. Zelda moved in front of him, waving her gun so he would back up. Micah complied. She tossed his Bible to the floor and planted herself in the chair. The woman stared at him through narrowed eyes.

Micah waited.

Zelda waved for Micah to get on his knees. He obeyed. Whatever she wanted him to do, he'd do. Up to a point. To the point where his sons would be coming in. Micah would not allow them to be put in danger again. No, he would see this farce ended before then.

The arsonist glowered at Micah. He wondered if Zelda had a plan before she came in or if she even knew what she wanted. Keeping the weapon firmly trained on him, she pulled out her phone. Zelda punched the talk-to-text feature and spoke several sentences into it. Finally, she tossed it down in front of Micah and signaled for him to pick it up.

Talk to text. Micah read, "You murdered me. I wasn't hurting anyone. You had to have your cake, and now I'm dead. I will get even."

Micah texted back, "You can turn yourself in. They could decrease the sentence. If you go in before anything else happens." He laid the phone between them and inched it back to her.

Zelda took it, looked at it, and scoffed. She talked again.

"Sure, they'll reduce a murder charge. Not in my lifetime."

"You don't know. All you know is if you keep running,

the police will find you. The longer you run, the worse the charges." Micah took a chance. "Aren't you tired of running?"

Zelda read the text, then stared at the floor. She pushed the phone back to him. Micah took another chance. "What's your name?"

"So you can tell the police?"

"If I'm dead, I can't tell anyone."

Zelda thought about it, then said, "Stick with Zelda. It works."

Micah had to know. "How did you find me?"

Zelda huffed. "I have a source. She's not too bright, but she had all the information I needed."

"Did she help you kidnap my son?"

"What does it matter?"

Micah shouted, unsure what his voice would sound like, "It matters to me. That's my son you threatened. I want to know who helped you."

Zelda pointed the gun at Micah. She sighted it at his head, then dropped it to her side. "You're going to be dead. It won't make any difference, will it?"

"Then tell me, and I'll die happy."

Zelda snarled into the phone. "Always about what you men want. Always your feelings. Always your way. You you you." She paused. "I don't care about you. I certainly don't want you to die happy. I want you to be as miserable as I am."

She slid the phone to him. He read her text, then slid the phone back without commenting.

Zelda lifted her back, straightening it. "The little game you tried to play. Sending me to Rock Island. Like you would ever go there."

"How did you know?"

"You're Boy Scouts. You wouldn't be within a mile of that place. I know men better than that."

Micah didn't try to absolve her of her notion. He'd spent

many an hour playing darts at Points and Pints. Truth be told, he'd enjoyed a pint on occasion. Sobriety was not the same as abstinence. Which was all beside the point.

"What happened, Zelda? What made you turn to arson?"

Zelda stared at Micah. She flung the phone at his head. Micah ducked, then retrieved it and handed it to her. She banged it on the carpeted floor, then shouted into it. Micah waited until she finished her tirade. He slipped his hand out for the phone. Zelda slammed it into his palm, all the while keeping the gun leveled at his middle.

"He canceled the wedding. One week before the date. Said his mom told him marrying me would be a mistake. He'd be better off with the girl who lived next door to her. His mom always liked her best."

Zelda's eyes burned. Micah didn't need the text to relay the emotions. They were written across her face. Hatred. Anger. Disgust. Craziness? Undoubtedly. Micah handed her back the phone.

Zelda's eyes narrowed. She shrieked into the phone. "I made up my mind I would save others from going through what I did. I would make sure no one suffered the soul-crushing heartache ever again." She eyed Micah sideways. "I'm guessing more than half the weddings I ruined will never be rescheduled. You wanna bet?"

Micah texted back. "I'd have to be alive to see if you were right or not."

The woman snorted. She stared at the floor and shrugged. Micah continued typing. "You don't want to kill me. Not really. You planned all this so no one would be physically hurt. You're not a killer."

"Tell the police."

"I will." Micah slid the phone back to her. Zelda stared at it, lowered her eyes, and extended the gun out, pointing it at his middle. Micah reached for the gun.

The backdoor light flashed. Micah didn't react. He laid

his hand on the barrel...

Zelda swung around. Micah heard a muffled shot. Then another. He dove to knock the woman down.

Quinn joined the scrum. Three bodies struggled on the floor. Someone kneed Micah in the jaw. He grabbed at Zelda's arm. She kicked at his chest. Micah's wounded shoulder ached and burned as he fought to control the arsonist. Quinn barrel-rolled and came behind the flailing woman. The gun went off a third time. Everyone went still.

Micah rolled to the side and off his assailant. Quinn held her from behind. Zelda no longer struggled. Quinn caught the gun from her hand and tossed it aside. Zelda lay still. Micah knelt beside her, looking for a bullet wound.

He found it in her chest. Zelda's eyes rolled back in her head. Micah sobbed and sat back on his haunches. He signed, "She was surrendering. She was handing me the gun."

Quinn closed the woman's eyes. He caught Micah by the shoulders and signed. "I didn't know. I didn't. I saw her threatening you. She shot at me."

Micah repeated, "She wanted to surrender." Guilt washed over him. "Which one of us shot her?"

Quinn shook his head. "I don't know. Does it matter?" He pulled out his phone and punched in a number. Probably the police.

Micah slammed his fist down. "It matters to me."

Quinn squeezed Micah's good shoulder. "We were all fighting for the weapon, Mick. She could have pulled the trigger herself. We can't know."

Tears streamed down Micah's cheeks. "I have to know, Quinn. I have to know if I killed her. She trusted me. In the end, she trusted me. Did I murder her?"

Quinn shoved Micah back. "No. No. She did this, Mick. It's her responsibility and no one else's. Whether she pulled the trigger or I did, she still started this whole disaster. Don't blame yourself for someone's actions." The mentor caught

Micah by the shoulders. "Be grateful you're alive. I am. I'm grateful we're both alive."

Micah looked at the still figure. He closed his eyes. "I don't even know her true name." He let Quinn lead him from the house.

* * *

Micah and Wendy sat on the porch swing at Wendy's house. Micah stared at the ground, morose and withdrawn. Wendy held his hand and said nothing. After minutes of not moving, Micah signed, "She was surrendering. Handing me the gun. Why couldn't God have waited one more minute to let Quinn in? Tripped him? Slowed him down? Why? I don't understand."

He stared at the sky. "I know, there's no why. I'm not supposed to understand. But it's like time ran out. If she'd surrendered a moment sooner, she might have had time to learn about Jesus. Even in prison, I know many who come to Him. But she'll never have the chance." He looked at Wendy. "Did I do that? Did I take away her last opportunity? Is she on my head?" He looked at his hands, then signed, "I still don't know if I killed her. Quinn won't say. Forensics may not be able to tell. I may never know." He lowered his head. His entire body shivered. Micah closed his eyes. "Can I let it go?"

Wendy leaned into his chest. She tapped him gently. He opened his eyes. She signed, "God knows. He loves you, Mick. He loved Zelda. God did everything to give her a chance at life beyond this world. He sent His Son to die for Zelda. You're not responsible if she chose not to accept Him. No, you don't know if she knew Him or not. You can't know. But it's not your fault. We serve a God Who is love. He says it's not His will any perish without knowing Him. He will do everything it takes to bring someone to Himself. Whether they accept Him or not is their free will."

She kissed him lightly. "You know this. You taught me

this. Do you trust God at His Word?"

Micah looked deep inside. What answer could he make? Only one. "Yes."

"He gave Zelda every chance to accept Him. You didn't deny her the opportunity to be saved. You're not responsible for her choices."

Maybe. Maybe he could accept the truth. But there remained one question. "Did I kill her?"

Wendy took hold of his head and forced his forehead to hers. She let go and signed, "You did not kill Zelda. You may have pulled the trigger. But she put herself in the position. She broke into your home. She held you at gunpoint. She fired at Quinn. Twice, from what I'm told. Zelda put herself in that position. Not you. Not Quinn. You have no responsibility for her death, even if you did pull the trigger."

She held his eyes. "Do you believe me?"

Micah stared deep into Wendy's gaze. He weighed her words, weighed what he knew to be true. Faced the emotions which wanted to cripple him. Drew in a deep breath and let it out slowly. He nodded. Signed, "I believe you. Now. Remind me of this conversation when I start to doubt."

Wendy kissed him full on the mouth. She hugged him, then signed, "I will. No monsters in our house."

Not another one, anyhow. Plenty are living in it as it is. Micah kept the thoughts to himself.

* * *

FRIDAY

Another week passed. The police investigation revealed Zelda to be Esther North. Twenty-six. Police interrogations of Mitzy proved she'd been working with the arsonist. Mitzy had been passing information using her insider knowledge from the floral warehouse to give Esther targets and times. When Esther went after Micah, Mitzy was there with the intel the arsonist needed. All of it passed by an unwitting BB. Mitzy confessed everything but the why. That, she kept to herself. And no one could guess the reason. Micah left word he wanted to be notified when Zelda would be buried. No one tried to talk him out of it.

With three weeks to the wedding, preparations geared up. Micah, Tav, and the rest of the Knights took over decoration duties. Wendy and Jen came to Micah's house to give them their instructions. The women laid out a floor plan of the ballroom and directed what they wanted in the manner of flowers and greenery. Ben sat at the table sketching pictures of life-like flower arrangements.

Anticipation made Micah's stomach flutter. He decided comic relief needed to come into play. He'd moped over Zelda's death long enough. Time to suck it up and get back into the game. "Quinn told me they have at least one suit of armor in the house."

"And they will stay fully assembled. You are not to even think about dressing in chainmail, you got it, Andres?" Wendy glared at him in mock anger. She moved cutouts along the walls of the floor plan.

Micah forced a grin. "Not a chance. I'd jingle all night, and even if I couldn't hear it, I'm sure it would get annoying."

"It's annoying thinking about it. No swords, either." Jen placed another cutout in the center of the floor of the ballroom.

"Not even as an arch?" Now he thought of it, it sounded good. Or signed good.

"No. We're not going that far with our Knight analogy. Promise me." Wendy practically pleaded.

Micah bowed his head. "I promise. I make no promises for Tav, but I promise."

Jen signed, "I'll make promises for him. Trust me. There will be no sword arch."

Micah pouted. "You take all the fun out of weddings." The play felt foreign. But he could see in Wendy's eyes her gratitude at the "old Mick" being back. Even if he wasn't.

Jen and Wendy exchanged glances. After a moment, Wendy relented. "One sword. You two can fight over who gets to carry it."

Jen asked, "Why not two?" She placed representations of floral units in the floor plan.

"Can you see them setting up a mock duel to see which one of us gets selected?"

Micah drew an X over his heart. "Wouldn't happen. Not with Quinn standing between us. We could let Quinn carry the sword. Then you know we'll behave." Quinn carrying a sword would keep things in order.

Jen motioned to Quinn's new portrait. "Does he have the face of someone who will keep you from playing? He'll be the worst of you lot."

Wendy shook her head. "We'll discuss it. Later."

Micah kissed Wendy on the cheek, mindful of Ben's watchful eye. Even focused on a drawing, Ben could still interrupt a kiss if he chose. Which he always did.

Wendy and Jen hugged BB and Ben and left. Micah sagged on the couch. "No swords."

BB chuckled. "Safer that way." He sat across the living room in the rocker.

"True. And no chain mail." Micah thought a moment. "I could wear gauntlets to throw down."

"Play it straight, Dad. At least at the first one. If you clown around at the second, you're already married, and she can't change her mind at your antics."

Micah pointed at his son. "Wise man. Wise man."

"My dad didn't raise a fool." Micah watched BB's eyes for any hint of self-doubt. None showed. They could continue the play with the proper response.

"I hope not."

* * *

MONDAY

The gift of the funds took more than a few days. Moving that kind of money around proved to be a significant undertaking. Yes, the Knights could receive it without cost. However, the taxes on the gift had to be paid, and the transactions had to be approved. It all had to be looked at and contemplated and otherwise investigated by the powers in charge. The banks that received the money held the deposits as well to verify the veracity. And make sure it wasn't some ill-gotten gain. In the end, the monies were all moved and accepted. Given with a willing heart and received with grateful hands. What more could there be?

Quinn and Grace sat on the couch in their living room. They held hands as they finished praying. Quinn slipped his arm behind Grace's shoulders and sighed. "I have never felt so much peace."

Grace smiled. She leaned in and kissed her husband. "Neither have I."

"Is this what you wanted?" Quinn slipped his fingers through her silvering hair.

"A husband at home and at peace? Yes. I would have settled for you at peace whether you were here or gone. But I know this is where your heart is."

Quinn chuckled. "I never wanted anything to do with

the estate. Never. I wanted it to go to someone else. My brother. My sister. Anyone."

"But they both died before you."

Quinn nodded. "Right. We didn't have anyone else. Not while Grandfather lived." He sighed with contentment. "But now it's the boys' and girls' problems."

"Which you'll still be around to oversee, right?" Grace tipped her face to catch Quinn's eyes.

"We'll be around to help. But if one of them runs off the rails, it's not our problem. We'll counsel, we'll suggest, we'll pray, but we won't take responsibility." He kissed Grace. "If I thought these kids couldn't handle it, I'd never have given them the burden. But I believe in them."

Grace lay her head on his shoulder. "I do, too. Except for one."

"Chay?" His step-daughter. Grace's daughter.

"When she comes back to the fold, I'll give her the portion that is hers."

"She has to move back to Galt?"

"She has to get her life together. She's miserable where she is. She doesn't have to come here. She has to show me she's responsible enough to handle this kind of wealth." She nodded. "I'll know when."

Quinn kissed the side of her head. "I trust you will."

They sat quietly for several minutes until Grace asked, "Do you think Lorna will leave the Knights alone now?"

"I think my ex is a shrewd woman. She knows there's no advantage for her to go after anyone now the money is gone. I wouldn't have distributed the money if I thought otherwise."

"Of course not." Grace snuggled closer into Quinn's arms. "I love you, Quinn Magary."

"I love you, Grace Magary."

Quinn's phone rang. He picked it off the table and looked at the number. His eyes narrowed. Grace eyed him. He shook his head and lifted the instrument to his ear. "Say what you have to say."

Quinn didn't put it on speaker. Grace didn't need to hear what Lorna said. At least not how Lorna said it. Quinn listened. He waited. "You done? Now you listen. Call off your henchmen. Not one more attack. The money is gone beyond your reach. There's plenty left for you and Denner when I'm gone. Unless I meet an untimely end. Then you get nothing. Call off your people, or I will call in the Feds. You're dead right I will. I don't care what happens to me. I've got all I need. You do what you have to do to make peace with it. But the estate is gone, and it isn't coming back. Call 'em off. Got it? It is now."

Quinn disconnected the call. Grace waited. Quinn snuggled back against her. "That went better than I thought." He nuzzled her neck. "I'm going to have extra protection for you for the next month. Be very careful."

Grace lay her head on his shoulder. "My only outings will be to address wedding affairs. And the girls pretty well have those wrapped up. We're at the 'waiting for the day' stage, I think."

Quinn chuckled. "I'll be glad when it's over."

Grace kissed him. "I'm sure you will be."

* * *

MONDAY EVENING

Late in the evening, car engines revved from the lane. Micah heard them. He felt them in his chest. The vibrations were clear and present. He peered out the window and saw cars three abreast at the top of the street. Except they had a two-lane road. He grabbed Ben from the table and shouted, "BB!" at the back of the house. He couldn't hear his own voice but prayed it carried the panic he wanted. He shoved Ben toward the patio door and yelled, "Go! Go!"

The cars revved again. BB came out of his bedroom, a look of alarm on his face. Micah pointed and yelled, "Out!" Mialma followed close behind, barking and whining.

Micah felt the thunder of the wheels. As he shoved his sons out the door, he saw a flaming bottle come smashing through the front window. He hovered over his family, sheltering them from flame and debris.

The cars circled the block, tossing Molotov cocktails at every turn, hitting all eight houses in a single pass. The Smothers family spilled out of their back door. Micah grabbed Tim and Ury, Wendy's brothers, and huddled with them. Wendy, Jen, and Mrs. Smothers came coughing and choking into the quadrangle.

Realization of the tactic hit Micah. They were sheltered inside a ring of burning buildings. He shoved everyone closer to the center and turned on the sprinklers full force. BB had his phone and called 911.

Wendy raced between the houses to get a look at the cars. She sprinted back to huddle with Micah and the others and signed, "No plates. I got some models, but none of them had plates."

Micah surveyed the quad for an opening, a way to get through the flames. But what waited for them on the other side? Life? Or were they to be picked off one by one? Was the property destruction enough? Or were the attackers ready to finish off the Knights?

Why hadn't anyone come from Quinn or Tav's house? Were they gone? Micah texted Tav. No answer. Flames engulfed the Vaughn house. Were Tav and his brothers still inside? Could he live with himself if he didn't find out?

Micah started for the back door, but Wendy grabbed him by the shoulders. She shook him hard and shouted in his face, "No!"

He tried to break free. Wendy grabbed him around his middle. She swung him around and shouted again, "No!" She signed frantically, "They're gone. Not home. Safe."

Micah nodded. Back to the safety of the group in the middle. Stay where they were and pray the sprinklers kept working? Or make a break for it? Crash through the raging inferno, risk immolation, or wait?

Wait. BB redirected the sprinkler heads to point in one direction. Everyone stood as close to the spray as possible, letting the water wash down their clothes and bodies. Would they risk being boiled or steamed?

BB shook Micah and signed, "Sirens. Fire engines. Police. We're saved."

The intensity of the fire lapped the water pooling on the patio. The blaze burned swiftly toward them. Heat and steam engulfed the group sheltering in the quad.

Torrents of water poured into the houses and over the tops of the roofs. It knocked the flames down, but not out.

The group bunched in the water, Ben in the center, Tim, Ury, and Arlene next, BB, then Micah, Wendy, and Jen. Micah, on the outside, tried to encircle the two women, but his arms could only reach so far. *God, cover what I can't. Keep them all safe.*

More water cascaded into the courtyard. Firefighters in burly fireproof garb broke through the flames. They motioned for the group to split up to allow them to carry the Knights through the fire to safety. Micah shoved the youngest boys toward them. Time would be wasted arguing. He knew Wendy and Jen's preferences. He would honor them. Mrs. Smothers, then BB. The women. Micah last, carrying Mialma in his arms. Leave no man—or dog— behind. No questions from anyone.

Micah coughed and hacked in the smoke. By the time he'd been rescued from the yard, the others were all sucking in life-giving oxygen. His savior shoved a bottle of air to him, covered his mouth, and turned the cylinder on. Micah breathed, choked, breathed, coughed, breathed, cleared his lungs, and breathed some more. Finally, he lowered the canister and nodded.

There was no saving anything except lives. Firefighters didn't try to put the flames out. They focused on not letting the conflagration spread. All the Knights huddled together and watched their lives burn away. For the second time in two years, they would be starting over. With less than they had after the earthquake. At least then, they'd saved the irreplaceable. This time, they would save nothing.

Ben looked at his dad. He mouthed something Micah couldn't hear. BB translated. "He says the monster came to all of our houses. He wants to know if the monster will win?"

Micah signed, "Tell him no, the monster will not win. As long as we have each other, the monster will never win."

Ben nodded his single nod, then knelt and hugged Mialma. The dog whined and wiggled. Micah checked her for burns and found none. She remained unscathed, as had they all.

Micah watched unmoving as the fire destroyed their homes. What now? Where would they go? What were the chances of finding another eight-plex? If they didn't live together, didn't share all things in common, were they destined to fail as a family?

Wendy hugged his arm. She touched his face. He looked at her, his heart a stone. She signed, "We will come back. We will stay strong together. This isn't the end, Mick. It's not."

He sank to his knees and sat on the ground. Micah lowered his head into his hands. How many times could they rebuild? How many times did they have to start over? He told Ben the monster hadn't won. Wouldn't win. But had it?

Tav walked beside him. He knelt and rested his hand on Mick's shoulder. Mick looked at him. Nothing. He felt nothing.

Tav signed, "We have each other. We have the Lord. We will survive."

Micah nodded. Closed his eyes. Prayed. Lord, I'm lost. You knew this would happen. You could have stopped it. You could have turned the hearts of the attackers. You could have protected us. I know. You did. We're all alive. We have the resources to start over. I don't know if I have the strength. Help me. Please.

He wanted peace to sweep over him. Wanted to feel assurance all would be well. The only answer that came, the only answer there would be, was "Trust Me."

Micah lowered his head. *I do. I will. Help my weakness.*

Tav squeezed his shoulder and signed again, "We have each other. We will make it."

Micah looked. "Where were you?"

"Blowing off steam. None of us could relax. So we went out to Kensies."

"Were Quinn and Grace with you?"

"Peter and Kevin. Quinn and Grace went out on their

own. They wanted to celebrate their new freedom."

Micah shook his head. "Freedom. When will it be? The bad guys wanted to kill all of us this time. Did they really think it would get them the money they wanted?"

"I don't know, Mick. I don't. The police need to nail these guys."

Wendy joined the conversation. "We can trace them. The Molotov cocktails leave a distinct chemical signature. We can isolate it and track it to its source. From there, we find the buyers. We'll catch them. We've got them this time."

Micah kissed Wendy on the forehead. "I hope so."

The Red Cross showed up with blankets, coffee, hot chocolate for Ben, and a list of places they could stay for the night. They also had lists of organizations that could aid the refugees with clothes and supplies until they could get into something semi-permanent. Micah took the list. They would need the residences. Until they could figure out what they were going to do.

Quinn and Grace walked to the huddle. Both mentors embraced the group. Ben took one look at Quinn and declared, "The monster is back."

Quinn stared at Ben, then hugged the boy hard. BB translated Quinn's response for Micah. "No, it's not. I won't allow it to come back. It will not win. Not now, not ever."

Micah drew in a deep breath. He signed, "Right. No monsters." He looked at Grace. "You have your notepads for our lists?"

She pulled out her phone. "I can make lists right here."

Wendy noted, "The Red Cross has a list of documents we need to get. Licenses, birth certificates." She smiled. "Marriage licenses." She went on. "Social Security cards. Credit cards. We're going to be very busy."

Micah nodded. "I still have my wallet and my phone." The vibrations kept him alerted to texts.

"That's a start."

He breathed in and out. "I'll have to file extensions for all my clients. At least everything is on the cloud." Especially important since any disk drives were destroyed in the fire.

Micah banished the thoughts from his head. He was homeless, but he worried about filing taxes? Priorities, man. Priorities.

Quinn signed, "First, we get accomodations for the night for the bunch of us."

BB signed, "Kenmore has room for Ben and me. We can stay with him until you get other arrangements made." He held Micah's eyes. "Ben's been to Kenmore's before and stayed the night. I think he'll do better there than anywhere strange."

Micah nodded. "Good thinking." He turned to Luke. "Can you take BB and Ben to Kenmore's?"

Luke nodded. "You want me to take Mialma with them? She'll be better with someone she knows."

"Right. Take her." Kenmore had a German shepherd Mialma loved to play with. And being with Ben would make things easier. Especially when it came to finding a place for the humans to stay. Though the Red Cross had a list of places approved for animals, it didn't mean Mialma would approve of the places. Better she go to Kenmore's with Ben and BB.

Micah gazed at Arlene, trying to gauge her state of mind. She stared at the embers that had yet to be extinguished. She looked at Jen and Wendy, non-comprehending. Wendy interpreted for Micah. "How terrible. I wonder whose place this is?"

Jen hugged her mom. "We'll find out in the morning. Right now, we need to take you to Aunt Sherry's. She wants you to spend a few days with her."

"Aunt Sherry? I don't have an Aunt Sherry. I have a sister, Sherry."

"That's who I mean, Mom. To your sister Sherry's home. She wants you to come stay with her."

"Oh. That will be nice. But won't you girls need me to stay and help you?"

"No, Mom. We'll be fine. You can go and have fun talking to your sister."

"My sister? Do I have a sister?"

Jen bit her trembling lip. "Yes, Mom. Sherry."

"Oh. Yes. Sherry. Do you know her?"

Jen barely whispered, "Yes, Mom. I know her. We'll take you over to her."

Quinn stepped forward. "We'll take you all. And Grace can get some clothes for her tomorrow."

Jen shook her head. "Just Mom and the boys. Sherry doesn't have room for all of us."

Grace nodded. "Then just your mom and your brothers. Your mom will be fine.'"

Wendy's eyes overflowed with tears. "She wasn't this bad earlier."

"This will be hard on her. Losing everything." Micah dropped his hands. *Why, Lord? Why, on top of the dementia?*

Trust Me.

I do. I have to. I don't have anywhere else to turn.

Micah accepted the offer of a ride from the Red Cross to the nearest hotel of repute. He was bone weary. Ready to collapse somewhere. Anywhere. He even accepted the survival package they offered him of a change of clothes, toothbrush, toothpaste, and other essentials for the remainder of the night.

The hotel was lonely. Quiet. The Red Cross had scattered the group all across town out of necessity. The night marked the first time in two years he couldn't walk across a yard and be home with a fellow Knight. Alone. Truly alone.

Micah hit his knees. Not alone. You're here. You're with me. You will make it all make sense. Eventually. Tonight, I need to hold on to You. Your love. Your peace. Your strength. I don't have any. I'm empty. Fill me with You, Lord. Fill me.

In Jesus's Name, amen.

He climbed into the bed, pulled up the duvet, and closed his eyes.

* * *

TUESDAY

Morning came. Micah checked in with BB and Ben by text. Both were doing well. Ben's text read, *Pancakes.* All was well in Ben's world.

BB asked, *Can we go clothes shopping?*

Micah texted back. *I need a ride to the shops. I'm staying at Fall Mountain.*

Is that the best they could do?

On short notice. Micah grinned at BB's umbrage of the placement.

BB texted, *Where are the rest of the guys?*

I don't know. I'll check in with them. Stay safe.

You stay safe. Watch for bedbugs.

The place is not bad. Give the Red Cross a break. They do good work.

Fine. KO.

Knight out. Micah hoped not permanently.

He texted Tav. *Where are you?*

Mountain West.

Fancy digs.

Not this room.

Can we go clothes shopping?

Pick you up where?

Fall Mountain.

See you in thirty.

KO.

Next would be Wendy.

Morning, beautiful. Where are you?

Glory Hills. Jen and me. We're ready to head out to Aunt Sherry's.

Can we meet for lunch?

Will have to see. Only if Mom is okay.

Right. I'm running errands today. Clothes first. Micah needed to be presentable to get all the IDs and licenses and whatever else he needed.

Wendy had not lost her sense of the absurd. *The apostles were told take no extra shirts. Not this child of God. Need clean unmentionables.*

Micah chuckled. Silently. *Heard. Read, anyhow. Love you.*

Love you.

Micah texted back, *KO.*

True, Jesus did send His apostles out with nothing but what they had on. Different time and place. Different culture. First-world problems. He needed underclothes. And a place to wash them.

The only check-in left was Quinn. Micah hesitated to text the man. But there wasn't any other way to get hold of their mentor. It might be early, but Quinn never rejected a text.

Where are you and Grace?

The answer came almost immediately, as had all the others. *Spring Landing.*

So they hadn't gone high class, either. Everyone was staying in a Red Cross-designated accommodation. Like real people.

Plans for the day?

Shopping for essentials. Lunch later if we can pull you all together.

Micah reached for a response. Wendy, Jen might be out. Depends on Arlene. How she's taking the change.

Understood. She seemed very out of it last night. She didn't know where she was. I will check with them soon.
KO

Micah clambered to his feet. Straightened out his shirt. Walked to the front desk. Smiled at the desk clerk, who waved as he headed for the door. Outside, he leaned against the wall, waiting for his ride. Who would take him to breakfast first, he hoped. Priorities. Biscuits would be great. And fast.

Luke pulled up and flashed his lights. Micah climbed in the car and signed, "Thanks for picking me up. Where's breakfast?"

Tav answered, "Pancake Palace. Over by the mall. We can eat, then shop."

Micah heard the drone of Tav's voice but read the sign language. "Just us?"

"Addison has his car and will join us later. He wanted to hit the gym first."

Micah knew Addison kept a change of clothes in his locker at the gym. No sweaty mess when the youngest Vaughn joined them.

The three Knights ate breakfast, then went to the mall to shop. Kenmore dropped BB off to meet up with his dad and the Vaughns. The group bought three pairs of everything (except underwear. Six pairs.) Two pairs of shoes, plus the wedding shoes. Since they were shopping, they may as well get it all in one fell swoop. Micah bought emergency clothes for Ben as well. Three outfits, complete with shoes. Extra tee shirts and shorts. The soft kind. They each bought a duffle bag to store the items. Gotta have someplace to put things.

They met up with Wendy at noon. Micah hugged his fiancée. She appeared worn. He touched her cheek and signed, "How was it last night?"

Wendy's eyes moistened. "Mom got up about every half hour and walked around the house. She said she was looking for her dog." Wendy bit her lip. "We don't have a dog. She insists he's in the house. She can hear him whining."

Micah lowered his eyes. "I'm sorry, Wendy. What can we do? What can I do?"

Wendy shook her head. "Nothing. We called her doctor for a refill on the meds she lost in the fire. They'll take a while to kick in, but the trauma may have sent her over the edge. We may not get her back again."

Micah embraced Wendy and held her for several minutes. She straightened, gave him a taut smile, and signed, "I'm fine. I took the brothers shopping already. They have clothes for a few days. They're back at Sherry's washing them. We've got work to do. Let's do it."

He kissed her, grateful Ben could not break them. They both needed this.

Tav tapped them on the shoulder and signed, "We're in public. Let's get moving."

Micah sneered at his best friend but nodded. The group moved on about their business. Addison joined them shortly after. Micah kept checking his phone for any word from Quinn. Nothing. They hit a grocery store to stock up on food to keep at the motels. They kept it fast and simple.

By two, they had done all they could. Next trip, the laundromat to wash everything before wearing it. The group had no dissension about the need. Or whose clothes went in what load.

As they watched the clothes spin in the dryer (and took bets on which sock would make it first around the tub,) a realization hit Micah. He looked with horror at Wendy. "Your dresses. The wedding gowns."

Wendy gave him a straight-lipped smile. "At the dry cleaners. They've had them since last week. I wanted to storm down and get them back, but Jen said they would be fine there." Tears filled her eyes. "At least we still have those."

Micah put his arms around her. She leaned into his

chest, then stood, straightened her shoulders, dried her face, and drew in a deep breath. She signed, "I'm fine. This will not beat me." She managed a genuine smile. A little one, but a real one. "No monsters."

"Right." Micah looked around. "Where to next?"

Tav signed, "We need to get copies of the marriage licenses. We should be able to have them replaced without standing in line again."

Luke sniped, "Call Jake from County Ranch. Home insurance."

Micah nodded. "Right." He looked around. "What else would we need to buy right away?"

"We need housing. Right away housing." Wendy signed the obvious.

Micah added, "Transportation. I need a vehicle."

Wendy nodded. "I need one for Mom as well."

Addison asked, "Any idea how long we can stay where we are?"

"We'll have to check with our insurance. I'm guessing we can do long-term corporate housing until we find places. Cheaper than motels and more like a real home."

"Good plan. Maybe we should look for it now. We can all stay at the same place."

Micah felt a check in his soul. He shrugged. "Cars first. We can stay another night where we are. I can, anyhow." Not that he wanted to. But something needed to be assessed. Prayed over. Asked.

Quinn texted around four. *Where are you?*

Car shopping.

Meet at Aunt Sherry's for dinner. Seven p.m. All call.

Wendy side-eyed Micah. "Isn't that going to be a lot for Aunt Sherry to handle?"

Micah texted, *We bringing food?*

Arranged. Be there.

Micah shrugged at Wendy. "I'm sure Quinn has cleared it with your aunt. He's not the type to just bust in on someone." Not an outsider, anyhow. Micah stared at the upside-down finance papers the car salesman had pushed to Wendy.

Wendy ducked her head. "Yeah." She looked at the royal blue SUV and told the dealer, "I'll take it. Write it up."

The man smiled wide. "You'll be delighted with this vehicle. We have excellent financing options and great interest rates."

Wendy nodded. "I'm sure you do. Let's do the paperwork." Micah squeezed her hand. No show of wealth. No flaunting what she could do. Let the man get his sales quota for the day.

While the dealer processed Wendy's papers, Micah wandered around the lot and looked at vehicles for his family. Who would soon be Wendy's family. Did they really need two cars? Three, with BB needing something for school?

With Quinn retired, Micah would receive no more forensic investigations. Back to regular tax accounting. Was that really what he wanted to do? What the Lord wanted him to do? Another question to lay before the Lord tonight.

And speaking of, did they all have their answer to the "be ready" command? Did the firebombing of the houses fit the bill of what they were to be ready for? Or could there be more to the Lord's word to them? What was Micah missing?

He and BB rode with Wendy in the new car to Aunt Sherry's house. Luke picked up Ben and brought him with the others. All the Knights, plus the Smothers boys, presented themselves to Quinn.

Tav quipped, "Yeah, we even ran through a car wash so we'd all be presentable. And sparkling clean."

Quinn rolled his eyes. "Clowns. You're all a bunch of clowns."

Grace smiled. "Better than crying in our cups. This is huge for all of us."

Quinn leaned in and kissed his wife. "Yes, it is." He

motioned for everyone to circle in. He signed, "We would typically hold hands, but I need mine to be free to talk. We should bow our heads and close our eyes, but Mick and Tav would be left out. So, we'll keep it simple. Lord, thank You for our lives. You protected the one thing we can't replace."

Micah's heart caught at the irreplaceable. Jeremiah's pictures. The original Knights together. Incredible grief swept over him. He lowered his head and looked at the floor. Quinn continued signing, but Micah missed it. A sob tore through him. His shoulders began to shake. The sheer weight of the incredible loss bore down on him. He looked up, expecting condemnation or ridicule.

Instead, he saw men and women, his brothers and sisters, all expressing the depth of the pain they had come through. Eyes were filled with tears, flowing down cheeks, dribbling over noses, being wiped on the backs of hands or sleeves. They had suffered as a group. Now, they would mourn as one also.

Quinn stopped signing. He turned and embraced Grace. Then he clasped Tav, who stood on his other side. Tav passed the hug to Luke, who passed it to Addison and on around the circle. Some hugs lasted longer than others. Wendy and Jen were last in the circle. The two women held each other the longest. Micah sensed they had perhaps lost the most. Arlene. Would she come back from the shock? How could they help her?

Quinn waited until the group returned to a semblance of decorum before continuing. "I called, and Sherry graciously agreed to let us gather here so we could be together. To prove the monsters will not win." He motioned to the kitchen. "We brought take-out. Everyone, grab some food and find a place to sit. Sherry has chairs out back on the patio as well."

The Knights filled plates, found places to sit and tucked into the meal. They exchanged small talk and banter until everyone had enough to eat. Quinn called them to order again.

All eyes studied the senior Knight as he announced, "I made a severe error, and I owe you all an apology. I underestimated Lorna's hate and overestimated her rationality. Because of me, you're all targets of her vitriol."

Addison signed, "Bring it on. Because of you, we are who we are. She comes after one of us she gets all of us."

Quinn signed, "I think that's her intent."

Micah repeated Addison's avowal. "Bring it on. She's one person."

Wendy corrected, "Who has hired multiple assassins." She looked around the room. "Who we don't know."

"We also don't know how she's getting her information on where we are." Tav threw in another issue.

BB protested. "We thought we identified the leak. Isn't that enough?"

Micah clapped a hand on BB's shoulder and signed, "I don't think Mitzy could be passing information to both parties."

Addison's face darkened. "Unless it's one of us, all spying ended when we were burned out. We don't have anyone left to talk to."

Quinn disagreed. "Beyond the bakery, I've been thinking about the other two attacks against you. What did they have in common?"

The room emptied of all but silence. Quinn raised his eyebrows. "The Vaughn cars. Specifically Luke and Tav's." He signed to Addison, "I'm not discounting yours may be chipped as well, but theirs were used in attacks." He pointed to Luke. "No one knew we were going to the tux place." He continued to sign, pointing to Tav. "No one knew you were going downtown. But the bad guys still found you. They knew because they had a tracker on your car."

The silence deepened. Hands went still. Eyes cast around the room. Quinn nodded. "I could be wrong. But the surest way to be safe is not to use Tav's SUV. From now on, you ride with someone else. Find a parking lot and leave the

SUV."

Tav nodded. Wendy's eyes widened. She signed, "What about Aunt Sherry? They know we're with her."

Quinn held a hand in peace. "We'll have protection for your aunt. She'll be safe. I promise."

Micah knew Quinn never made promises lightly. Sherry would be as safe as any of them. But how safe were they?

Quinn signed, "I think we're scattered enough. Once the Vaughn cars stop moving, the perps will have to use some other means of finding us." His eyes narrowed. "We'll do a sweep for trackers and bugs. In the meantime, I suggest we not talk to anyone about locations and activities. If someone asks, tell them we're fine. We have to be strategic." He looked around the room. "Until I can figure out a way to draw Lorna out and make her come after me."

Micah couldn't hear the words, but the protests translated through the body language of the Knights. No one agreed. And they put some vehemence in their actions.

Quinn held both hands and waved them. "Down. Down. I'm not saying I'll face her one on one. I'm saying I want her to come after me where we can take her out. On our playing field. On our terms."

Micah signed his question. "What about the hired goons? If we catch them, will they turn on her?"

"If the DA does his job right. I'd rather entice Lorna to come herself. That way, there's no chance of her skating."

"How do you do that?"

"Make the stakes high enough. She'll have to come. She'll want to see it for herself."

"I ask again, how?"

Quinn stared out the window. "I appeal to her base nature. I tried to use reason with Lorna. My mistake, and now we're homeless. She's operating from her base nature. I can work with that."

Micah caught several sets of eyes narrowing. Including his own. What did Quinn have in mind?

Quinn motioned to Wendy and Jen. "We might need to change the venue. And not tell anyone."

Micah gave an exaggerated sigh. He signed, "No suit of armor? No swords? No gauntlets to throw?"

Wendy shoved him. "No. And we discussed it. No, no, and no."

The atmosphere in the room took a one-eighty from the darkness to the light. Micah smiled. "That's better. We can do this, people. We're God's children. Persecution wasn't anything new to the disciples back in the first century. It's still going on in our times. We can overcome and bounce back. As long as we stay in His will."

Quinn's shoulders dropped. He managed a relieved smile at Micah. "Thank you for the reminder of Who is in control. We'll pray about what comes next. Before I get us into something stupid." He looked around the room. "It's getting late, and people need to get back to their hotels. Let's break and meet again tomorrow. Time and place to be determined." He stopped, then asked, "Who doesn't have transportation yet?"

Micah raised his hand. He circled a finger to indicate BB and Ben as well. "We don't. Wendy has a new van for after the wedding, but she needs it for Arlene."

"First thing tomorrow, get wheels." He looked to Jen. "You?"

"Not yet." The weariness in her face spoke heart-breaking volumes.

"When you're able. Wheels will be the first priority. They're easier to come by than a house. And more useful right now."

Jen ducked her head. "When I can. I need to be here."

Grace offered, "Give me a breakdown of what you're looking for, and I'll shop for you. I'll video anything I find." Grace flashed an "I love you" sign across the room.

Jen smiled and relaxed. "Thanks, Grace. It would take a load off my plate."

Grace nodded to her. "I understand."

Quinn stood. "Prayers, then go home. Relatively speaking. And be thinking about where we can make this wedding happen. Even if it has to be under military guard."

As they walked out the door, BB signed, "Maybe Kensies?" He grinned.

Micah shoved him.

* * *

Quinn and Grace returned to their motel room. Quinn tossed the keycard on the dresser, then turned and embraced his wife.

Grace's smile turned down at the corners. "What's this all about?"

"I need you to help me with something. I have an idea of how to trap Lorna. But it will take all of us to pull it off."

Grace eyed Quinn. "Without endangering anyone?"

"Absolutely. I'm not going to put anyone in harm's way. I'd never do that to them." He dropped his head. "I already did, didn't I?"

Grace put her arms around his neck and squeezed him. "No. You were being who you are. You can't take on the crazies of the world and let them determine your actions." She took his hand and led him to the couch. They sat side by side. Grace laid her head on his shoulder and curled her feet on the seat. "Tell me this plan of yours."

Quinn kissed her. "It will be hardest on you."

She shrugged. "I'd expect no less. Because however hard it will be on me, I know it will be even harder on you. So I'm ready. What do we have to do?"

They talked and planned late into the night. Then held each other close the rest of what was left. And knew there wasn't enough time to say all the things they needed to say. But it would have to do.

* * *

WEDNESDAY MORNING

The group met at Blueberry's for breakfast. The restaurant had an empty conference room. Wendy and Quinn picked up the group, leaving Tav's SUV parked at the nearest "Park and Ride." (Luke's vehicle remained at the shop, awaiting repairs for the bullet holes.) With the foster brothers, the crowd swelled to fourteen. Arlene stayed at the house with her sister, too fragile to do anything else.

With fourteen, they got the crowd special: pancakes, bacon, sausage, eggs, biscuits, and gravy. All you can eat, but no takeout. Chatter and laughter filled the room. Smells of bacon and pancake syrup overpowered all but the coffee. Gallons of coffee. Some with creamer. Most without. Compared to Micah's coffee, no one complained.

Once the assembly had been well-fed and the tables cleared, Quinn closed the doors to the room and called the group to order. Everyone looked to the mentor for what came next.

Micah listened to the drone of the voices. They were becoming clearer. Not enough to say he could follow the conversation. But if the speaker enunciated succinctly or stressed a word, Micah could catch it. He remained grateful his comrades all continued to sign for him and Tav.

Quinn stared around the room, catching each person's eyes. He said and signed, "We need to draw Lorna out. Make her think she's hit the jackpot for revenge. We're going to go to Points and Pints for a day out. Everyone. All of us." He eyed Wendy and Jen. "Except for your mom, of course."

Micah felt his heart surge. "Ben?"

Quinn shook his head. His mouth didn't move. But he signed, "He will stay behind." He looked at Wendy and signed, "You choose for your brothers." He began speaking again. "We all go out in one boat. We make it clear we're going for the day, going to blow off steam. And won't be intimidated."

Tav raised his hand, then dropped it to sign, "How do we communicate the idea to Lorna? Call her and tell her?"

Micah wondered how Tav made signing look sarcastic, but he managed. Quinn accepted the rebuke. "Okay, that's my take on it. What she thinks of it will be anyone's guess. But I'm guessing she'll see us all together in one place, so soon after losing everything, as a signal we're fighting back."

Micah dipped his head back and forth. Made sense. Quinn continued. "What she won't know is we're all leaving just as quickly as we arrive."

He looked around the room. "We'll have security—invisible security—scouting the island. They'll keep us abreast of anyone approaching the island. And from which side."

He pulled out a rough map of the island. "This is the entrance to Points." He pointed to the back door. "The pub is in the basement. Underground. The exit is here, on the far side of the island." He smirked. "Used to be a bootlegger's paradise."

Micah raised his eyebrows. A little fact the pub kept to itself. Quinn continued, signing, "There is a tunneled exit that comes out in the trees on the far side. A group of people could enter the pub, follow the tunnels, and come out on the beach on the other side. Then climb into a boat and motor home." He added, "Electric motor, which is silent, of course.

No one on the near side would know the island had been vacated.

"I expect Lorna to send her goons onto the island to trap or cut down the lot of us. We won't be there, but the Mounties will be. Once we have them, we have Lorna."

Tav asked, "They'll turn?" He pulled the map closer to get a better look.

Quinn's face filled with disgust. "Hired help has no honor. They'll turn state's evidence in the first five minutes. Probably before they get off the island."

Micah turned the plan over and over in his mind. And over and over. And over… BB? Was the young man old enough to decide for himself?

BB held his father's eyes. Micah read his son. Read the drooped shoulders, the lowered head. The longing. The shame. Would Micah treat him like a child, like Ben? Or would Micah trust his son to be safe and do what he was told like all the "adult" Knights? Was BB a Knight in name only?

Micah swallowed hard. His guts trembled. He forced himself to steady his hands. He signed, "You can come."

BB didn't gloat, didn't shout, or throw a fist in the air. He tapped his knuckles with his dad. Signed, "Thank you." Micah reached out and put a hand on BB's shoulder. He squeezed it. Then let him go. BB nodded once. Ben-like. And turned back to listen to the conversation.

Micah prayed, Don't let me make a mistake, Father. I have to let him grow. Have to let him be who he is. But don't let me make the wrong choice. Protect him. Protect all of us.

Did Micah trust Quinn? Yes. But Quinn was human. Did Micah trust God?

Trust He *could* protect BB? Yes. Trust He *would*? That was a different question.

One which required the same answer. Yes. Micah trusted God to care for BB. And love the young man more than Micah could. So yes, BB would be safe. One way or another.

Quinn wrapped the meeting. "That's it, people. Monday, the thirtieth, we're going to Rock Island. I'll have the place hired out so no one but us is there. No management. No one gets on the island except with a reservation, so there will be no stragglers to worry about. No one there except the Knights. We'll meet at the dock. I'll have the boat rented, and we'll be ready to go." He held Tav's eyes. "I want your keys."

Tav dug in his pocket and tossed the car keys to Quinn. Quinn caught them with a nod. "Thanks. I'll be careful. I have two beautiful daughters to give away soon."

Wendy pointed at him. "You better remember. You promised."

"And I keep my promises. We'll get through this, people. We will. For now, we're going to shift from scattered housing to long-term housing. I've made the reservations. Let's move. All of us."

* * *

Wendy drove her brothers and Micah and his crew to the Express Inn. Micah walked into the living area and immediately breathed easier. He strolled to the kitchen, turned around, and grinned. Finally, a place for a home-cooked meal. With his sons. His family together again.

Wendy promised to deliver Mialma to the suite after she got her brothers settled. The four fosters would live in the suite opposite Micah's. Quinn and Grace would be to the left, Tav and his brothers to the right. Wendy and Jen would stay with Sherry and their mom. Now would not be the time to move Arlene anywhere. Nor to leave her unaccompanied.

It didn't take long to get settled. When you don't have anything, you don't have to unpack it. Micah sat down and made a list of items he needed to get his business up and running.

Or not. He sat back at the desk and thought. Maybe he wouldn't do tax accounting anymore. Maybe he would...

Maybe he would finish with the clients he had, get them settled with someone else, and *then* quit. He still had responsibilities. Right.

Micah watched Ben getting acquainted with the new space. The boy ran his hands along every ledge, every wall, every window, and every door. Getting the feel of the place. Micah didn't try to decipher what Ben needed from his examination. It mattered to Ben.

Ben stopped at the window overlooking the courtyard. He stared for a long time. He turned to Micah and declared, "No mon-sters in this space." BB translated.

Micah nodded. "Right, buddy. No monsters. We left the monsters behind. They can't come in here."

Ben walked into the kitchen area. "The mon-sters will not win."

"No, they won't. Ever."

Ben looked around. "I need pen-cils and pa-per."

Micah wrote them down on his list. *Car. Sketch pads. Charcoal pencils. Food. Laptop. Two laptops.* BB would need one for his schoolwork in the spring, as Micah would need one for his accounting business. One step at a time.

He called out to BB. "What's on your list of needs? Besides a laptop?" And hoped his son could decipher his words.

BB came out from the bedroom he would share with Ben. He enunciated, "Pajamas."

Micah grinned. "Yeah, I forgot about those. Been sleeping in my clothes."

"More clothes." BB plopped down on the sofa. He leaned back against the top. He signed, "Do I need to cancel going to school next term?"

"No." Micah's voice sounded harsh to himself. He tried to moderate the tone. "No. You are going. We…this family…will be fine. We will move ahead with life." He sat opposite his son and stared out the picture window. After a moment, he turned to BB. He signed, "I am getting married any day now. As soon as Quinn says it's safe. Wendy and I will find a house, we'll all four move in, and things will be fine." He eyed BB. "Do you believe that?"

BB bounced it back to him. "Do you?"

Micah nodded. Once. Ben-style. "Yes, I do."

Ben tugged at Micah's arm. "What are you and BB saying?"

Micah hoped Ben would understand him. "Wendy and I are getting married. We will buy a new house for us all to live in. And there will be no monsters."

Ben stared at the floor for a long time. He seemed lost. Or lost in thought. After several moments, he looked up. "Wen-dy will live with us. We will be fam-i-ly. Right?"

"Right." Micah waited for Ben to resolve whatever issue he had.

Ben thought for several more minutes, then nodded once. "Fam-i-ly. All of us. And Mi-al-ma."

Micah smiled. "And Mialma. We will all be family together."

"Will Wendy come to stay with us here?"

Micah hadn't thought about Wendy moving in with them in the hotel suite. Maybe not. Too close quarters. And she needed to be with her mom until Jen and Wendy could get Arlene settled somewhere. Micah punted. "We'll have to see about it."

He held the paper with his list. "What food do we need?"

Ben jumped. "Cereal. Milk. Bread. Pea-nut but-ter. Jel-ly. Lit-tle cake rolls."

Micah held up his hand. "I know what's on your list, bud. Let's think about real dinners."

Ben jumped again. "Piz-za!"

Life.

* * *

MONDAY

Carly stayed with Sherry, Arlene, Ben, and Mialma. Ben pouted about being left behind. Micah told the boy he needed to help with his grandmother. She needed people to talk to. And Ben talked to her better than most people. It didn't make up for having to stay when BB got to go, but it did make Ben feel better.

The fact the two youngest Smothers boys stayed behind as well made being singled out less of a burden. Ben understood it had to do with age, not with any weakness on his part. Tim and Ury were as unhappy as Ben. But staying with their mom made it less of a trial.

The other boys, Peter and Kevin, went with the Knights to Rock Island Landing. Quinn drove Tav's van with just him and Grace. Luke drove Quinn's van and ferried his brothers. Wendy drove the new van with Jen, her brothers, Micah, and BB. Eleven people climbed on the chartered boat.

Quinn signaled for prayer before leaving shore. "Lord, we're here to have a good time and honor You in all we do. You know our plans. You have Yours, and they are infinitely better than our own. Have Your will and way, Lord. In Jesus' Name, amen."

Eleven "amens" followed. Micah breathed his own

prayers for safety if God willed it. And this whole debacle would soon be over, and they could get to the wedding and the "happily ever after." He was so ready…

The ride took ten minutes. The air rushed past the boat. Water splashed over the gunwales. Lake birds dove after bugs skittering on the water. Sunlight reflected off the liquid droplets, creating prisms of rainbow colors.

Micah breathed in the pine-scented air. He could almost believe they were going to picnic or have a day at the lakeside beach. He could almost relax and smile.

If he didn't know they were trying to trap a murderer who had destroyed their homes and wanted to kill them all. He sighed.

Quinn wore an earpiece and a microphone. He spoke into it and signed, "All clear. The island is free of any trouble."

Micah signed to Tav, "I don't know what to hope."

Tav nodded and tapped knuckles with Micah. They stood in the bow and let the spray wash over them.

They pulled the boat to the wooden dock, slid it into place, and tied the vessel to the piling. Luke jumped out, followed by the rest of the group. Quinn came out last. He stood tall on the deck, stretched high, and laughed loud. Like he wanted to be noticed. Which he probably did. Wasn't that the point of this whole charade? That Lorna and her goons would see them on the island? Micah shook his head. Time would tell.

The group filed into the pub, down the steps, and into the basement area. Glasses lined rows of shelves. Dartboards hung on the walls. Pictures of winners past adorned the spaces between targets. Benches were pulled alongside slab tables. The checkerboard floor gleamed.

Quinn pulled out his magic box. "All phones in here. If the bad guys have some tap I don't know about on your phones, all they're going to see is you here, having a good time."

The Knights slid their cell phones into the box. Quinn shoved it behind the bar, then moved directly to the backdoor of the room and pulled it open. He pointed into the darkness. "Here. Now."

As the group filed in, Quinn turned on a single overhead bulb to light the way. Two doors met them at the end of the corridor. One said, "Exit." One said, "Storage." Quinn unlocked the one marked "Storage" and motioned for the group to file through.

Grace went through first and led the others around a set of barrels and through a six-foot crate marked "Cleaning solution." She pulled at one panel. It opened. She stepped through and continued down a tunnel. The floors were hewn rock. The ceilings were rock and clay. A thin light ran the length of the subterranean shaft. Several twists and turns later, Micah had no sense of which direction they had come. Grace continued to lead with confidence, with Quinn bringing up the rear.

Suddenly, the tunnel stopped. Ended. No further passage. Grace waited until the group gathered around her, then she shoved against the earthen barrier. The hole creaked open, and daylight flooded through. Micah peeked his head out and gazed around at a wooded area. He stepped out and tried to get his bearings.

Yeah, good luck with that. He pulled on Quinn's arm and signed, "Where are we?"

Quinn smiled a tight-lipped smile. He spoke and signed, "About half a mile from the pub on the west side of the island. The side away from the beach where we landed. No one will see us here."

Quinn took the lead again and led the group through the trees down to the water. A boat sat anchored off the shore. Quinn directed, "Everyone, shoes off unless you want to lose them in the mud. Carry them out to the boat. Yes, you're going wading."

No one grumbled. At least not so Micah could hear. And

no one's mouth moved. Everyone bent down and removed their shoes. Micah tied his laces together and slung the shoes over his shoulder. He noted Tav did the same. Great minds and all that.

Quinn caught Peter and Kevin's arms and directed them in first. Wendy and Jen next. He signed and called, "Down the stairs into the cabin. Out of sight." BB waded out next, followed by Addison and Luke. Finally, Micah and Tav waded in the chest-high murk out to the boat and climbed aboard. As they were settling in, the boat pulled away from where it sat. An electric motor pushed soundlessly through the water.

Micah realized Grace and Quinn hadn't followed them into the boat. He grabbed the captain and yelled what he hoped sounded like, "Go back! Go back."

The captain shook his head. He said something Micah didn't understand. Micah looked at the shore and saw Quinn and Grace walk back to the tunnel exit. Micah fumed and said, "I'll pay you double!"

The captain huffed, waved Micah off, and kept steering the boat through the murky water away from shore.

Micah locked eyes with Tav. His friend nodded. Together, they slipped over the side of the boat and started mucking back to shore.

They'd gotten a good fifty yards away when Luke came from the cabin. He flashed ASL signs at Tav. Tav responded, "Watch the women and kids. We'll be back."

Luke held his fist in the air. Tav did the same. They stood frozen for several seconds, and then Tav turned back to the task at hand…walking back to shore. Micah pulled himself along with tree branches or bushes that jutted out into the murk. It exhausted him.

They reached the shore, climbed up, and laid down for several moments. Breathing felt good. Not pulling your feet through two or more feet of mud and muck every step felt even better. Micah knew they weren't done. Whatever Quinn and Grace had in mind, they would not face it alone. One for all and all for one.

Micah and Tav put their shoes on and walked through the shoreline littered with broken pinecones and prickly pine needles. It would have been torture barefooted. They tried to keep the crunching to a minimum. Yes, they could hear music being pumped through loudspeakers. Quinn wanted to cover the noise of the boat, no doubt. And give the impression all was good at the party.

Micah heard the drone of voices. Not clearly, and no words. But to their wounded ears, it sounded like people talking. Micah wondered what it sounded like to a normal-hearing person?

They reached the secret entrance. *Does it have a secret password to open it? Speak "friend" and enter? Open sesame?* The two felt around the rocks and stumps until Tav grabbed hold of an iron ring the size of his hand. He looked at Micah. Micah nodded. Tav pulled, and the door yawned open.

The lights were out. The tunnel sat in pitch darkness.

Tav signed, "Great. Now what?"

Micah shrugged. "I don't remember any openings except the one we followed. We will feel our way along."

Tav grimaced but nodded. "Guess so. You want to lead?"

Micah stepped into the burrow and waited for Tav to close the tunnel. They walked side-by-side, careful not to lose each other. Micah was reminded of the underground labyrinth he and Wendy were trapped in when they first worked together. That had worked out well. He grinned. Yeah, good things can come from the bowels of the earth. He prayed this would be as positive an outcome.

They had no sense of time in the tunnel, only winding the way left, right, left, left again…twisting and turning through the underground. Micah refused to compare the current journey with what he thought they'd traversed the first time. Had it taken this long? Could there have been a branch in the passageway they'd missed? Were they hopelessly lost? Would they die down here in the blackness?

He wanted to hum. Wanted to sing. Wanted to shout. But he kept walking in silence. The idea was to keep the element of surprise. Whatever Quinn and Grace were up to, they didn't need Micah and Tav alerting the bad guys help had arrived. Stay quiet. Stay calm. You will get through this. You will.

A glow ahead shone like bright daylight to their eyes. The door to the basement had been left cracked open. An inch, maybe less, allowed light to shine into the blackness. Tav and Micah tapped knuckles again. They'd made it back. Now...

Now what? Tav peered through the gap. He stepped back and shook his head. Micah stepped forward and put his eye to the crevice.

Grace stood at the top of the stairs. She called to someone. Micah saw her mouth moving but heard no sound. Too far away, and too much peripheral noise from the canned music and laughter. Micah watched for several moments. Grace seemed relaxed, not on alert or stressed. She leaned against the doorpost, letting it support her.

Micah signed with Tav. "Stay here? Go in?"

Tav stared at the light. His hands twitched, but not in intelligible words. Micah waited. Tav looked up finally. "We go in."

"Together? One at a time? One stay in reserve?"

Micah's best friend studied the floor. After several moments, he signed, "One in reserve."

Which could only be settled with a Ro-Sham-Bo competition.

They counted to three.

Micah threw rock.

Tav threw rock.

They counted to three.

Micah and Tav both threw paper.

Count to three.

Micah threw paper again.

Tav threw rock. He threw his hands in the air and signed, "Two out of three."

Micah signaled thumbs down. Rules were rules. He signed, "Stay safe. Use your head."

Tav grabbed Micah by his shoulders, shook him, then shoved him toward the door.

Micah slipped through the opening, prying it wide enough to fit his body sideways. Grace was focused on the events upstairs and didn't see Micah. He considered how to approach her. If he walked and tapped her on the shoulder, she would likely scream. He didn't want to distract her from whatever plan she and Quinn had going…but he did want her to know he had come. Micah reached behind the bar and picked up a soda can. He laid it on the floor and rolled it toward her.

Grace heard the clatter and turned around. She spotted Micah. Her eyes flew wide. She yanked the door closed, scrambled down the steps, and grabbed hold of him by the shoulders. She shoved him hard. She pretended to box him in the ears. She shoved him back and signed, demanding, "What are you doing here?"

Micah gave her a self-conscious grin. "Cavalry."

Grace groaned, rolled her eyes, and threw her hands. She looked behind him. "Are you alone?"

Micah signed, "Do I look like I'm alone?"

Her eyes narrowed, and she glared at him. "Where is your back-up?"

Micah hesitated, then motioned over his shoulder. Grace stalked to the basement door, jerked it open, and grabbed Tav by the arm. She yanked him into the room and proceeded to dress Micah and Tav down in sign. Micah didn't bother to interpret most of it…he waited until she ran out of ways to tell them how stupid they had been.

When she finally quit signing, Micah and Tav exchanged glances, then signed, "We love you."

Grace turned away from Micah and Tav and threw her fists in the air. She shook them hard at the sky. Only when she had released her frustration did she turn around and address the men..

"You will do exactly as you're told. You will obey everything I tell you, or you'll get someone killed. Do you understand me?"

Micah and Tav nodded. Tav signed, "We came to help, not get in the way. We didn't want you to be alone."

Grace hung her head, dropped her shoulders, and then kissed both men on the cheek. She nodded once. She signed, "I don't have time to tell you the plan. Just stay behind me. Whatever you see, stay behind me."

She climbed the stairs again and opened the door. Micah heard her voice addressing someone on the other side. Her tone stayed calm. Must not be ratting them out to Quinn. Maybe he didn't need the stress at the moment.

Micah could smell smoke. The kind of smoke from a campfire. He missed the crackle of the bark popping and snapping. Maybe one day again. *Lord?*

He heard the sharp pop of a rifle report. He snapped his head toward Grace. He watched her pause, holding the door. Micah and Tav both jumped forward. Grace held the fort against them, preventing them from getting past her. She thrust them back, indicating they should remain where they were. She waited. Waited. Waited…

…then screamed and tore the door open. Grace rushed through the entryway and out into the front of the building.

Quinn lay on the ground. Blood spatter colored his chest. Grace fell on top of him and continued screaming.

More shots were fired. Micah watched as security guards rose from the bushes and riddled a fast boat with bullets, tearing a gaping hole in the side. The watercraft flooded and swamped, leaving the occupants floundering in the water. Speedboats flew from their hiding spots in the brush and captured the hapless gunmen.

And still, Grace wailed. Micah and Tav knelt beside her. Quinn lay motionless. Grace covered his body with her own, wailing. Micah tried to pull her off. She fought him with surprising strength. One of the security guards approached and leaned down. He put his hand on Quinn's neck, looked at his compatriots, and shook his head.

Grace refused to move. The sodden assassins were marched, their hands cable-tied behind them, past Quinn's body. Micah jerked to his feet and tackled the lead man, ready to pummel him into the dust. The guard kicked Micah aside. Tav grabbed him and pulled him away. Micah screamed. He heard his own voice yelling words he would never in his right mind repeat.

Except he was, and he did.

Micah crumpled to the ground in anguish. He'd failed his mentor and friend. Dishonored his Lord. Destroyed his testimony in a moment's rage. Who was he?

Human. Human enough to need a Savior. And forgiveness. Even at this point in his "perfect" walk. Micah came to his knees and wept. Open. Unashamed. Filled with remorse. He repeated over and over, "I'm sorry. I'm sorry. Forgive me."

Tav knelt beside Micah. He put his arm around Micah's shoulders. Everything in Micah was hollow. Empty. He'd failed. Quinn was dead.

Grace turned from Quinn and caught Micah in her arms. A guard threw his jacket over Quinn's head and chest. Micah wept. Noiseless sobs wracked his body. He closed his eyes. Grace tried to murmur in his ears, but he couldn't make out the words. It wouldn't matter if he did. There was no consolation. He failed.

Grace bumped her forehead against his. Micah opened his eyes. She mouthed, "I'm sorry. I'm so sorry." Tears lined her face, but her eyes shone. Micah stared at her. What?

The guards hustled the goons away, loaded them in a boat, and roared off to the far shore. Only as they disappeared from view did motion behind him catch Micah's attention.

Quinn sat.

Micah's jaw dropped. He glanced at Tav. Tav glanced back. The two Knights grabbed Quinn in a tackle hold and knocked him back to the ground. Quinn laughed.

Micah signed, "How? How?"

Quinn shoved the two younger men. "It was Grace's idea. Let Lorna think she'd killed me. Then, let the hired goons turn on her. The police would round her up, she'd go to jail, and we'd be finally free of her."

Grace sat in the dirt beside the guys. "I didn't have time to tell you, Mick. I am sorry. But you certainly added realism to the act."

Micah's face fell. Life drained from him again. Quinn clapped him on the shoulder. "Get over it, Mick. You're human. The human nature, with all its flaws, is still in you. We need the Lord just as much today as we did the day we accepted Him. We never stop needing Him. Remember that."

Micah stared at the ground. Did I forget, Lord? I'm nothing without You. Worse than nothing. Wretched. Forgive me, and keep reminding me who I really am.

Micah stood to his feet. Quinn eyed him closely. "You okay now?"

Micah nodded. "Yeah. I'm a fool. But a humbled one."

"Wise the man who figures it out before the end."

Tav climbed to his feet as well. "Is it over? Really over? Can we have our wedding now and get to the happily ever after part?"

Quinn nodded. "I do believe we can." He put his arms around Tav and Micah's shoulders and intoned for their hearing, "Let's go home."

Grace put an arm around Micah's shoulder, leaned in,

kissed his cheek again, and signed, "Home."
Wherever it was.

SATURDAY

The group gathered at the Hemming house. Wendy, Jen, and Grace laughed and giggled and snuck their gowns into the designated dressing rooms. Arlene and Carly went with them to supervise and help where they could. Arlene understood her daughters were getting married. Today. In gorgeous gowns. But what "married" meant confused her a little. She couldn't grasp the concept of where the girls would live once they were married. Micah and Tav had become strangers to her. But the girls were beautiful, and that's what mattered to the woman.

Wendy's stomach twisted and turned and gurgled in regular revolutions. The old camp song, "I Know an Old Lady Who Swallowed a Fly," wouldn't stop replaying in her head. Wendy could believe she'd swallowed the spider, the bird, the cat, and the dog, all in an effort to catch the fly. Her hands began to shake. Tremor. Not shake. Not that bad. Yet.

Jen was no better. She stepped on her gown three times, tripping twice. Only Grace managed to be calm and calming.

After the third time Jen failed to attach her necklace in the proper place, she pitched the pearls on the floor and shrieked, "I've had it!" She buried her face in her hands and sobbed. "I can't do this. I can't. I'm a mess."

Grace wrapped her arms around Jen and held her. "Yes, you are. But it's going to be okay. I promise you. You'll go out to the chapel, you'll trip over Quinn's feet, you'll forget your vows, someone will be in the wrong spot, the pastor will read the wrong scripture, and at the end of the afternoon, you'll be just as married as if it went perfect. So suck it up, straighten up, and relax. I can guarantee you Tav is having as hard a time as you are."

Jen looked at Grace. "You think so? I bet they're over in the other room cutting up and telling jokes."

Grace shook her head. "I'll take that bet. After the service is over, you ask Tav how many times he almost ran out the door."

The older woman laughed at Wendy. "Micah, too. I know those boys. And they are boys. They're as scared as you are. What you all need to remember is God has this. He has you. It will be fine. It will be. The wedding doesn't make the marriage. The marriage makes the marriage. The work you put into it makes the marriage. Any of you four could have walked away when the going got hard. When the boys lost their hearing. When the quad burned. When Lorna tried to have you murdered. Those were hard times. This is a breeze."

Grace kissed Jen, then kissed Wendy. "You four are already committed to each other, ceremony or not. This is a party for to celebrate and confirm your happiness."

The fly in Wendy's stomach—and all its companions—settled. She breathed out, letting her shoulders drop. She kissed Grace. "Thank you, Grace. I needed that."

"What you need is makeup, your veil, and your shoes. Now, get to it."

"Yes, ma'am." Wendy risked a quick kiss on her mom's cheek.

Mom smiled at her. "Grace is right, Wendy. You need your shoes." She snickered a bit. "I married your father in my bare feet. I left my shoes at home. But under my gown, no one could tell. I think I must have been the only one who didn't have sore feet that night."

Jen laughed. "Mom! You never told us that story."

"Didn't I? Oh, well, I'm sure there are stories I haven't told you." She looked off to the side and stared away. "I don't know what they are, though."

Carly leaned forward from the dressing bench. "They'll come to you, Mrs. Smothers. What did your husband wear that night?" She took Mom Smothers' hand and said, "Why don't we go into the living room, and you can tell me all about it?" She led the woman away and out of the dressing room.

As Carly and Mom talked, Wendy completed putting on the finishing touches. Her phone buzzed. Time to move it along. She yawned.

What? Yawn? Since when? Maybe she had become too keyed up. That must be it. Overexcited.

Which explained why Jen yawned as well. And Grace...Grace would be surprising Quinn in her stunning gown. Wendy could imagine Quinn's look when he first set eyes on his striking bride. She could be excused for being overstimulated...

Jen sat down and leaned against the wall. "I need a nap."

Wendy shook her. "Oh, no, you don't. Don't do this."

Grace slumped against the dressing table. "I'm so tired."

Wendy's eyes opened wide. This wasn't the way it was supposed to go. No naps. No tired. Excitement. Happiness...

But a few winks? Just a moment or two. She slipped down on the floor. Wendy leaned against the wall, then slid down to a prone position. She rested her head on her arms and closed her eyes. In moments, she was out.

* * *

Quinn stood at the door, guarding it from any runners. He glared hard at Mick and Tav as they suited in their tuxedos. Both BB and Luke had to help dress their respective grooms fasten buttons and cufflinks. Mick continually ran his hands through his hair, swallowing hard and trying not to hyperventilate. Ben sat on the floor sketching the men. Addison sat beside him on a bench, commenting on the artwork.

Quinn checked his watch to ensure they were on schedule. The pastor should be arriving in the next half-hour. He had a prior wedding to do, so he would be a little delayed. Not late for the actual nuptials, but he would miss all the dressing room drama.

The mentor made a circling motion with this hand. "Let's speed it up, boys. The girls will be waiting for you, and that's never good."

Addison quipped, "Yeah, the guys are supposed to wait on the girls. And wait and wait."

Mick made a rude comment in ASL. Addison returned the favor. Tav looked at Quinn and shook his head. He signed, "How did you do this? Weren't you afraid?"

Quinn suppressed a yawn, then laughed. "Terrified. With the first one. But not with Grace. We knew. And we hired a pastor and had a simple ceremony on the beach. You've both got performance anxiety. This is a big deal."

Mick stared at the floor. "It's the Knights. It's the Smothers boys. It's a few young women we hardly know. What's to be afraid of?" He held out his hand, and Quinn saw it shaking. Mick continued, "Everything in me wants to run."

Quinn nodded. "That's why I'm standing here." He swallowed another yawn.

Mick glared at him. "Are we keeping you awake?"

Quinn sat down. "Now that you mention it."

Tav dropped down beside Quinn. "Why am I so tired?"

"Too much anxiety. Take some deep breaths. Both of you."

Quinn breathed with them. In. Out. In. Out… He closed

his eyes. The mentor sensed Mick, Luke, and the others also sinking to the floor. Time. Time to move. Time…

Everyone went still and silent. No one moved. Breaths became shallow. Slow.

Stopped.

A gas mask-wearing shape walked into the room. The figure looked around at the crumbled bodies. He waited five minutes, then five minutes more. Finally, the assailant moved to the side of the area and flipped a toggle on a ventilation unit. He waited as clean air pumped into the chamber. Satisfied, the man pulled his mask off and sniffed the quality of the atmosphere.

He strode to where Quinn lay prone on the floor. The man stared at Quinn, his eyes narrowing. He gave a self-assured smile. "You're dead. You and all your precious children. This is for Mom. We win."

He stepped forward, putting his foot on Quinn's neck.

In an instant, Quinn twisted and jerked the man's foot off his throat, upending the hapless assailant. Quinn ground the man's face into the tile and sneered, "Who wins, Denner?"

The Knights all bolted upright, coming to their feet.

Denner's eyes flew open wide. "How? I used carbon monoxide. You should all be dead."

Quinn yanked Denner to his knees. "We found your gas. And your cameras. We decided we'd give you a last show. Only one gassed is you."

The ladies walked out of their dressing room and joined the Knights. Quinn pulled Denner upright. "It's over, Denner. You're going down. No more blackmail." Quinn called, "Take him out, men."

Three burly gentlemen in dark suits entered the area and took control of Denner. They escorted him out of the room.

Quinn rubbed his hands together. He grinned wide at the Knights and signed, "Let's have a wedding."

Cheers, high-fives, and hugs met the pronouncement.

Tav, Luke, Addison, Mick, BB, and Ben all moved to the ballroom for the presentation of the brides. The women lined up in proper order for the walk down the aisle. Carly brought Arlene out from the safety of the living room to join the others in a place of honor at the front of the area. The pastor signaled the pianist, who began the wedding march.

Quinn stepped out with Wendy and Jen. He muttered, "Right, left, right, left," as they walked to keep them in cadence. He was aware someone followed him, but decorum forbade him to look around. Instead, Quinn stayed focused on the two grooms ahead of him. The mentor passed Wendy to Mick with a kiss on Wendy's cheek, then gave Jen to Tav with another kiss for Jen. Only then did he turn and see who stood behind him.

Grace. Looking exquisite. She carried a small bouquet, slipped her hand into Quinn's arm, and joined his side. She whispered, "It was the girls' idea. They wanted to see us get married, too."

Quinn chuckled but couldn't wipe the smile off his face. His cheeks hurt.

The pastor spoke, and vows were exchanged. The moment came for the command, "You may now kiss the bride." Mick looked at Ben and tapped him on the shoulder. Micah spread his hands wide.

Ben nodded once. "Now you can kiss."

And they did.

* * *

The after-party was a joyous event. The cake proved to be beautiful. Elegant and smooth and standing tall. When Ben received the first chocolate piece, he set it down and danced in circles. He hugged Wendy and Jen, jumped up and down, and did zoomies around the room. Wendy stared in amused confusion. She signed to Micah, "Why?"

"Ben didn't feel like he was an important part of the wedding. Getting chocolate cake proved to him he mattered." He kissed Wendy. "You did great. Thank you. For everything."

Quinn received his gifts of framed portraits of him and Grace with a grateful heart. Ben shared his sketches with the men and made sketches of the women to pass around. His gifts. Other gifts would have to wait until they had a place to put them. But where would they live?

Micah clapped his hands over his head for attention. He pulled out his phone and pulled up a scripture to read. He signed it for Tav.

Great persecution came to the church. And all except the apostles were scattered. They preached the word wherever they went.

Micah continued to sign, "We were right to gather and share all things like the early church. But now, like the same church, we need to scatter and go out preaching the word."

He lowered his head, then lifted it. "I'm not saying we need to move to the ends of the earth. Wendy and I need to stay close to Tav and Jen to help with Arlene. We all still need each other. But we need to spread out and preach the Word in our going."

Quinn caught Micah in a bear hug. The mentor roughed Micah's head, then nodded. "Wise words. We start house hunting tomorrow." He grinned sideways. "But I will know where you all live."

Fifteen thumbs went into a circle (the Smothers boys had a say in it, too). Fifteen thumbs went up. Measure carried. Forward to life.

If you enjoyed ***Knights of the Octagon,*** sign up for Colleen Snyder's newsletter to keep up with new books and projects. It will also give you a place to talk to the author directly. And she loves to talk to her readers. Trust me!

Emails will NOT be sold, shared, or used for any other purpose. Promise.

Go to: **colleensnyderauthor.com** and leave your email to sign up.

Also connect with her at Facebook, **Colleen K. Snyder, Author**.

Also out now:
Knights of the Octagon: The Christmas Stalker
BOOK V

I can't wait to be with you. Friday can't come soon enough.

Chay Waylon is receiving threatening messages from her own email account. Someone is mimicking her address. Someone who wants more than her attention. He's pursuing an imaginary relationship. A Christmas romance.

But why? And most important, who?

Ken, her boss, thinks she's sending the messages to herself to create drama. No big deal. Get back to work.

Then, the entire office system is locked out with Chay's picture on every screen throughout the accounting company. Ransom is demanded. Ken is convinced Chay is behind the theft.

How can she clear her name of the holiday hoax and catch the stalker who wants to make her his own?

And when the once love of her life makes a second appearance, will she let him go again? Or will she admit she needs help and welcome him back in her life…this time forever?

Did you miss the first books in the Knights of the Octagon Series?
Find them here:

Knights of the Octagon: Benefactor
Book I

It's life or death. Can they pull together to survive?

Dumped from a raft in the middle of God literally only knows where, four friends are stranded in the wilderness. No cellphones. No maps. No food. Three pocket knives, a compass, and each other are all they have.

Until two shadowy figures lead Micah and his friends to a stash of survival equipment scrounged from the river. Who are these mysterious benefactors? What do they want?

Then rescue comes with a catch. Micah and his friends can wait four days to be taken to civilization or join a real-life quest for a million dollars. The Magary treasure hunt—going on its fiftieth year with no winners—has seen deaths before. With a murderer in the field, will the men become victims?

Is the reward worth the risk? Can the Knights work as a team to not only survive but find a treasure no one else has found? Where is God in their search? In their lives?

Join the Knights of the Octagon on their first adventure.

Also find...
Knights of the Octagon: MIA
BOOK II
Q is missing.

Quinn Magary, patron, supporter, champion of the Knights of the Octagon, is missing.

Five days late from a three-day personal assignment, and no one can find him.

Then Grace Painter, another member of the Knights, disappears without warning.

The remaining Knights—Tav, Luke, and Micah—vow to find their friends and mentors.

Then someone runs Tav off the road. And Micah is nearly murdered at Grace Painter's worksite. An innocent lunch date becomes a conflagration as a shadowy figure blows up the restaurant.

Dead bodies appear. Knights are battered, kidnapped, and left for dead. Who is after them? Why? What can they do to end the attacks? And above all, where are Quinn and Grace?

Join the Knights for their next adventure in:
MIA

<u>Knights of the Octagon: Quake</u>
BOOK III
The Quake is Coming

Impeccable research from a brave geologist predicts a major earthquake for the local area. Soon. Within thirty days soon. Not all his colleagues agree with his conclusions. The quake is coming? Absolutely. But three weeks? More like three years. Maybe.

A group of young men are convinced of the geologist's calculations. They're preparing for it. Frantically buying food and supplies for the survivors. But will there be any? Of the five thousand people in town, how many will believe their report? "Orton's Crazies," people call them. "Cultists" who want to sit on a hilltop and wait for the end to come.

It would be easier for the Knights not to tell anyone and simply get out of town. But then how many deaths will be on their heads? How do you convince people—family, friend, and foe alike—of a truth they don't want to hear??

The quake is coming. What would you do about it?

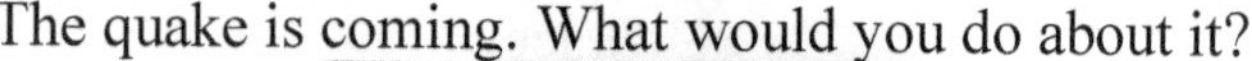

ABOUT THE AUTHOR

Colleen K. Snyder has always had a passion for writing. She authored two previously published books: *Journey to Amanah: The Beginning* and *Return to Tebel-Ayr: The Journey Continues* (B&H Publishing). In 2020 she published the first book in the *Collin Walker* series: *Verdict at the River's Edge*. There are now seven books in the series. She lives on a "ranchette" in California and is the juniorest ranch hand. She serves on her church prayer team, and exercises a ministry of intercessory prayer. She has worked as a factory line worker, pharmacy technician, USAF missile systems analyst, janitor, nanny, teacher, accounting manager and anything else the Lord required. Her son, Bear and his wife Krystal, their two daughters, Mara and Kaylynn, and her daughter Katie all live in Ohio.

Colleen's story is for His glory, always.

**Read on to learn more about Colleen's books in the
Collin Walker series.**

The Collin Walker Series

Seven books of action and suspense for your reading
enjoyment. Follow Collin Walker as she follows the Lord into
murder, intrigue, mayhem…you know, Life.
Available on Kindle, KindleUnlimited, and in paperback.
(Also hardback, but why??)

www.ingramcontent.com/pod-product-compliance
Lightning Source LLC
Chambersburg PA
CBHW070416310726

48977CB00003B/718